MARK HUCKERBY & NICK OSTLER

■SCHOLASTIC

Scholastic Children's Books
An imprint of Scholastic Ltd
Euston House, 24 Eversholt Street, London, NW1 1DB, UK
Registered office: Westfield Road, Southam, Warwickshire, CV47 0RA
SCHOLASTIC and associated logos are trademarks and/or
registered trademarks of Scholastic Inc.

First published in the UK by Scholastic Ltd, 2017

Text copyright © Mark Huckerby and Nick Ostler, 2017

The right of Mark Huckerby and Nick Ostler to be identified as the authors
of this work has been asserted by them.

ISBN 978 1407 16424 3

A CIP catalogue record for this book
is available from the British Library.

CONTENTS

FOR OUR PARENTS
RICHARD AND BARBARA
STEPHEN AND CHRISTINE

I

RAISING THE DEAD

Richard would never forget the day he began to hate his brother.

They were eight years old, playing hide-and-seek in the grounds of Buckingham Palace. Alfie had never been very good at hiding; the flowers would set off his hay fever, and all Richard had to do to find him was follow the sound of muffled sneezing. That afternoon their game was interrupted when their father came marching across the neatly trimmed lawn. Richard remembered being surprised. They hadn't seen much of their dad in the months since he had become king. Dressed in military attire, King Henry had clearly come straight from some formal event. His face was red and flushed in the sun.

"There you are! We've been looking everywhere. The King of Saudi Arabia has asked to meet you. Come on, quickly."

The boys started to follow their father back to the palace, but he put his hand out to stop Richard.

"Not you. Just Alfie."

Alfie looked at his brother and shrugged, embarrassed. Richard stood there on the lawn and watched as the king took his brother's hand and led him away. It felt like he had been punched in the stomach and he couldn't catch his breath. At that moment Richard realized something. No matter what he did, no matter how hard he worked, or what great things he achieved in life, he would always come second in his father's eyes. Alfie was the heir, and he was the spare. A nobody.

Richard decided to bury his hurt feelings as deep down as he could. He didn't want people to feel sorry for him. What was the point of that? There was nothing anyone could do about it. So he pretended he was happy to be Alfie's younger twin, to enjoy the relative freedom it gave him. He excelled in his studies and at every sport he tried. In the eyes of his family and his friends he was the easy-going, carefree one, the winner. Even when their parents divorced and he cried himself to sleep every night for a month, all anyone talked about was how it was affecting Alfie and their little sister, Ellie. No one paid much attention to Richard; he was the mature one, he was strong. Richard would cope.

By the time the brothers were teenagers and attending Harrow School, Richard was becoming aware of how the outside world viewed his family. The days when the royal family was popular, when his much-loved grandmother Queen Grace was still on the throne, were long gone. His father was seen as cold and distant, a bad husband and an out-of-touch monarch. Then there was Alfie and his *mishaps*: watching the Trooping of the Colour with his flies open, accidentally sneezing in the face of the President of the United States, being photographed in a bin down a dingy alleyway. It was as if Alfie were on a one-man mission to bring down the House of Arundel. Out of loyalty, Richard kept his mouth shut, but it was clear his family had become a laughing stock and there was nothing he could do about it. Or so he thought. That was before he met Professor Lock.

"Window up, please, Your Highness."

Lock's commanding voice shook Richard out of his memories. They were in a car, speeding out of London. They'd set off two hours earlier just as it was getting dark, but nightfall had brought little relief from the temperature. A summer heatwave had fallen over Britain like a heavy rug, and it was no time to be cooped up inside an old sports car with broken air-conditioning. Not to mention the one-hundred-and-fifty cheeseburgers piled up in a sack on the back seat. They had visited six different drive-through takeaways to avoid arousing suspicion, but Richard still had no idea who the questionable feast could be for. Between the heat and the meaty stench, the atmosphere was beyond stifling. And then there was the company.

"I can't breathe in here," Richard said.

"If you are spotted we will have more to worry about than a bad smell," hissed Lock. "Window up, if you don't mind."

Professor Lock may have sounded like he was being polite, but there was no mistaking his tone of voice. It was an order, not a request. Richard sighed; he couldn't really argue. It would be hard to explain what Prince Richard, brother of the king and first in line to the throne, was doing driving into the depths of Suffolk at night in a car driven by Professor Cameron Lock, a man officially listed as "missing, presumed dead" after the events of the coronation. Unofficially, the only thing waiting for Lock, should he ever be caught, was a cold cell deep down in the dungeons of the Tower of London.

"Where are we going, anyway?" asked Richard as he wound the window up. "What could possibly be worth slogging all the way out here?"

"You'll see. Not far now," replied Lock, turning left at a battered road sign that read: HADLEIGH, 3 MILES.

Richard slumped back into the sticky leather of the seat, frustrated. This wasn't the way it should be. By now *he* should be the one on the throne. And he should be the one with the powers that came with it – the Defender of the Realm. Not sneaking around in the dark like a rat. He could feel the anger burning deep inside him again, bubbling up like poison, preparing to unleash that other side of him that lurked in his bones like a disease – the Black Dragon.

The car pulled off the road on to a gravel track and crunched to a halt in front of a weathered sign that read: St Mary's.

"Is this it?" asked Richard, peering up at the silhouette of an old church framed against the dark sky.

"Yes. Don't forget the burgers," replied Lock, clambering out of the car.

Richard hauled the heavy sack round the church and deep into the overgrown graveyard, where the professor was waiting for him, leaning casually against an old tomb. In a neighbouring field, sheep bleated, unhappy at having their sleep disturbed by the arrival of these outsiders. Lock reached into his jacket and pulled out a curious pair of chunky glasses. He put them on and adjusted the thick, protruding lenses, which clicked as he turned them, and scanned the graveyard.

"Aha, there!"

He pointed and hurried past crumbling headstones towards a large mound in the far corner.

"What is it?" asked Richard, dragging the sack of burgers with him through a tangle of brambles.

"Take a look," said Lock, handing him the odd glasses.

Richard put them on and saw through the fuzzy lenses that the thick carpet of moss covering the mound in front of them was glowing bright green. He'd never seen anything like it.

"It is called fairy fire," Lock went on. "Invisible to the naked eye. Very rare. And rather useful. Now, if you don't mind, we're going to need our scaly friend. . ."

"What? You never said anything about me transforming tonight!" Richard protested.

When Lock had told him they were going out for cheeseburgers, he'd expected a quiet chat, not a mission for the Black Dragon. There was nothing easy about changing from a human boy into a huge monster; the pain was excruciating, like every bone in his body was breaking at the same time. But worse than that, every time he turned into the Black Dragon it felt like another piece of Richard, the human side of him, was being chipped away. When he was the Dragon, his mind was so clouded by rage that it was hard to think straight, like trying to recite your times tables just after you've stubbed your toe.

"I can wait all night," Lock said, hoisting himself up on to an ivy-covered gravestone.

Richard sighed, resigned. He had learned that there was no use in arguing with the professor. He closed his eyes and focused, relaxing his body and allowing the monster to rise inside him. Richard gasped as, with a sudden *crack*, his legs and arms bulged and reshaped. He fell on to all fours and dug his hands into the soil as black scales erupted across his skin in a sickening ripple. As his clothes fell away in tatters, his tail emerged, flicking back and forth. He let out a high-pitched howl as his jaws elongated and sharp teeth burst through his gums. Finally, a single, leathery wing stretched out behind him. The stump where the other had been severed by the Defender in Westminster Abbey was sealed with a thick scar. His transformation into the Black Dragon was complete. In the field the sheep fell silent, as if sensing the presence of some primal predator.

"Well? What do you want from me?" growled the Black Dragon, scraping the earth impatiently with his heavy claws.

Lock smiled and scooped up a handful of fairy fire from the mound, walking behind the monster. "This will sting a little. . ."

Lock reached up and rubbed the glowing

substance on to the Black Dragon's scabby wing stump. The beast roared with pain and a jet of fire erupted from his jaws, incinerating a nearby tree. The professor backed off and watched as the Dragon fell to his knees, doubled over in agony. Then, with a sickening *snap*, a new wing burst from the stump on his back. Breathing easier, the Black Dragon got back to his feet and flapped his new-grown wing, impressed.

"Is this why we came here?" he grumbled.

"No. This is just a bonus. Fairy fire only grows on very particular kinds of burial sites – X marks the spot, as they say," replied Lock. "Now, dig. Please."

Blowing smoke from his nostrils, the Black Dragon turned to the mound, fell on to all fours and speared his long claws into the earth. As he dug, black clouds gathered above them with unnatural speed, blotting out the stars. Lightning crackled across the sky and rain hammered the gravestones. Lock, his hair plastered to his head, didn't seem to notice; he only had eyes for the deep hole that was growing in front of him.

THUD.

The Dragon stopped – he had reached something solid. Gripping with his claws he hauled out something massive from the sodden ground. Huge clods of soil fell away to reveal a long, rotted wooden ship. Its pitted, majestic prow topped with a serpent's head curled high into the air, the sleek lines of its hull fanning out like the contours of a whale's throat. A simple timber mast stood in the centre and half a dozen oar-holes dotted each side.

"We came here for a boat?" laughed the Dragon.

"Inside," sneered Lock.

The Dragon flew up and perched on the side of the longship. Lashed to the deck were ten coffins, caked in mud. They were large, the wood ornately carved, each held in place with several thick leather straps, as if in preparation for a voyage across stormy seas.

"Stand them up," barked Lock.

The Black Dragon hopped down, sliced the straps with his claws, and tossed the coffins out of the boat one by one, until they all stood upright in the graveyard like chess pieces on a board. His work apparently finished, the Dragon transformed back into Richard. Shivering in the rain, he hurried back to the car and pulled on his spare clothes. By the time he rejoined Lock, the storm was raging even harder, thunder rolling out across the countryside like an artillery barrage. Richard considered the rows of coffins standing before them. "If this is what we came for then we should have brought a van or something."

Lock smiled. "No need."

The professor pulled out a small book from his pocket. Its cover was rough and thick like cowhide, but it glowed with a faint golden hue. Shielding it from the rain, he opened it with great care to a stiff, yellowing page covered with strange runes and symbols. He read from the book in a language Richard didn't recognize.

"*Inn mesti hermenn!*" Lock cried. "*Vaknit ór úendiliga svepnit yðr! Rekjazk!*"*

And with that, Lock put the old book away, rapped his knuckles three times on the largest, most intricately decorated coffin and stepped back. Lightning struck the church spire, sending tiles clattering to the ground like giant hailstones. The air was thick with static electricity. Something had changed. Richard was startled to hear a long, rattling groan from inside the coffin. Suddenly the lid exploded, splintering to pieces, and out stepped the

---

* "Great warriors! Wake from your endless sleep! Arise!"

biggest man he had ever seen. An immense warrior clad in worm-ridden furs and cracked leather armour, with long red hair and a straggly beard falling from a face that was the bruised colour of a bloated corpse. But a corpse that was very much alive. The brute roared louder than the storm above and swung an axe into the ground, shaking the earth. As one, the other coffins burst open and more undead warriors emerged, shaking the soil from their bodies and grunting and howling like wild animals. There was no mistaking what these were: Vikings.

Lock stepped forward, raised his arms and shouted, "GUTHRUM!"

Was that the leader's name? wondered Richard. It certainly seemed to get his attention, as the giant Viking turned their way, glowering down through the pouring rain with dead eyes milky with age.

"*Hverr þorir at vakna mik?!*"* the warrior bellowed at them.

Richard flinched as he was hit by the wretched smell that hung over these things, like a bin bag of old meat and fish that had been left to fester in the sun.

---

* "Who dares to wake me?!"

12

"*Jarl Guthrum inn mesti! Fylgit mik enda skal ék færa þér góða gripi ór gull. En í fyrstu, búum til veizlu!*"* Lock replied calmly.

Guthrum stared at them for what felt like an eternity before laughing deep and long, exposing a mouth full of rotten teeth and blasting them with breath as fragrant as a blocked drain. But he seemed to like what the professor had said.

"I didn't know you spoke dead Viking," whispered Richard.

"It's called Old Norse," replied Lock. "This is Guthrum, the famous Viking lord."

"What's he doing in Suffolk?"

"He was buried here by the man who defeated him, Alfred the Great. Oh yes, best not mention you're a relative. Might not go down too well."

Guthrum's men stamped their feet and waved their arms. They seemed to be getting impatient for something.

"What did you tell him?" asked Richard.

"I said if he followed me, I could get him great riches. Vikings will do almost anything for gold. Oh,

---

* "Great Lord Guthrum! Follow me and I will bring you rich plunder in gold. But first, a feast!"

and I said we'd feed them. From what I've read, they tend to wake up quite peckish."

Richard grabbed the sack of burgers and emptied it at the undead Vikings' feet. They fell on it like a pack of wolves, pushing and snarling at each other to reach the feast. But none argued with Guthrum, Richard noticed, when he took the lion's share for himself. In seconds there was nothing left. Guthrum barked something at Lock, angry.

"It would seem they're still hungry," said Lock, a note of concern creeping into his voice.

Richard was just wondering how fast he could turn into the Black Dragon and fly them out of there, when a high-pitched whine came from the field next to the graveyard. One of Guthrum's undead warriors had picked up a sheep and was in the process of chewing its head off. Following his lead, the rest of the Vikings bulldozed through the graveyard wall and fell on the poor flock, finally satisfying their hunger.

"That was a stroke of luck," said Lock, relieved.

Richard winced and looked away as Guthrum plucked a sheep off its feet with one hand and snapped its neck before tucking in.

"Why do we need these . . . monsters?" he asked.

"You want your brother's throne? This is what we need to get it," replied the professor as lightning forked across the sky. "There's a storm coming unlike anything this country has ever seen."

THE TOR

We're falling too fast!

Clinging to Wyvern's back, plummeting from a star-filled sky, Alfie and Hayley were both thinking the same thing. It's not like they hadn't planned it this way. Reaching the cover of the small tower on the isolated hilltop without being spotted would not be easy, they knew that. Approach too slowly, and someone was bound to see them. Dive too fast, and the Defender's ghostly horse wouldn't be able to hit the brakes in time. Alfie wasn't so worried about himself; his magical armour would save him if they crashed. But Hayley, gripping on to his waist from behind, had no such protection.

Wind knifed into Hayley's eyes as she lifted her head to check their target. She wished she hadn't. Stone walls rushed up to meet them, and they seemed to be headed straight on to the top of the tower itself! This was going to hurt. But then, a split second from impact, just as they dropped through the roofless tower and into the shadow of its narrow walls, Wyvern lifted her nose and extended her legs, pinning her passengers flat against her back as she glided into the softest of landings. She shook her wispy mane and whinnied proudly, as if to say, "Don't know what you were so worried about."

Hayley laughed with relief, and patted the horse on her flank. "Never doubted you for a second, girl," she whispered.

Wyvern snorted and reared up, sending Hayley tumbling on to the ground.

Alfie stifled a smirk and thought *Spurs*, making Wyvern spiral back into his boots. He reached out his hand to Hayley. "We're lucky she lets you ride her at all. You should feel kind of honoured," said Alfie, voice muffled beneath his helmet.

"Honoured? Yeah, right," said Hayley, ignoring

Alfie's hand and brushing the dirt from her jeans as she stood up. "Remind me to get the bus next time."

From somewhere in the valley below they could hear the sound of chanting voices and a thousand feet stamping, like a great army on the march.

"It's started," said Alfie, nervous but excited. "Come on."

Together they crept out through a small archway, crouching low to avoid their silhouettes appearing to anyone who might be gazing up at the lonely tower from the surrounding countryside. It was yet another swelteringly hot, cloudless night and the moon was bright. Filling the fields below the hill was an endless sea of tiny lights, as if a thousand constellations had fallen from the night sky. Beyond that was a huge white tent illuminated by powerful, restless spotlights. A long cheer erupted from the crowd beneath the blinking lights and a deafening sound filled the air.

Music.

Alfie reached up and whipped off his armour, which shrank back into the form of the Shroud Tunic lying limp across his hand. He opened his backpack and stuffed it inside along with the golden spurs. To anyone who didn't know they would have looked just like a scruffy old T-shirt and a pair of novelty bottle openers. But in reality they were among the most important items of the United Kingdom's priceless regalia.

"I've always wanted to go to Glastonbury," Hayley said as she settled down to watch the gig.

"And here we are. Well, near enough," replied Alfie, sitting next to her.

On stage the lead singer launched into the chorus and the crowd joined in, swaying their mobile phone lights in time. Alfie hadn't heard of this band until earlier that day when Hayley had shown him a newspaper that said they were headlining the festival. To make up for his embarrassment he'd suggested they sneak out that night and fly to Glastonbury Tor, the name of the old church tower on the hill, which he figured would make a safe vantage point.

Neither of them had had much time off in the three months since the coronation. By day Alfie had been attending to his duties as the new King Alfred the Second of the United Kingdom, while by night he had been busy as the Defender, secretly investigating Professor Lock's escape during his transfer to the Tower of London. From what they could tell, his treacherous old teacher had somehow turned into the Black Dragon again and overpowered his guards – even though they'd been sure his monstrous side had been destroyed during the battle in Westminster Abbey. But now the trail had gone cold, and the Lord Chamberlain seemed happy to give Alfie the night off. Not that he knew Alfie had a secret Defender outing planned with Hayley; the fussy old man would NOT have approved.

As for Hayley, she had been busy reorganizing the information-gathering and communications side of the Keep's operation to drag it into the twenty-first century. The Lord Chamberlain wasn't too thrilled about everything she was changing – she could tell that by the way he kept shouting, "Stop changing everything!" By contrast, Brian, the king's bodyguard and the Defender's armourer, and the Yeoman Warders seemed up for a little modernizing, although they weren't that keen on Hayley's latest idea – Thursday night "Zumba" class. She wanted to encourage the beefeaters to lose some weight. Plus if she really had to spend every night cooped up in a cold, secret underground base, she figured she might as well try to liven the place up a little – although the way everyone suddenly found some urgent errand to go and run every time the class was about to start told her that she might have her work cut out for her. But besides terrorizing the Yeoman Warders with threats of compulsory exercise, the one thing there had not been much of in the last few weeks was FUN. Tonight was all about putting that right. At least, it was supposed to be.

"What's wrong?" asked Alfie. He could tell that Hayley was brooding about something.

"My gran. She'd love this."

"Your grandmother likes this band?"

Hayley scowled at him with half a smile. "No. Idiot. I mean being here. Somewhere with all this history. She's stuck in that stupid old people's home, and I'm out having fun. It's not right."

"Well, I'll ask Wyvern, but she's only just got used to letting you hitch a lift. I'm not sure she'd be up for another freeloader—"

Hayley grabbed Alfie's arm and twisted it behind his back.

"All right, all right! No more jokes!" promised Alfie.

Hayley released her grip. "You know, for a superhero, you're kind of a pushover."

Alfie rubbed his arm, regretting taking off

21

his Defender armour so soon. "Yeah, well, you're supposed to be on my side. I could have your head chopped off as a traitor."

"Uh-huh." Hayley had turned her attention back to the festival far below. The band was playing their next song.

"If it makes you feel better, I probably shouldn't be here either," continued Alfie. "I should be trying to see Richard."

He hadn't spoken to his brother for weeks. They always used to reply to each other's messages, no matter what, but ever since the coronation Richard had become more and more distant. He never came back to the palace for weekends any more, and he'd even stopped answering Alfie's calls.

"What's the matter?" asked Hayley. "Little brother still annoyed about the whole humiliation-in-front-of-the-entire-world thing?"

"I did him a favour!" replied Alfie. "He has no idea how lucky he is."

"Yeah, but he doesn't know that, does he? Anyway, he'll come round. You've got that whole twin thing going on, haven't you?"

Alfie smiled. Hayley was right. Richard couldn't stay angry with him for ever.

"Make you a deal," he said. "Soon as we get back, you go see your gran, I'll go and see Rich. Bit of quality family time."

"Deal." Hayley listened to the crowd cheering the band. The sound of the bass drum was thumping around the hills. "This is nice, Alfie. But it's not the same, is it?" She sighed.

"Same as what?"

"Being down there."

Alfie jumped up, swung his backpack on to his shoulder and pulled Hayley to her feet.

"Where are we going?" she asked.

"Where do you think?"

Laughing, Alfie and Hayley ran down the steep, grassy hill in the dark, hand in hand.

Soon they were in the throng of the crowd, jumping up and down to the music with their hands in the air. Alfie had put a cap on, just in case, but no one here was expecting to see him; he was just another kid in a whole field of happy faces. The throbbing bass beat filled their bodies, from the soles of their feet all the way up to their beaming smiles. In that moment he was no longer King Alfie, the secret superhero, and she was no longer Hayley Hicks, the runaway from the estate. Tonight they were part of something bigger than themselves, a joyous mass of humanity dancing as one, and it felt incredible.

Alfie sensed eyes on him. A growing unease jangling at the edge of his mind. Had someone spotted him? He scanned the crowd. It was OK, everyone was facing the stage. No, wait. There. Through the heaving forest of bodies, a hooded figure standing still, wearing a long red robe. Whoever it was, they looked like a monk with a cowl and while everyone around them watched the band, this Red Robe seemed to stare back, straight at him. Alfie blinked and suddenly the figure had moved, about ten people to the right. *How did they do that?* Alfie was unnerved – even though he couldn't see Red Robe's face beneath the hood, he could feel the strange figure's eyes boring into him. Spotlights swept across the crowd and *blink* Red Robe had moved again.

"What's wrong?" Hayley yelled in Alfie's ear, startling him out of his trance.

"Someone's watching me." Alfie pointed through the crowd, but Red Robe had disappeared.

Alfie looked around. There were plenty of other people wearing costumes, silly hats, faces painted.

And with the confusion of flashing lights, maybe he was just being paranoid.

"Forget it. It was nothing."

Hayley grabbed his shoulder. "Alfie! Your backpack!"

Alfie spun round, clawing at his back, finding nothing but a loose piece of strapping – it looked like it had been cut. It was gone and with it, the Shroud Tunic and spurs!

"Wyvern!" gasped Alfie.

They both scanned the ground, frantic. Alfie pushed people back and crawled on his hands and feet, desperate to find his bag. "Where is it?!"

People around them had stopped dancing and started staring at them. Hayley tried to pull Alfie up. "You're attracting attention," she hissed.

A high-pitched whinnying pierced Alfie's ears. He winced and held his head. It was Wyvern. She was scared, crying out. He could hear her. He jumped up and pulled Hayley back through the crowd. "This way!"

Alfie hated the noise Wyvern was making in his head, but he was sure it was her – somehow calling for help, urging him to find her. He fought to block out everything else – the music, the yells of people he was pushing past. As they broke clear of the scrum near a long line of portaloos, Hayley yanked at his arm.

"Where are you going, Alfie? We have to find your bag!"

"I can hear Wyvern – don't ask me how. She's calling to me. She's close!"

Hayley's eyes swept the dark corner of the field. People were milling about in all directions – carrying drinks, dancing in small groups, eating, heading back to their tents. Suddenly she spotted a tall man with long matted blond hair lingering near the queue for the toilets. He was looking around nervously and holding something tight under one arm – Alfie's backpack!

"THERE! STOP!" Hayley shouted and set off at a sprint. Alfie scrambled after her.

The man heard the yell and saw Hayley bounding towards him. He shoved his way through the queue and ran. The ground was uneven and Hayley stumbled, but she was soon back on her feet, eating up the space between her and the thief. She was confident she could catch him, as long as she reached him before he made it back into the main crowd. The man gripped Alfie's bag as he weaved his way past a guy on a unicycle and a pair of stilt-walkers. Then he stopped, turned back and kicked the unicyclist into the stilt-walkers. All three cried out and tumbled over in a heap, just as Hayley and Alfie reached them. By the time they'd dodged past the chaos of arms and legs and stilts, the thief was far ahead of them, nearing the main crowd. They were going to lose him!

But as the man looked back and grinned, the door of the very last portaloo in the row snapped open with ferocious force and smacked into him, knocking him out cold. Hayley ran up and knelt down, wrestling the backpack from the man's limp hands. When Alfie arrived a second later, he thought he caught a glimpse of red cloth through the crack of the open portaloo door. He heard a faint *POP* from inside and a felt a rush of warm air pass over him.

Hayley stood up and held out the backpack to Alfie. "What would you do without me, 'eh, Alf?"

But Alfie was holding the portaloo door open, staring at the empty space inside. "How did it open like that? I thought I saw—"

"Who cares?" said Hayley, holding her nose. "Shut the door before I pass out."

Alfie couldn't explain what he'd just seen without sounding crazy, but he was sure that whoever Red Robe was, they'd just helped stop the thief. Alfie took the backpack from Hayley, checking inside. The Shroud Tunic and spurs were both there, safe and sound. He touched the spurs and Wyvern's cry faded from his head, calm once more.

"That's it. I've got you, girl," whispered Alfie.

He couldn't believe he'd come that close to losing her, not to mention his armour. He had put a thousand years of his family's history at risk for five minutes worth of fun. His father would never have done that. As the thief slowly woke up, rubbing his head and groaning, Alfie and Hayley walked away.

"I guess we should call it a night," said Alfie.

Hayley took a look round at the dancing crowds, the food stalls, the tents full of life and laughter. She cracked a mischievous smile. "Are you kidding? We only just got here."

A ROYAL AUDIENCE

"Herne, get off me..." croaked Alfie, without opening his eyes.

His loyal Irish Wolfhound had got into the habit of creeping on to his bed in the middle of the night. Snoring erupted close to Alfie's ear once more.

"Herne, seriously. Move!"

Alfie forced open an eye and was surprised to see two things. One, he wasn't at home; he was propped against his backpack on the wet ground at Glastonbury. And two, it wasn't Herne's head lying on his chest. It was Hayley's.

"Um . . . Hayley?" Alfie coughed. "Wakey, wakey."

Hayley's eyes flicked open and she gazed up at Alfie, smiling for a moment before she realized where she was and jumped up, embarrassed. "Whoa, sorry," she stammered.

Alfie gave his best "no big deal" shrug even though he was blushing.

"My neck hurts. You suck as a pillow," Hayley said, regaining her composure.

"And you snore worse than Herne," Alfie said, stretching.

They were in the midst of a multicoloured sea of tents. Early morning mist hugged the ground.

"Wicked night though, right?" Hayley said, somehow smiling and yawning at the same time.

"Epic," Alfie agreed. After they'd got their hands back on the backpack and the precious regalia, they'd danced, eaten dubious burritos from a van, watched some comedy, tried their hand at unicycling and then danced some more until they virtually fell asleep where they stood. "I can't believe you got your face painted," Alfie laughed. Hayley's face was crisscrossed with stripes like a zebra.

"When in Rome." Hayley shrugged. "Anyway, what time is it?"

Alfie glanced at his watch and his stomach lurched. "Oh no. We have to go. Now. I'm supposed to meet someone back at the palace."

Alfie grabbed Hayley's hand and marched off, looking for somewhere they could use the spurs and summon Wyvern. He pulled Hayley behind a row of shuttered catering vans.

"Cancel them!" Hayley said, looking longingly at their surroundings. "Who's so important that you have to leave the world's greatest party?"

Prime Minister Vanessa Thorn drummed her bright red fingernails against the ornate armrest and emitted a tut just loud enough for the footman hovering in the doorway to hear. Dressed in her trademark dark trouser suit, her jet-black hair tied in a severe bun, Thorn was sitting in the grand drawing room of Buckingham Palace facing a dark, time-stained oil painting. It was of some king or other in a tri-cornered hat astride a horse in front of his massed ranks of troops, pointing in the direction in which he wanted them to advance. *Not that he'd do any fighting*, she thought. In Thorn's experience, the royals didn't have the stomach for real work and would leave it to the poor saps around them.

Unlike the young king, Thorn had fought her way to the top against all the odds. Born to a teenaged single mum in the shadow of a defunct Welsh steelworks, she succeeded in leaving school with enough GCSEs to get herself a job on the local paper. A fast learner and hard worker, in a little over ten years she moved from small-town newspaper to national TV station and became a prime-time newsreader. But the illusion of power was not enough for Thorn – she wanted the real thing. So she moved into politics, trading her charm and fame for a place in Parliament. Her tough start in life had made her determined and resourceful. It had also made her ruthless, as her rivals for the party leadership found out soon after.

The prime minister snatched another glance at her watch and took a sip of tea, grimacing. It matched her mood, cold and sour. Her weekly audience with the king was supposed to have started twenty-five minutes ago. As usual she would brief the monarch on what her government was doing, pretend to be interested in his silly questions, and then leave as fast as possible. She hated taking up so much of her precious time on such a ridiculous tradition, especially when it meant talking to some *child*. A feckless boy who was yet to be on time for even one of their meetings. Among the prime minister's advisors, the new king had earned the nickname "Alfred the Late".

Thorn sighed and once again shuffled through the papers on her lap. Most of it was the usual humdrum government business: the economy and taxes, new roads and hospitals. And then there was the other, more *unusual* stuff. Thorn's day had begun with a five a.m. briefing deep in the bowels of Ten, Downing Street by sombre-suited security experts about their hunt for what they liked to call "Exceptional Individuals". The prime minister had rolled her eyes at their jargon.

"You mean superheroes?" she had snapped, motioning for someone, anyone, to pour her another cup of coffee. "Let's call it like it is."

Standing in front of the briefing screen, Agent Fulcher nodded. She was, the prime minister decided, the most breathtakingly ugly woman she had ever seen. Not that she'd ever say that to her face, because Fulcher looked like she could crush walnuts with her bare hands. Next to her, Agent Turpin, small and oily in his neat, dark suit, smiled.

"Yes indeed, Prime Minister, sir ... er, madam. Super, ahem, heroes." Turpin grinned.

"Well, then, have you found them?"

"No," said Fulcher.

"Yes," said Turpin.

"Which is it?" the prime minister asked through gritted teeth.

"Sort of," Fulcher mumbled. "Not really."

"Shut up," Turpin hissed under his breath to his partner.

The prime minister exhaled, long and hard. First meeting of the day and already she had a headache. The security services had been given millions of pounds in extra funding to help track down and capture these super-freaks, and this was the best they could come up with? After the "fireworks" at Westminster Abbey three months ago, the country was still in a collective mental meltdown that superheroes could even exist. Every day across Britain, new sightings of the "Defender" and the "Black Dragon" were being reported. According to Turpin and Fulcher, 99.9% were "fakes, frauds and people just seeing things", which seemed to be true. Whoever these magical beings were, there hadn't been a confirmed sighting since the coronation. But the prime minister was still under constant pressure to provide answers. Who were they? What kind of threat did they pose? But what really bothered Thorn was the thought that she had struggled all these years to reach the top, only to find out that, when it came to them, her power was meaningless. What good was it being prime minister if a bunch of superheroes could fly around doing whatever they pleased? She would not rest until she had hunted down and destroyed every last one of them, starting with that absurd white knight.

"Prime Minister, His Majesty will see you now."

The gaunt frame of the Lord Chamberlain had appeared at a doorway, smoothing down his thin, grey hair. He was red-faced and flustered, like he'd just run to meet her. The prime minister smiled, as courteously as she could muster, and followed him to the king's study. As much as she would have loved to ask if the clocks still worked at the palace, it just wasn't the done thing.

Alfie sat at his father's old desk, out of breath, pretending to finish a letter. The prime minister swept in.

"Your Majesty," said Thorn, giving the shallowest of curtseys.

"Oh, hi. Sorry for the wait, PM. Stacks of

paperwork, you know how it is! So what's new?" said Alfie, doing his best to act natural.

Expertly hiding her disdain, Thorn smiled and passed him a folder. "I thought I should bring you up to speed on the search for the so-called Defender. Here is the latest, such as it is."

Alfie opened the folder to see a cheesy school photograph of Hayley, scowling at the camera, her hair pulled tight into bunches. He burst out laughing.

"Something amusing, Your Majesty?" asked the prime minister.

Alfie swallowed hard. *Play it cool*, he thought, *she has no idea*. "No, no. Just remembered a funny joke. Um, who is she?"

"Hayley Hicks. A runaway from some grotty estate. We suspect she is the key to understanding all of this, but she has gone to ground."

"You're so right," Alfie said out loud without meaning to, thinking of the warren of secret chambers and halls beneath the Tower of London. "I mean, where could she be?" he added, pretending to think long and hard about it.

"Rest assured, we have our best people working on it," the prime minister lied, thinking of Turpin and Fulcher.

She drew Alfie's attention to the next picture, this one of Hayley's gran, sitting on a bench outside the Whisper Grove Rest Home. It was a long-lens surveillance shot and Alfie reminded himself to warn Hayley about it before she tried to visit her.

"We hoped to find the girl through her grandmother," continued Thorn. "But the poor dear's rather lost her marbles, so she was carted off to this dreary place."

Alfie tried not to let his irritation show. Hayley's gran was one of the loveliest people he'd ever met and he hated Thorn saying something so insensitive.

"Can't be easy without any leads," said Alfie, handing back the folder. "Especially when you're so busy trying to improve the lives of all the people living in those estates and old folks' homes," he added.

Thorn flinched, then forced a smile. "There was one other item of business, Majesty. Have you given any thought to my idea for a royal tour?"

"Oh yeah, it's top of the agenda," Alfie said, trying to dredge up the details from his memory of their last meeting. Something about travelling the country to let the people meet their new king. It wasn't exactly a trip to get excited about.

"The public's memory is surprisingly short," the prime minster said, picking imaginary fluff from the cuffs of her jacket. "Take it from me. Your ordeal during the coronation no doubt endeared you to the country. But, since then, well, forgive me, but you've been rather inactive and the press are beginning to get restless."

The last thing Thorn really wanted was for the king's popularity to grow. In fact she was confident that he would make a fool of himself every time he stepped outside the palace, which is precisely why she had suggested the tour. As prime minister, she could not openly argue for an end to the monarchy, but that's exactly what she hoped to see one day.

Alfie stood up. "I'll think about it, Prime Minister. Promise."

"Your Majesty."

As soon as Thorn was gone, the Lord Chamberlain came in through another door. He'd obviously been listening in.

Alfie kicked his shoes off and breathed a sigh of relief. "Well, that was as much fun as ever."

"You did well, Your Majesty. But please do try not to antagonize her. The prime minister may be a trifle plain-spoken, but she can help you read the public mood."

"I'll try my best," conceded Alfie.

"She is a sharp young woman," continued LC. "If she picked up any hint of your superhero identity, she would surely hunt down the truth like a bloodhound savaging a fox."

"You have such a way with words, LC."

"Why, thank you, Majesty," smiled the old man.

"He's taking the mickey, you daft old coot," laughed Brian as he strolled in polishing off a bacon sandwich.

"Really, King's Armourer, this is a royal palace, not some roadside cafeteria," sniffed LC. "And I am not happy with His Majesty's unauthorized excursion last night. You're supposed to be his protection officer. Kindly stop him!"

"He was hard enough to keep track of before he had his own magic flying horse," Brian shot back.

Alfie waved at them, annoyed. "Hello? I am still in the room, you know."

"Then answer me one more thing, Majesty, before the royal bath. Are you supposed to be a lion or a giraffe?" LC asked.

Alfie looked blank until Brian indicated he check

his face. Alfie wiped a finger across his cheek and saw he'd spent the entire time talking to the Prime Minister of the United Kingdom with an orange-and-black face.

"Hayley, you are so dead," Alfie muttered.

4

KEEPER OF THE KING'S ARROWS

"May you never die a Yeoman Warder!"

Chief Yeoman Warder Seabrook raised his cup to the three new beefeaters as the walls of the Keep echoed with the reply of the spectators:

"MAY YOU NEVER DIE A YEOMAN WARDER!"

A throaty cheer went up as the fresh recruits had their hands shaken and backs slapped by their new colleagues. The ceremony had taken place once already that day, top-side on the sun-drenched Tower Green, for the benefit of the tourists and press. The three long-serving soldiers, two men and one woman, had sworn their oaths of loyalty to king and country and been officially appointed "Yeoman Warders of His Majesty's Palace and Fortress the Tower of London". But this, down in the Keep with only the beefeaters, the king, Lord Chamberlain and King's Armourer, plus Hayley, looking on, was the real deal – the secret investiture. Or the "after party", as Brian liked to call it.

Alfie chuckled to himself as the new recruits gazed around the vast underground hall, its walls draped with tapestries depicting the *real* history of the United Kingdom, Defenders from through the ages doing battle with all manner of super-villains and monsters. It wasn't so long ago that he had stood where they stood now, full of disbelief and wonder.

"Interestingly the Yeoman's oath does not derive from any concern about dying in combat," droned LC, "but rather an historical quirk to do with their pay—"

"Which you've told us about before, LC," interrupted Alfie.

"Not that this is boring or anything," added Hayley, "but don't you think it's time we got this party started?"

She took out a small silver remote control and pressed a couple of buttons. Suddenly the lights dimmed and a glitter ball descended from the ceiling, filling the Keep with strobing lights. Loud pop music blared from hidden speakers. The Yeoman Warders cheered once more and started to dance with alarming enthusiasm. The Lord Chamberlain clamped his hands over his ears as his face began to flush purple. "Wh-wh-what is THIS?" he spluttered.

"Modifications," shrugged Hayley, retreating to a safe distance.

A little while later, most of the beefeaters had decided to take a break from the dance floor and wage all out war on the buffet, filling their beards with pastry crumbs. After the main scrum had moved on, Alfie approached the table and picked up a lonely-looking sausage roll. But as he raised it to his mouth, it was plucked from his fingers by a raven.

"Hey, that's mine!" cried Alfie.

But the big black bird hopped under the table, where she gobbled the sausage roll down in one gulp. Yeoman Eshelby, the Ravenmaster, rushed over and shooed her away.

"Get out of it, Gwenn!" He turned to Alfie and

bowed. "Sorry, Majesty. That one thinks she's a human. Untrainable."

"No problem," laughed Alfie. "Ravens have to eat too."

Sausage-stealing aside, Alfie liked how the ravens were given free run of the Tower of London. Shortly after he had first arrived in the Keep, Alfie learned that the big, black birds were not just there for show. The Yeoman Warders took the ravens' mystical bond with the Tower very seriously. At least six birds had lived here ever since it was first built, and according to legend if they ever left then the Tower and kingdom would fall. Alfie had laughed when he first heard that – how could a few birds decide the fate of the whole kingdom? But Yeoman Eshelby had shown him that the ravens' wings were not "clipped" as it said in the official Tower guidebooks. In fact they could fly just fine and were free to leave any time they liked. They simply chose not to.

"Why not?" Alfie had asked.

"No one knows, Majesty. But if you ask me, ravens are just as smart as people. And just as loyal," the Ravenmaster had replied with a friendly wink.

More ravens were flapping towards the buffet. Seeing that he was outnumbered, Alfie left them to it and strolled past a group of Yeomen Warders huddled around a television in one corner. It was showing the Wimbledon Tennis Championships and the opening match of the big British hope, feisty young Kate Robertson.

Meanwhile Hayley was trying to tempt Herne out from beneath the ops table with a carrot stick. "Come on, you stupid mutt. You're going to like me one day, even if it kills me."

The silver-grey dog growled and bared his fangs. Alfie strolled over and whistled. Herne crawled out and trotted to his side, licking his hand. "What can I say, Hales? He's just a good judge of character. Or maybe it's because he's not a vegetarian."

"You'll see," said Hayley, crunching the carrot stick herself.

The music stopped and the lights came up. Brian clinked a glass to get everyone's attention. "Now that our merry band of beefeaters is back to full strength, there's one more loose end needs dealing with. And I'm sorry to say Yours Truly drew the short straw, so listen up."

Everyone exchanged worried glances. Brian looked deadly serious.

"The ancient rules of this place are clear. No

civilian without a formal position can reside in the Keep. Therefore, Miss Hicks. . ."

Gasps rippled through the hall. All eyes turned to Hayley. Could he really be talking about throwing her out?

Alfie stepped forward. "Brian, you can't—"

"I'm sorry, sir," replied Brian. "Rules is rules."

Hayley put her hand on Alfie's arm. "It's OK," she said. "I knew it couldn't last." Hayley turned to the assembled Yeoman Warders and did her best to smile. "Don't worry, I'll keep my mouth shut. Well, see ya, I guess."

The Yeoman Warders parted, heads bowed, as Hayley sloped past them towards the doors. Alfie looked around for LC – he couldn't let this happen! But the old man was nowhere to be seen.

"Hold up, miss!" bellowed Brian. Hayley turned back. "I ain't finished yet. No civilian without a formal position can reside in the Keep, *therefore* we have decided to reinstate an ancient post not held since the reign of Henry the Fifth."

Brian marched over to Hayley and handed her a long scroll.

"Miss Hayley Hicks of Watford, I hereby appoint you Keeper of the King's Arrows."

"Arrows? What arrows?" asked Hayley.

The Yeoman Warders giggled as behind them a curtain rose and a long metal rack filled with longbows and hundreds of arrows was wheeled in. Excited, Hayley took one of the bows from the rack. It was taller than she was.

"Sweet."

"That's a war bow. Made from an ash tree. But you'd be better off training with a half-sized one," Brian said.

"Nah. I can handle this big boy," Hayley replied.

She levelled the longbow and tried to draw back the string, but it was so stiff she could barely move it.

Brian laughed and slapped her on the shoulder. "Don't worry, we'll work on it. Now, the post comes with your own quarters in the Tower, so no more kipping on the sofa for you. Oh, and a uniform."

Yeoman Box, a female beefeater who had taken Hayley under her wing over the last few months, came forward with a red-and-black tunic complete with Tudor bonnet. "Looks like you're one of us now, love," she beamed.

Hayley, looking more flustered than Alfie could ever remember, took the uniform and brushed a tear from her eye.

"Thanks, Brenda. I don't know what to say," she whispered.

"Say yes!" shouted Alfie.

Hayley laughed. "Yes!"

The Yeoman Warders cheered and gathered round to congratulate her. She even let Alfie give her a quick hug.

"Nice threads," he said, admiring her new gear.

"Yeah, well, the longbow's cool. But I'm not wearing this. Seriously, you can't make me."

The ravens were fluffing up their feathers as they settled down to sleep and the party was winding down. Hayley had gone to check out her new room, which was at the top of a small spiral staircase from the Keep, and Brian was packing away the longbow rack. Alfie noticed candles burning inside the Training Arena and came in to find the Lord Chamberlain contemplating the shrine to the fallen Yeoman Warders. He had almost forgotten that the only reason they were having the party at all was because three new Yeoman Warders had been needed, replacements for those killed by the Black Dragon during Professor Lock's escape. The faces of the fallen smiled at him from their photos, each proud in their uniform, the very picture of loyalty. A loyalty that had cost them their lives.

"There is something I am missing." The old man's voice was quiet, like it was a thought he hadn't intended to say out loud.

"Like what, LC?"

LC bowed his head to the shrine, and crossed to a low stone table near the regalia cabinet. On it lay the dragon bones recovered from Lock's secret chamber at Harrow School. Curled up, as if sleeping, the creature was still huge. Even in death, its angular eye sockets and vicious teeth had the power to turn you cold with fear.

"The professor must have found a way to awaken the dragon magic using the power of Alfred's crown. But all our tests showed that there was no trace of the creature left in his body after the battle at Westminster Abbey."

"Maybe the tests got it wrong?" said Alfie.

LC rubbed his grey chin. He looked weary. "Perhaps, Majesty. But then why wait so long to transform into the Black Dragon again? He could have escaped at any time. Something does not add up."

Alfie didn't like seeing him so glum. LC might

be an annoying old pain in the neck most of the time, but he had stuck by Alfie and believed in him when no one else did, including himself.

"I wish Lock hadn't escaped. But at least he's gone now," said Alfie. "He wouldn't dare come back after what happened. We should forget about him."

LC covered the dragon bones with a cloth and chuckled.

"Why are you laughing?" asked Alfie. "You never laugh. Stop it. It's weird."

"I was just thinking, Majesty, about the wonderful optimism of youth." And suddenly his face was grim and lined with worry once more. "If history teaches us anything, it is that men like Cameron Lock do not simply go away. We must be on our guard."

RAIDERS

Roderick "Sultana" Raisin squelched towards his cottage on the Holy Island of Lindisfarne and glanced down the line of rough wooden poles that marked the route known as the Pilgrim's Path through the sand back to the mainland. It never ceased to amaze him how fast the sea came in here, cutting the island off from England for hours at a time. Every other month or so, some dozy tourist would ignore the big yellow warning signs at either end of the causeway and wind up with their car six feet underwater and a coastguard rescue, if they were lucky. When Sultana had first arrived on Holy Island years ago, the sea used to scare him. It still did, if he was honest. It was just so . . . indifferent. The sea didn't care if you were stuck in the sand; it came in all the same, uncontrollable. Back at the Tower of London, where he used to be stationed, the Yeoman Warders' barracks were ordered and neat, just the way he liked it. But, out here in this lonely outpost, if the sea wasn't trying to drown you it was keeping you awake, roaring through the night, washing in boat wrecks and strewing the beach with rusty rubbish like a monster spitting out the unwanted bones of its latest victim.

Sultana reached the safety of the island and stopped to catch his breath. His daily race against the sea was good exercise, but he was a heavy-set man and getting on a bit now. He peered through his binoculars at the glinting lights of the distant mainland and sighed. *If I wanted to live this close to the water, I'd have joined the Navy,* he thought for the hundredth time and fumbled in his pocket for his house keys.

"Evening, Rod," said Trisha Harald as she rattled down the lane on her bike. She was the landlady of the Ship Inn, on her way to open up for the evening. "Darts tonight, remember?"

"Wouldn't miss it for the world," he replied.

"Looks like it might be a big one blowing in!" Trisha shouted back as she peddled off, the wind whipping her words away.

Sure enough, a storm was gathering in the east, the skies behind the turrets of Lindisfarne Castle were as black as pitch and the sea was rough and rolling. *You sprung up quick,* thought Sultana, gazing at the bank of clouds, puzzled. It had all the making of an "earplug night"; you hadn't heard wind until you'd spent a night on Holy Island during a force ten northwester. Back inside his cozy fisherman's cottage, Sultana drew the curtains and put the kettle on.

"Now, then, Imp, how are you? Been keeping lookout?" he chuckled.

Imp was his tabby cat, who spent all day on the windowsill watching the sea and purring. And she was the only other living creature who knew what Sultana was really doing on Lindisfarne. As far as everyone on the remote island was concerned, he was just plain old Rodney, ace darts player and not particularly brilliant local fisherman. But Sultana didn't even like fish. *They don't call us beefeaters for nothing,* he was fond of saying to himself. In truth, he was one of the "Burgh Keepers", a secret band of semi-retired Yeoman Warders stationed up and down the coast of Britain – an undercover early-warning system, working for the Defender of the Realm.

Checking over his shoulder like he always did to make sure no one was spying on him, Sultana stepped into the kitchen's small pantry and twisted a fake tin of baked beans around. A hidden door slid open to reveal a small, windowless room beyond. Sultana stepped through and hung up his binoculars on a peg next to a faded "Spotters' Guide to Monsters" poster. It showed the silhouettes of all kinds of horrible creatures that had attacked Britain in the past – sea monsters, giants, dragons and more – and how to identify them. As a Burgh Keeper, it was Sultana's job to watch the skies and seas for anything unusual and report back to the Lord Chamberlain at the Keep.

At the centre of the cramped, musty space was a strange little brass instrument on a wooden stand, like a cross between a compass and an old-fashioned light fitting. It was called a sortilegic meter and it monitored ley lines: the invisible tracks of magical energy that crisscrossed Britain like veins under the skin of a body. Every Burgh Keeper in every secret watch house across Britain had a meter. If any supernatural monster crossed one of the ley lines or even passed nearby, it would set off the closest meter's alarm like a tripwire.

That was the theory anyway. In reality, in all the years Sultana had done his duty as the Lindisfarne Burgh Keeper, his sortilegic meter had never made so much as a peep. In his days as a beefeater back at the Tower of London, he'd seen his fair share of action, including fighting alongside the late King Henry, Alfie's dad, against an army of seventeenth-century zombies under the streets of London. Everyone said he'd enjoy his retirement as a Burgh Keeper, but truth be told it was all too quiet for Sultana. Every Christmas, he would travel down to the Tower of London and have a drink with all the other Burgh Keepers from across the country and listen jealously as they swapped their latest war stories. Kenny "Kettle" Davies stationed up in Loch Ness was always busy, what with the famous local monster regularly setting off his alarm. And Phil "Talc" Powder out on the Suffolk coast had once seen Black Shuck, the legendary ghost dog which haunted that part of the country. Talc loved to boast about it and even called it "the famous Battle of Blythburgh", but Sultana hadn't seen it in any of the official histories yet. Still, the fact was his mates had all had cause to pick up their pikes in retirement, while all Sultana had done was patrol the windswept island, watch his silent meter and drink tea.

Imp snaked around Sultana's legs, purring. She wanted feeding.

"Come on then, you."

Riiiiiiiiing!

Sultana spun around, trying to place the sound. Had he set his alarm clock by accident? What on earth could it be? The sortilegic meter! He scrambled into the secret room and stood, gawping, barely believing his eyes. Sure enough, the meter's hammer was smacking back and forth between the shrill little brass bells. Fear mixed with excitement trickled down his spine like ice water. Sultana took a deep breath and grabbed his halberd, a kind of axe on a pole that was leaned up against the wall. He ran his finger across it, checking it could still do some damage, but remembered he hadn't sharpened it in a long while.

Riiiiiiiiiing!

No time. Sultana shrugged at Imp.

"Sorry, petal, dinner will have to wait!"

And with that, Sultana sprinted out of the cottage, into the storm.

Back at the Keep, Alfie was just about to head back to the palace and bed when the alarm went off. A light was flashing on the north-east coast of the ops table map.

"Holy Island, Lindisfarne burgh," Yeoman Box relayed. "Fifty-five degrees, forty seconds north; one degree, forty-eight seconds west," she added, pushing a miniature Defender counter up the east coast of Britain on the massive map.

"Duty calls, Majesty," LC replied, looking at Alfie. "I think you'd better suit up."

Alfie slipped the Shroud Tunic over his head and the Defender armour enveloped his body in a second. He couldn't help smiling. This was his first combat mission since the battle at the coronation, and his stomach was knotted with excitement. He barely had to murmur the word "Spurs" and Wyvern sprang out, bearing him out of the Keep and into the night, streaking up in a powerful climb, as fast as a fighter jet. Wisps of cloud streaked past Alfie's head like someone had set the world in super fast forward. They'd be at their destination in minutes.

LC's voice crackled in his ear. "Sir, we're getting reports of a violent storm ahead."

Alfie scanned the sky. It was a perfect, star-filled summer night. But as the Defender neared his destination he saw that the island was swathed in dark clouds. There was something about the way they swirled and churned that Alfie didn't like. And they weren't just black like normal storm clouds; they were flushed with putrid greens and purples like a nasty bruise.

"Yeah, it's a big one, all right," Alfie replied. "I'll go around and see if I can approach it from another direction— Whoa, WYVERN!"

The Defender's magical horse snorted with derision and plunged straight through the towering thunderheads. Lightning bolts arrowed down as if racing them earthwards, and hailstones battered Alfie's armour like bullets. Before he knew it, they had landed with a *squelch* in the middle of a ruined, rain-wrapped abbey. Wyvern let out a satisfied whinny and disappeared back into Alfie's spurs.

"The Defender has landed," Alfie said weakly,

mentally noting that he needed to have a quiet word with his horse about just who was in charge.

The ferocious storm raged on as he patrolled the crumbling walls, broken columns and empty arcades of the abbey. With the claps of thunder overhead and the lightning flashing off the tall walls, it was a spooky place in a Halloween, trick-or-treat, sort of way, but there didn't seem to be much to be seriously alarmed about here.

"Looks clear," Alfie reported back to the Keep. "Could the storm have set off the alarm?"

Some instinct made Alfie duck, spin around and unsheathe his sword, which glowed with near-phosphorescent light. He just about registered the blade of an axe as it whistled past and buried itself in the ground next to him. Alfie readied his sword to strike back, but the tubby, bearded man in front of him fell to his knees, arms wide.

"Majesty, I'm SO sorry!" Sultana said, shocked, pulling strands of his soaked hair out of his eyes.

"It's all right," Alfie said, catching his breath. He pulled the man to his feet and handed him back his rusty halberd. "I don't think that old thing would have done much damage anyway. You're the Burgh Keeper?"

"Yes, sir. Yeoman Raisin, at your service. They call me Sultana," he said, bowing.

"At ease, Yeoman. Seen anything unusual tonight?"

"No. Not yet. But I'd bet my beard there's something out here," Sultana growled, scanning the dark abbey with keen eyes.

He took a whetstone from his pocket and began to sharpen his halberd with glee. Alfie walked a few feet away and contacted the Keep.

"Nothing going on up here. Just a freak storm and a homicidal Burgh Keeper. I think it might be a false alarm."

"Very well, Majesty." LC sounded relieved. "I have your sister on the line if you wouldn't mind talking to her?"

"Sure," Alfie sighed.

This was another one of Hayley's many improvements to the armour's communications: patching through calls when he was out on duty. Of course, Princess Eleanor would have no idea he was standing in a suit of magical armour in the middle of a ruined abbey. He tried to keep his voice neutral.

"Hey, Ellie. What's up?"

"You haven't replied to my email!" Ellie barked.

"And neither has Richard. You do know what RSVP at the bottom of an invite means, don't you?"

Her birthday party at Windsor Castle was coming up, and she was desperate for her brothers to be there.

"Yeah, El, I'm sorry. I've been a little busy."

"You know who used to say that all the time? Dad."

Blooooooooooo!

The low blast, like an eerie foghorn, shook the ruins around them. Alfie spun around, alarmed. Sultana was standing bolt upright, holding his newly sharpened halberd, at the ready. At first Alfie thought it must have been thunder, but then it came again.

Blooooooooooo!

"What was that?" Ellie said in Alfie's ear. "I thought you hated drum and bass? Do yourself a favour and turn the bottom end down—"

"Sorry, Ellie, got to go!" Alfie said, breaking the connection.

He knew he'd pay for cutting her off next time they spoke, but he had a feeling the Defender's work was not done after all.

Alfie and Sultana crept forward, keeping low behind a ruined wall. On the path ahead a trail of enormous, slimy footprints led up the beach towards a low, modern building with picnic tables arranged outside it. Over the wind, they could just hear the sound of crashes and bangs from inside, as tables and chairs were overturned and windows smashed. A whiff of decay hung in the air, like old eggs, dead fish and off milk all whisked together in a bowl.

"I'd know that niff anywhere. It's the undead," Sultana whispered. "Back in the old days, I fought at the Battle of the London Plague Pits with your father."

Alfie nodded, even though that was yet another event in the Defender's past he'd never heard of.

"That's the gift shop. National Trust," Sultana said, pointing at the building. "They do lovely shortbread," he added, as if it might help.

"I really don't think the undead are going to come here looking for shortbread," Alfie said.

The gift shop door flew off its hinges as five bloated, dead-skinned Vikings emerged, carrying armfuls of new wool blankets, "I Love Lindisfarne" mugs and what looked like packets and packets of shortbread.

"Then again, I might be wrong," Alfie said, astonished.

The undead Vikings were huge and stinking, but

there wasn't that many of them. If they surprised them, Alfie reckoned they might run. But even if they didn't, what kind of Defender would he be if he let them get away with a smash and grab on his turf?

"Hey, you up for a scrap?" Alfie whispered to Sultana.

The Burgh Keeper stuck his chin out, proud. "Let me at 'em, Your Majesty."

"Spurs!" Alfie said and Wyvern emerged beneath him as Sultana looked on, excited.

Alfie drew his sword and kicked the spectral horse into a gallop, aiming for the centre of the small group of Vikings, scattering them like skittles. Up close their stench was overpowering, and they were screaming in surprise and anger in a language Alfie had never heard before.

An axe sliced through the air, but Alfie knocked it aside with his shield and brought the lion-head pommel of his sword down on the top of another Viking's helmet with a *clang* that rang across the beach.

"The gift shop is closed!" Alfie shouted. "Get out of here! Leave!"

Another mammoth undead Viking, half his

face rotted away to reveal the yellowing skull beneath, made a leap for Alfie, but Wyvern saw it coming and kicked him with her powerful hind legs, sending him tumbling backwards. With a yell, Sultana sprang to his side. Wielding his long halberd with skill, he clobbered a Viking on the head and tripped over another with the handle. He had a huge grin on his face. "Wait until I tell old Talc about THIS!"

Alfie had no idea what Sultana was shouting about, but he was more concerned with fending off the axe blows that were raining down on him from all angles. He hoped he hadn't underestimated these undead brutes – they showed no sign of retreating. And then there was the small matter of how to defeat them.

"How do you kill something that's already dead?" Alfie yelled.

Sultana swung his halberd over his head and sliced it through the air. "Cut anything into small enough pieces and it doesn't keep moving for long, sir!"

Blooooooooooo!

The mysterious horn blast echoed across the beach again. Hearing it, the Vikings stopped attacking, turned and ran towards the sea.

"Where are they going?" asked Sultana, disappointed.

They watched the Vikings splash into the sea up to their chests.

BLOOOOOOO!

This time Alfie didn't so much hear the deep horn blast as feel it shake his entire body. Even Wyvern staggered back under the audio assault. Alfie watched astonished as a rotting longship the colour of algae emerged from the sea mist and carved through the surf towards the retreating Vikings, its tattered, wet sails flapping in the wind. At its oars sat two more pairs of undead Vikings. At its serpent-head prow stood Guthrum, blowing into his walrus-tusk war horn, summoning back his raiding party. The Viking lord fixed Alfie with his milky white eyes and grinned, revealing his jagged black-and-yellow scattershot teeth.

On the beach, Wyvern reared up, and Alfie raised his sword above his head in reply. *Whatever, dead bloke. And don't come back.* Together, Alfie and the Burgh Keeper watched the Viking ship turn and disappear beneath the waves, taking the raging storm with it. The rain petered out, the wind dropped and all was suddenly still.

"We showed those dead-uns a thing or two, didn't we, sir!" Sultana said as he sat down heavily on the sand to catch his breath, a huge smile plastered across his face.

Alfie smiled and tossed something into Sultana's lap. A packet of shortbread.

"Don't eat them all at once."

HIDEOUT

Richard was puzzled the first time he received a summons to the professor's study. Lock wasn't one of his teachers, after all. Richard had Mr Ramsden for history, while Lock was Alfie's teacher – there was a policy of keeping the brothers in separate classes, partly, Richard suspected, to stop Alfie being embarrassed at always getting lower grades. So it was with some trepidation and not a little curiosity that he sat down opposite the young professor in his dark, ramshackle room. He waited while Lock skimmed through Richard's latest essay,

"The Dissolution of the Monasteries by Henry the Eighth". Finally Lock tossed the papers on to his desk and leant back, examining Richard with his piercing blue eyes.

"Very good. Clear. Concise. You clearly know your stuff."

"Thank you, sir."

"Of course it's utter fiction."

"What is, sir?"

"Henry the Eighth had nothing against the monks. But when you're trying to hunt down a pack of hibernating werewolves, monasteries are the first place you look. They like the singing apparently – lulls them to sleep."

Richard laughed, then stopped as he saw Lock wasn't joining in. He was staring at Richard with an intense expression.

"The history of the United Kingdom as most people know it is a lie," Lock continued, pushing back from his desk and crossing to an over-stuffed bookshelf. "Churchill's histories of Britain, rubbish." Lock pulled several volumes out and threw them into a bin. He grabbed another book. "AJP Taylor, nonsense! And don't even get me started on this Simon Schama fellow." Another history book flew across the study and hit the wall. "If you want to know the real story of our country's past then I could fill you in, but you must swear not to tell a soul, least of all your brother."

"Alfie? Why not?" asked Richard, still half suspecting this was some kind of joke.

"I don't want to sound unkind, Richard, but your brother has certain ... shall we say, limitations. In you, on the other hand, I see something more. You could have a great future, if you chose to. Shall I show you?"

Richard knew the professor was flattering him on purpose, but he couldn't help feeling pleased and curious. He nodded. Lock opened a cupboard and lifted out a large object covered with a black velvet cloth. He placed it on his desk and removed the cloth to reveal a very old, oval mirror with an ornate silver frame, perched on a heavy wooden stand. The mirror's glass was dark and covered with long scratches.

"A mirror? So what?" Richard was getting annoyed. He hated practical jokes, if that's what this was.

"Patience. It takes a few moments..."

Lock took a tall black candle from a bookcase

and set it down next to the old mirror. He waved his hand over the candle and it seemed to light by itself. The study lights blinked off, again without Lock touching them. Richard wanted to ask how he'd done it, but his words were catching in his throat. If this really was a trick, then it was a good one. The air inside the room suddenly tasted thick and musty, like a newly opened tomb.

"Come and see what could be," Lock whispered, beckoning him.

Richard rose unsteadily on his feet and crossed to the desk.

"I call it my 'seeing mirror'. The ancient alchemists would often use them."

Feeling like any second the professor was going to laugh and tease him for being so gullible, Richard nevertheless leaned down and peered into the speckled glass of the mirror. At first, he couldn't see anything, just his reflection picked out in the candlelight and behind him Lock smiling like he knew a great secret. But the more Richard gazed, the more the reflection of the study seemed to fall away like a stage set being struck; the book-stuffed walls winched up and out to reveal a vast blackness before they were replaced with new walls. The grand interior of Westminster Abbey. A robed figure was kneeling as a priest placed a crown on his head. It was a coronation.

"How did you— Is that my father's coronation?"

Lock didn't need to answer. Because as Richard watched the strange vision in the mirror, the figure wearing the crown stood up, gazing out over his subjects, who chanted, "God save the king! God save the king! God save the king!" In the dark of the study, Richard gasped. It was not a magical recording of his father's coronation. It was *his*. He was the one being crowned king. An event that had not happened. At least, not yet.

The vision faded and Professor Lock placed the velvet cover back over the mirror. Richard stared at him, his mind racing.

"Now perhaps you are starting to believe me," said Lock with a smile. "I have so much more to share with you, Your Highness."

After that, Richard started to visit Professor Lock in secret every night for private tutorials. The teacher laid it all out for him – the true history of the kingdom, how the monsters of myth weren't myths at all, but very real; how kings and queens had wielded immense superpowers ever since

Alfred the Great, the first Defender of the Realm; how they had used them to protect the nation from all manner of supernatural terrors and to wage war overseas. Then he told him how things had gone wrong. How weaker Defenders had lost their nerve, decided to draw back, to reserve their powers for only the most extreme crises; how the Defender of the Realm had become a hidden hero, concealing his or her identity as if it were something to be ashamed of, and how the country and its people had become lazy and ungrateful as a result.

Despite what he had witnessed through the professor's seeing mirror, Richard still struggled to believe any of it. Lock was talking about magic and monsters as if they were everyday things all around them. Richard's dad was supposed to be some kind of superhero. It was ridiculous. And yet the professor spoke with such belief and passion that it was hard to dismiss. Richard decided that the only way he could be sure was to see it for himself. So he hatched a plan.

It was the week before Christmas, and the royal family was staying at Balmoral Castle in the Highlands of Scotland. It had been snowing for days, and the roads had become impassable. But they had more than enough supplies to see them through, and everyone had enjoyed a quiet day indoors playing board games by the fire. One night, Richard sneaked into the porter's lodge and took the keys for his father's Range Rover. Being careful not to spin off the slippery road, he drove it to the lake in the woods where they sometimes had their summer barbecues. The lake was thick with ice and eerily still. Richard turned off the engine and took out his phone. He dialled the direct line for the king's study, where he knew his father would be working.

"Yes?"

"Dad, it's me. I did something stupid," Richard kept his voice fast and breathless just like he'd practised. "I took the car, but I came off the road. I'm on the lake. I think the ice is cracking. Dad, help—" and he hung up.

He turned the engine back on and drove out on to the ice. Two seconds later the car jerked to the side as the ice cracked. Freezing water gushed in around Richard's feet. In moments it was over his knees. The water was already up to the windows outside. The car was sinking fast. Richard thought about unbuckling his seat belt, kicking out the back window and swimming to shore. Even now he was confident he could get out of this, if he acted fast. But no, he had to follow through with the plan. He had to know whether Professor Lock had been telling him the truth. The water was up to his neck now. Richard fumbled for the door but in his panic he couldn't find the handle. The water was past his mouth and still rising. There was no way out. How could he have been so stupid? It was the last mistake he'd ever make—

THUD.

Something heavy landed on top of the car. Richard just had time to close his eyes and fake being unconscious before the roof was ripped aside and he was hauled out. Wind rushed past his face and he had the sensation that he was moving fast, but he stayed limp and kept his eyes shut. The next thing he knew there was a crunch of gravel and he felt himself being laid gently on the ground. A gloved hand touched his face and he heard a low, muffled voice say, "Foolish child. . ." Then he heard the doorbell being rung twice. Only now did Richard open his eyes. What he saw rising away from him and disappearing over the castle roof told him that every word Professor Lock had said was true. It was a translucent horse flying into the air, and astride it sat the Defender – his father.

"*HVAR ER ENGILSMAÐR INN LITILL?*"*

Guthrum's guttural voice echoed around the church's cold catacombs, scattering the image of his father from Richard's mind. It was a relief; he didn't like thinking about him. Guilt flickered somewhere within his chest, but weakly, like a guttering candle near the end of its wick, the memory of a feeling from long ago, when he was still completely human.

In the streets above him, cars rumbled by and people made their way home from a night out, unaware of the evil lurking just beneath their feet. Richard had got used to hideouts like this in the past few months, as Lock kept moving to avoid detection. From the dungeons of ruined castles to the damp cellars of abandoned country houses, Lock had skulked like a fugitive plotting his next move, sending secret messages to Richard at Harrow about where to meet him next. But he had promised that this old church crypt was to be their last hiding

---

* "WHERE IS THE PUNY ENGLISHMAN?"

place. Soon they would no longer need to live in the shadows like animals – or so the professor said.

Exhausted after their skirmish on Lindisfarne, the undead warriors slumped to the floor in the stone passageways and fell into a deep, noisy sleep. Only Guthrum didn't seem to need to recuperate. Ducking his huge frame under a stone arch, the Viking lord tossed several packets of National Trust shortbread at Lock's feet.

*"AUÐ HEITAÐU OSS!"**

With surprising coolness, considering the angry Viking monster looming over him, Lock opened a packet and took a bite. "Mmm, not bad," he said.

Richard watched Guthrum warily as he stamped around them, grumbling and glaring. "What's wrong with him?"

"It appears our friend isn't that impressed with the spoils from his raid," said Lock. "I did try to tell him that Lindisfarne wouldn't be quite how he remembered it a thousand years ago. Not a lot of monks' gold there these days. But Vikings just won't be told."

---

* "YOU PROMISED US RICHES!"

*"Var hvitr riddari á strǫnd,"** Guthrum ranted.

"The white knight?" Lock smiled, and then answered in Guthrum's tongue, explaining to him that it was someone called the Defender, but that he wasn't important.

Guthrum spat on the floor. *"Hestr hans jós miklu hermǫnunnum mínum!"*

"What was that?" asked Richard.

"Something about the Defender's horse kicking one of his men in the backside," Lock laughed. "Stupid Norseman probably deserved it."

"Careful," said Richard. "He might hear."

"Don't worry. Vikings don't understand English – they're pretty thick."

CRUNCH! Guthrum smacked his axe into the floor between them, sending sparks flying past Lock's startled face. The Viking roared a final insult in Old Norse and stormed off to rejoin his men.

"Maybe they understand more than you think," Richard smirked.

The stench of the Viking undead sleeping around them was overpowering that night. It worked its way into Richard's hair and clothes like smoke from a

---

* "There was a white knight on the beach,"

bonfire. Unable to sleep, he paced up and down. He would have to get out of here by dawn and head back to school before anyone wondered where he was. But the idea of having to go back to faking his day-to-day life again filled him with frustration.

"I still don't get why we're messing around with these stinking corpses," he protested to Lock. "Why can't we just deal with the Defender ourselves? I'm ready!"

"*Hafðu við þol,*" Lock replied.

Richard shrugged, more annoyed than ever.

"It means 'have patience', Your Highness. Your time will come."

Richard's eyes flashed red, briefly giving Lock a glimpse of the dragon sleeping inside him. "You'd better be right."

7

BACK TO SCHOOL

Alfie landed in the Training Arena, ruffled Wyvern's mane and recalled her into his spurs. He removed his armour and tossed the Shroud Tunic to Brian, who was waiting by the regalia cabinet.

"What, don't I get a 'well done'?" asked Alfie.

"Just a tick and I'll fetch your medal, sir," said Brian.

"Really?"

"No, not really," Brian guffawed. "Those Vikings didn't scarper because of you, chief. They left because there wasn't anything decent for them to nick."

"Unbelievable. Some people are never happy."

With a frown at Brian, Alfie abandoned the Arena in favour of the Map Room, where he found the Lord Chamberlain poring over the ops table, while Hayley was glued to her laptop. The Yeoman Warders were busy studying screen grabs from the Defender's video feed of the Lindisfarne encounter.

"Not bad, huh?" said Alfie once he realized no one was going to look up. "You know, me, fighting loads of Vikings, driving them into the sea – 'argh, no, it's the Defender, ruuuun!'"

"Yeah, yeah, very impressive," Hayley muttered without looking up.

Herne trotted over and jumped up at Alfie, excited. He scratched the dog's ears. "At least someone appreciates my awesome Viking-butt-kicking skills."

"Actually I think he's just hungry," said Hayley.

"This is no joking matter," said LC. "Those were not ordinary Vikings. They were *draugar*."

"Come again?" said Alfie.

"It means 'again-walkers'. The undead," tutted LC as if it was incredible that Alfie didn't somehow know this already. "There hasn't been an attack like this on British soil for centuries."

"Sheep!" announced Hayley, turning her laptop round for everyone to see.

"I beg your pardon?" said LC, squinting at the news story Hayley had found online.

Hayley continued: "I simply cross-referenced the Viking historical timeline with the locations of all recent burgh alarms, plus every local newspaper report in the last three months."

"But that would take days," said LC, confused.

"Nah, it's just a basic search algorithm," began Hayley before clocking the blank stares of LC and the beefeaters. "Never mind. But look at this – there was an unexplained sheep attack in Suffolk and a graveyard was vandalized – St Mary's, Hadleigh, rumoured to be the resting place of . . . how do you say that name?"

"Guthrum, the Viking warlord," said LC darkly. "A thousand years ago, he led an army south from Scandinavia, and drove King Alfred the Great into exile."

An uneasy hush descended over the Keep, as if a long-forgotten nightmare had suddenly been remembered.

"But . . . that could be a coincidence, couldn't it?" said Alfie.

LC was looking at the photos of the graveyard, the great hole in the ground where Guthrum's longship had been unearthed.

"I fear there is nothing accidental about this, Majesty," he said. "Guthrum and his raiding party were exhumed for a reason. By someone who knew how, and who wasn't afraid to do it."

"It's that traitor, Professor Lock," snarled Brian, joining them in the Map Room. "He likes digging up stuff he shouldn't."

Alfie looked to the Lord Chamberlain, hoping he would say it wasn't true, but the old man was staring into space, deep in contemplation. *Could Lock really be striking back so soon?* he wondered. Alfie had already defeated the Black Dragon once, at the coronation, and even then only just. The truth was he didn't know if he could do it again, especially not if Lock had an army of mad Vikings backing him up.

"Why can't it just be a one-off?" pleaded Alfie. "Bunch of Vikings got bored being dead, made some trouble, got a smackdown Defender-style? Why does everything have to be part of some big conspiracy?"

"Put an alert out to all Yeoman Burgh Keepers," LC ordered the beefeaters. "Double all patrols and report back any supernatural readings, no matter how small. We shall soon see if this was an isolated event, or . . . something else."

As the beefeaters flew into action, Alfie slumped on the sofa, next to Hayley.

"Something smells fishy," she said.

"Yeah, LC seems to think so," replied Alfie.

"No, I mean something really does smell of fish," she said, sniffing his shoulder. "I think it's you, Alfie."

Alfie sniffed his T-shirt. Sure enough it reeked of undead Viking. "Eww. How does it get through the armour?"

Alfie said goodnight, made his way to the secret underground carriage and sped back to his bedroom at the palace. He threw his clothes in the bin, took a twenty-minute hot shower and went to bed. The next morning, after a restless night and another steaming-hot shower, Alfie decided he needed a change of scene. He wanted to see a friendly face and talk to someone who knew nothing about superhero battles and Viking zombies and evil dragons. He would go to see Richard.

Mist clung to the clock tower like a warm duvet as Alfie made his way up the familiar steps of Harrow's

Old School Building. A first-former wearing a straw boater hat yelled an "Excuse me!" as he ran past, late for class. Alfie was surprised how good it felt to be back here. A few months ago he would have given anything to escape school – he had even called it "the Prison". But although being the Defender was exciting and fun – apart from when some horrible monster was trying to kill him – he sometimes missed how much simpler life had been when he was at school.

The downside of going back to his old school was having to see the headmaster to talk about his GCSE exams. Because according to the Lord Chamberlain it wasn't enough to be king AND the Defender at the same time. No, Alfie was also expected to know that $E=MC^2$ and that the Latin word for "spoon" was . . . OK, he had no idea what that was. So Alfie pretended to listen as the headmaster waffled on about study schedules and private tutoring – he couldn't help finding it funny how much nicer Mr Lang was to him now that he was, well, king. But it was worth putting up with for the chance to find his brother. Whatever grudge Richard was still bearing, he felt sure he could make it up to him.

After half an hour (that felt much longer), Alfie

escaped the headmaster's study. *Right, time to find Richard—* A large, sweaty hand landed on his arm.

"Hi, Alfie!"

Alfie recoiled on seeing the hand's owner smiling at him. It was Sebastian Mortimer, the overgrown thug who had made Alfie's life hell from his first day at Harrow School: the meathead he had finally put in his place by hurling him across the lunch table using some of his Defender skills. Surely Mortimer didn't want to reboot his bullying campaign against Alfie?

"Mortimer! Er ... hi," gasped Alfie.

"What are you doing here?" asked Mortimer, still grinning like a happy idiot.

"Exam chat with Lang. Well, nice to see you, Seb..." Alfie hurried off, but Mortimer kept pace with him like an over-friendly, giant puppy.

"The thing is, Alfie, mate, I wanted to say sorry for, you know, giving you such a hard time before."

Alfie was astonished. "You? Wanted to say sorry? To me?"

Either Mortimer had had some sort of brain transplant, thought Alfie, or else he was one of those shallow people who couldn't help sucking up to him now that he was king.

"Seriously, Alfie. I have seen the error of my ways. Look at this!"

Mortimer shoved his lapel towards Alfie. On it was a shiny silver badge in the shape of the school crest with the words HOUSE CAPTAIN printed on it. Alfie felt like he should say something encouraging to mark his former enemy's miraculous transformation.

"OK, then. Um, keep up the good work!" said Alfie, quickening his pace towards his brother's boarding house.

As he glanced back, he saw Mortimer actually giving him a cheery thumbs up. *Wow*, thought Alfie, *maybe people really can change.*

Alfie knew that seeing Richard might be awkward, but he was still excited as he took the steps to his brother's room two at a time. They would make up and then it would be just like the old days, sharing palace gossip, having a laugh together, brothers reunited. Alfie knocked on the bedroom door and tried to open it.

"Rich? It's me—"

It was locked. *That's weird*, thought Alfie. His brother never locked his door. He rarely even closed it. Alfie knocked again.

"Are you in there? It's Alfie."

Alfie pressed his ear to the door. He couldn't hear anything, but he had the weirdest feeling that someone was on the other side. Checking that no one was passing by in the corridor, Alfie took the Ring of Command out of his pocket and slipped it on to his finger. Brian had given it to him at the palace that morning "just in case" and told him not to tell the Lord Chamberlain. He was surprised that Brian was breaking the rules by letting him keep a piece of the regalia on him outside of Defender missions. But Alfie figured that seeing as he had it, he might as well use it. He pointed the sapphire-and-ruby-encrusted ring at the metal of the door's lock and closed his eyes. *I hope this is made from British steel*, thought Alfie, as he focused his mind, channelling his thoughts through the ring, "commanding" the bolts to slip back into the door. With a gentle *click*, the door swung open.

Alfie stepped into the small, neat bedroom. Unusually neat, it occurred to him. Where were the piles of muddy rugby boots? The scattered books? His brother might be an overachiever, but no fourteen-year-old boy was this tidy. The bed didn't even look slept in. Maybe he'd had an away match against another school. The only thing out of place was the window, which was wide open, creaking in the soft breeze. Alfie stepped over to it and gazed outside. He could see a class under way in the art department across the lawn. Of course, that was it. It wasn't quite break time yet; *Richard must still be in lessons*, thought Alfie.

He wasn't.

Richard had been inside his room when Alfie had arrived. He had heard his brother calling out for him. Part of him had wanted to open the door and talk to his brother: to act like everything was normal and pretend that he wasn't living a double life, plotting Alfie's downfall. But playing the good, loyal brother had become harder and harder over the last few weeks. Every smile he had willed himself to fake and every laugh he had forced himself to share tasted bitter in his mouth. So he had avoided seeing Alfie as much as he could, had stopped answering his calls and texts. What was the point in pretending, when Alfie's fate was already sealed? Richard would sweep him aside the same way he had their father. But not yet. Lock had been very clear about that – their plan required Alfie to stay in place for a little while longer, just until they were ready to strike. So when he had heard the knock at the door and Alfie's voice outside, Richard had climbed out of the window, transformed into the Black Dragon and flown up on to the boarding house roof.

Perched there now in the mist, like an oversized gargoyle, the Black Dragon gazed down. He could just see the top of Alfie's head as his brother leaned out of the window. How easy it would be to take him by surprise, to finish it here and now. Lock would be angry, but so what? He wasn't the one who had been humiliated at the coronation. He hadn't lived in someone else's shadow his entire life, the way Richard had. His thoughts were different when he was the Dragon – less human and more primal, devoid of conscience or empathy for anyone else. The Dragon's mind was that of a predator. He felt his claws release themselves from the roof and, before he knew it, he was diving down head first towards Alfie. The Black Dragon's mouth opened, fire gathering in his throat. Fire that would extinguish his brother and give him the revenge he craved.

Alfie felt himself being grabbed from behind and pulled back into the room. Outside, the Black

Dragon saw his brother disappear from the window. It jolted him back to his senses for a moment. What was he doing? If he killed Alfie now their plan would be ruined. He banked away from the building, swooping back up to the cover of the roof before anyone could see him.

For a second, Alfie thought Mortimer had hunted him down again. But then he saw who it was. "Tony! Where did you come from?"

Alfie's friend gave him a tight hug, beaming with excitement. "I spotted you from art. So I told Mrs Fry I was going to be sick and ran out to see you!"

Tony's real name was Hong-xian but like most of the Chinese boys at the school he had adopted a Western name when he arrived in England. He was the only one of Alfie's fellow pupils who had never seemed to care that Alfie was a member of the royal family. Everyone else had either been nasty, or too nice, or just didn't know what to say to him. Tony, however, seemed to like Alfie just because he was Alfie. Tony never failed to make him laugh, usually because he was on another planet and would say random things like:

"I found a dead owl behind the science block last night. I put a hat on it. Want to see?"

"Wouldn't want to miss that," said Alfie. "Hey, have you seen my brother today?"

"Richaramus?" said Tony – he liked to add bits to people's names, Alfie had no idea why. "Nah, I keep out of his way these days. He's been a grumpy-pants since he came back. He's not still mad at you, is he?"

"Maybe. I don't know. I just wanted to see him," said Alfie.

He thought about leaving a note for his brother, but then he'd have to explain how he'd got into his locked room. Besides, Tony was pulling him out, chattering away. Alfie laughed as, behind his back, he swiftly passed his ring finger over the lock, commanding it to slide shut.

"This place has been so boring without you, Alfie-bet. Are you back for good?"

"Afraid not, Tony. I'm kind of busy these days, remember?"

"Whatevs. So, this owl, I'm thinking of calling it Hootenanny. Either that or Monsieur Midnight."

Two minutes later, Richard pulled on a fresh shirt and watched from his window as Alfie and Tony crossed the quadrangle below, laughing together. *He has no idea of what's coming*, thought Richard. *No idea at all*.

EYES DOWN

The drawbridge over the moat had been the Tower of London's main entrance for over seven hundred years. But it wasn't the only way in and out of the ancient fortress. By Hayley's reckoning, there were at least another three secret entrances that she'd heard about from Brenda. Yeoman Brenda Box had been one of the first-ever female beefeaters, and it had taken a while for some of the older, stuffier Yeomen to accept her. But she had served her time in the army, just like them, and she was tough too – they soon learned not to say anything sexist about women not being suited to some jobs if they didn't want a kick up the backside from Brenda. Her two grown-up daughters had both joined the army too, so when Hayley arrived in the Keep, Brenda couldn't help but act like a mum to her. Usually Hayley hated being treated like a kid by anyone, but with Brenda it was different. She missed her mum and her gran, and although Alfie was her best friend now, it was nice to have a woman to talk to sometimes.

It was Brenda who told Hayley about the secret "sally port", which sounded nice but was in fact a cold, damp, pitch-black tunnel that led from the Keep, all the way under the moat and out of the Tower grounds. While the Lord Chamberlain had said to Hayley that, of course, she was not a prisoner in the Keep, he had made it clear that any unnecessary outings put them all at risk. The government agents who suspected that she knew the Defender's true identity and who had tried to snatch her before the coronation were no doubt still hunting for her. Fortunately Brenda had agreed with Hayley that never seeing her gran again was not an option – she just needed to be careful.

"The Keep is like Swiss cheese," Brenda had

said. "I don't think anyone knows how many secret passageways there actually are."

Hayley shivered as she found the torch app on her phone and shone it into the gloom of the tunnel. She would never admit it to Brenda, but this place gave her the serious creeps. The stones themselves seemed to radiate a nasty chill, the way it felt when you walked down the freezer aisle at the supermarket. It wasn't just the cold down here that got to you; it was the sounds as well. The dull rattle of a distant Underground train shook the tunnel, an old sewer pipe dripped and a rat's squeak echoed. Rodents and dodgy plumbing she could deal with, just as long as she didn't hear—

Werughhhhhhh!

Yep, something like that. Heart thumping, Hayley stopped in her tracks and shone the phone-torch around, but it barely cut a sliver in the blackness. She could not tell whether the ghostly moan had come from behind or in front of her, or somewhere below. She knew, of course, that the Tower was haunted. Not that she'd seen anything herself yet, but the longer-serving beefeaters talked about it in such a matter-of-fact way that she had come to believe it must be true. Whether it was the

Grey Lady – the headless spirit of Anne Boleyn, the "disloyal" wife beheaded by Henry the Eighth; or the crying figures of two young boys – the Princes in the Tower, believed to have been murdered by their own uncle; or even the spectre of a bear, once a resident of the Tower's private zoo, one thing was clear: sooner or later, Hayley was going to run into a ghost. *Just not tonight, please not tonight!* she thought.

Hayley hurried along the tunnel, humming a cheery tune as loud as she could, and trying to not think about the fact that she'd have to come back this way later after she had seen her gran.

She emerged through a secret door on the Merchant Navy Memorial opposite the Tower of London and took in a grateful gulp of hot, polluted air. As she waited for her heart rate to return to normal, she looked around, squinting in the daylight. It was just as Brenda had said it would be; the old war memorial was at the side of the busy Tower Hill Road and there were a few tourists milling around taking pictures, but they didn't see her. Whoever had designed this secret entrance had concealed it brilliantly. If anyone had by chance seen her emerge, it would have looked like she was just stepping out from behind a stone column. The other awesome thing about this sally port (nope, that still sounded silly) was that it was right by the bus stop she needed.

Hayley did her best to look like just another bored teenager hunkered down on the back seat listening to music as she secretly checked out her fellow passengers. None of them looked like a government agent, and the one guy in a suit, who she was slightly worried about, got off at a stop without giving her a second glance.

You're a wanted girl, Hayley, she laughed to herself. *Who'd have thought it?*

But at least Hayley knew what she was up against. Sure, Fulcher was a great beast of a woman, but she looked like she might forget to breathe if someone didn't remind her to. And Agent Turpin was all front; no way was he as smart as he looked. As far as Hayley could tell, their entire plan to catch her was to stake out the old folks' home where her gran lived and wait for her to show up. But today Hayley wasn't going there. Today she was playing bingo.

Max's Mega Bingo Hall was a giant, gaudy temple of greasy food, noisy slot machines and of course, the main event: bingo, played in a vast hall that could fit hundreds of players. The road outside had been turned into a car park of minivans and coaches from all the local old folks' homes, and Hayley easily slipped past the bored-looking security man on the door. Skirting the back of the hall, she bought two cups of tea from the cafe and then found an angle on the massed ranks of grey heads all intently marking their cards.

"Unlucky for some, thirteen!" The bingo caller yawned into the microphone that he was holding far too close to his mouth. "Winnie The Pooh, forty-two."

Hayley's heart leapt – there was Gran, sitting with her back to her, scribbling on her card with a big pen. Her hair had been freshly permed. One of the nurses at the home must have done it specially and something about that made Hayley's heart ache – she used to be the one who would help her gran do that before they went out. There was something else bothering her, but she couldn't put her finger on what it was. Besides, she couldn't hold back any longer. Checking that everyone was still engrossed in the game, Hayley squeezed between the tables and slid into a free seat beside her gran.

"Two fat ladies, eighty-eight." Hayley whispered into Gran's ear.

Gran looked up at her, but frowned, confused. "Have we met before?" she asked.

Tears sprung up in Hayley's eyes. "It's me, Gran."

The old lady's expression suddenly cleared. "Hayley!" Gran beamed, hugging her tight and kissing her cheek. "But what are you doing, child? Do you work here now?"

"No, Gran. Just thought I'd come and check you weren't cheating!" Hayley said, laughing with relief.

As the bingo caller droned on and Hayley's gran marked her card, they spoke non-stop about what she'd been up to: Jackie from across the hall kept borrowing Gran's kettle and forgetting to bring it back. They'd all watched a film together the previous night, or was it last week? But anyway, the sound was too low. Friday they always had fish and chips and it was the best Gran had ever tasted.

"Well, it sounds great. And you're looking amazing," Hayley said. It was true. If anything she'd put on a bit of weight. "Maybe lay off those fish and chip suppers once in a while, though, yeah?"

"Child, when you get to my age, you can eat and drink whatever you bloomin' well please." Gran laughed, and Hayley joined in.

It was just like being back at the flat. But as

Gran dabbed her eyes with the sleeve of her dress, it struck Hayley what it was that had been bothering her. Gran was wearing a baggy orange dress that she had always wanted to throw away.

"I thought you hated this old thing?" Hayley laughed. "You said it made you look like a pumpkin?"

"Don't talk nonsense, Lawrence. You only got it for me yesterday," grumbled Gran.

"Gran, it's me," said Hayley, a bolt of fear lancing across her stomach. Lawrence was Gran's husband, and had been dead for twenty years.

"Lawrence, hush now!" Gran said and smiled. But there was no recognition in her eyes; they'd clouded over again. "Hang on a tickety-tick, I think I've got bingo! BINGO!"

There were some excited shouts from the crowd as Gran raised her hand. Hayley looked at the card and her heart fell. It was like a child had scrawled all over it with their crayons. All the time they'd been talking, Gran hadn't been playing properly at all. A lank-haired employee in a stained Mega Bingo polo shirt sloped over, took the card from Gran with a cursory glance and gave her a new one.

"Yeah, yeah, well done, love. Now you can sail away on that yacht you've always dreamt of," he said, smirking at Hayley like she was in on the joke. It took every ounce of her self-control not to leap up and punch him in the mouth.

Gran was completely lost in the past now, rambling about holidays from years ago as if she had just come home, pets she needed to feed that had long since died, and how she was looking forward to going back to her job as a Tube driver on Monday even though she had long-since retired. After a while, Hayley didn't have the heart to correct her any more. *I've left it too long,* she thought. *I should have been there for her, not hiding out in some medieval castle. And now my gran is gone.* She wiped her eyes dry and looked up to see a figure in a suit heading straight towards her.

"How lovely to see you again, Miss Hicks." Agent Turpin smiled, flashing his sharp-looking teeth.

Hayley sprang from her chair and backed away – straight into the meaty arms of Agent Fulcher. "Where do you think you're going?"

"Get off me!"

Hayley dropped into a crouch and spun a leg against the back of Fulcher's knees, knocking her off balance and forcing her to let go. She reminded herself to thank Brenda later – she'd been giving

Hayley self-defence classes once a week and some of it must have stuck. Hayley leapt on to a chair and sprinted over the tops of the tables, scattering bingo cards, snapping pencils and spilling cups of tea. People shouted at her, but she wasn't stopping. Ahead, the exit Hayley was aiming for was suddenly blocked by a security guard. She changed direction and made for the stage. Maybe there was a fire exit or—

"Just remain calm, everyone!" The bingo caller squealed, sounding anything but.

Hayley barged him out of the way and grabbed the microphone. "Hi, everyone! Can I have your attention please?"

Turpin and Fulcher were striding down the main aisle towards her.

"Put that down, Hayley, and come here. Right now." Turpin ordered, sounding like one of her old teachers.

"Um, these two government agents are here to do a really, really bad thing," Hayley said, ignoring him. The elderly players were intrigued, staring at her. "They're here to shut this bingo hall down. For ever! NO MORE BINGO!"

Uproar. A sweet-looking old lady in a headscarf

stuck out a walking stick and tripped Turpin. He sprawled on the floor as Fulcher trampled over him, straining to get at Hayley. But the central aisle was now full of irate pensioners surrounding the agents, smacking them with handbags and poking them with pencils.

Hayley dropped the microphone, ran to the back of the stage and crashed through a fire exit out into an alleyway. She didn't stop running until she had covered the entire five miles back to the Tower of London. It was only when she was safely back in the frigid dark of the secret tunnel that she let herself relax. She was safe. But there it was again, the ache of sadness deep in her tummy; if it had been hard to see her gran before, it would be impossible now. Then again, if Gran didn't recognize her any more, maybe it didn't make a difference? She felt guilty for even thinking it. And, suddenly, even though she knew she had made new friends like Alfie and Brenda, she felt more alone than she ever had before.

Footsteps in the tunnel ahead. *Seriously? Now is when I have to see my first ghost? I'm trying to have a cry!* Hayley pinned herself into an alcove and turned off her phone-torch. Maybe, if she pretended not to be there, the phantom wouldn't bother her. The footsteps grew closer, followed by a gruff cough. Hayley was just wondering whether ghosts got colds when she peeked out of her hiding place to see Brian hurrying away down the tunnel towards the exit at Tower Hill. Hayley couldn't think why he would need to use her secret exit, but right now she didn't care – she was just relieved he wasn't some headless apparition. She gathered herself and hurried back towards the safety of the Keep.

Meanwhile, sitting in a car opposite the bingo hall, Turpin was peering at his reflection in the rear-view mirror, attempting to rub the imprint of Fulcher's shoe off his face.

"Do I look like a doormat to you?" he hissed at his colleague.

"Maybe," said Fulcher, trying not to laugh. "Anyway, don't worry, we'll get the little brat next time."

"There won't be a next time, numbskull," snapped Turpin. "She's wise to us now. Nah, enough with the girl. What we need to do is go after the big fish."

"What, the Defender? Not likely, mate," said Fulcher. "And even if we found him, how do you reckon we'd catch him? He has got superpowers, you know."

"Yes, I am aware of that, thank you. But how about we start spending some of that lovely money her ladyship the PM's given us? See if we can't buy ourselves something to catch a superhero. . ."

OLD YORK

"This is freaking me out," said Alfie, peeking through the curtains at the fields rushing past outside.

"What is?" asked Hayley, sitting opposite him looking glum.

"Never been on a British train that ran on time before."

Hayley smiled faintly at Alfie's corny joke. But he'd take it; he had been trying to cheer her up all morning without even the hint of a giggle. Alfie could tell she was feeling down about her gran, but he knew better than to push Hayley. She'd talk about it when she was ready. Brian leaned across and pulled the curtain closed, blocking their view. "Sorry, no sightseeing. You ain't here, Hayley, remember?"

They were on board the royal train, which was reserved for ferrying senior members of the royal family to the further-flung parts of the kingdom. The smart, claret-coloured locomotive dubbed *King's Messenger* pulled six luxuriously appointed carriages as they sped north. There was a sitting room with velvet-cushioned sofas and two ultra-high-def televisions, a bathroom with full-sized bath and golden taps, and a large dining room where they had already been served a freshly cooked breakfast. Paintings of hunting scenes, chosen by the late King Henry the Ninth, lined the walls. The carriages were so grand that it felt more like staying in some five-star hotel. Indeed, the extra suspension the coaches were fitted with made the ride so smooth it was easy to forget you were moving at all.

Alfie, however, was nervous. This trip to York had been the Lord Chamberlain's idea.

"We can't just sit back and wait for this band of Viking brigands to strike again!" LC had said earlier, gazing at the ops table in the Keep, deep in thought. "We must take the battle to them."

Reports of possible supernatural activity had trickled in from Burgh Keepers all over the country and there was one good lead: the York burgh had come back with a faint reading at the edge of the Humber estuary where the Rivers Ouse and Trent ran into the North Sea. It could just mean that Guthrum's longship had passed that way as it travelled south from Lindisfarne. Or it could mean that the Vikings had put ashore and gone to ground, lying low somewhere inland.

"The City of York was founded by the Vikings. They used it as a base from which to launch their invasion against Alfred the Great all those years ago," LC said.

By now Alfie was used to hearing tales of his namesake's glorious reign – the first and greatest British monarch. Personally, Alfie thought he'd settle for getting into the top forty.

"If the raid at Lindisfarne is anything to go by," continued LC, "then these undead monsters have long memories; they might be drawn to familiar surroundings. York is as good a place as any to start a Viking hunt."

The plan was to use the cover of a royal visit to the city to see if they could flush them out.

Alfie was going to open a new exhibit at the Jorvik Viking Centre, the popular attraction where hordes of tourists every year got a taste of what it was like to live in a Viking settlement a thousand years ago. For once, Alfie had congratulated LC on his sense of humour, though the old man swore it was a coincidence. Meanwhile, Hayley would get out and about in the city with a portable sortilegic meter and see if she could pick up any supernatural readings. At first, the Lord Chamberlain had been against her going on the trip at all. He didn't see any reason to risk her being spotted by the authorities. But seeing how fed up Hayley was, Alfie had insisted she come along; a break from the Keep would do her good.

Prime Minister Thorn had said she was delighted to hear that the young king had taken up her suggestion to get out there into the country and meet his subjects. Although the second she had put down the phone to the palace, she'd quipped to one of her advisors, "Be a nice change for him to see what it's like to work for a living."

On the train, Brian opened the long leather case at his feet and checked its contents. Nestled in the silk-lined interior was the Shroud Tunic, along with a selection of the regalia – the Great Sword of State, the sceptres and spurs. Alfie was already wearing the Ring of Command.

"Now, remember, boss, when we get there, it's business as usual. Shake a few hands, bit of small talk. But if anything does kick off Viking-wise, then we have everything we need right here."

Satisfied, Brian closed the case and handed it over to two Yeoman Warders, who were dressed in dark suits that looked a size too small for them.

"Oh, and if it's not too much bother," continued Brian, "try to look like you're enjoying yourself."

Alfie sighed. "I'll do my best."

As the train pulled into York station, Hayley leant across, straightened Alfie's tie and punched him on the arm. "Good luck. Don't mess up too much."

"Thanks. You too." Alfie laughed. Then, imitating Brian's gruff voice, he added, "You ain't here, remember."

Hayley flashed her first genuine smile of the day.

A welcoming party of dignitaries was waiting at the station to greet the king. Alfie worked his way down the line, mustering a few polite words for each one. Judging by the lobster-pink colour of some of their bald heads, they'd been waiting in the sun for a while. It still seemed weird to him that anyone would want to meet him in person. What were they expecting? He was just a fourteen-year-old boy. But as LC always reminded him, "It is not you they have come to see, Majesty. It is the Crown." And no, he didn't mean that Alfie was expected to stroll about wearing a crown (which was a relief – those things weigh a ton). He meant the institution of the monarchy; Alfie himself wasn't important, it was what he represented that mattered. Alfie couldn't decide whether that was a compliment or not, but it sort of helped him understand why these people four times his age were so interested in clapping eyes on him.

Hayley, meanwhile, pulled up her hood and slipped off the rear carriage, unnoticed. She darted past the station entrance and hopped on to a waiting bus. The doors closed with a *hiss* and the bus moved forward, but suddenly lurched to a halt again as two police motorbikes swerved in front of it. Hayley's heart raced – had she been rumbled already? But then a fleet of black cars rushed out of the station car park ahead of them, and the police riders moved off. They had just been waiting for the royal visitor to depart. The old woman sitting next to Hayley tutted.

"Flippin' 'eck, why should we wait for the likes

of him? Lad don't do 'owt for us!" she grumbled in a thick Yorkshire accent.

Hayley smiled to herself; she'd tease Alfie about that one later. The bus set off, carrying them over a bridge into the half-timbered heart of old York. She could see the grand towers of the cathedral York Minster ahead as they passed by the medieval walls that still ringed much of the city centre. Minutes later Hayley stepped off the bus and checked her watch. She was under strict instructions to carry out her recce and be back on the train in two hours, or she risked being left behind. That wouldn't be a disaster, but this was the first solo field operation she had been entrusted with, and she wanted to show she could be relied on.

Making sure that she wasn't being watched, Hayley felt inside her hoodie pocket for the little brass box she was carrying. Brian had given her the mobile sortilegic meter on the train and told her to practise using it without looking, so that she wouldn't have to walk around with it in plain sight. It was much lighter and more compact than the ones stationed at each of the burghs. Brian had showed her how to flip the box open, exposing the delicate filament.

"The insides are fragile," he'd said. "Another good reason to keep it in your pocket."

"How does it work?" Hayley had asked.

Brian had shrugged. "Above my pay grade. Some sort of ancient magic thingamajig, I expect."

"Useful. Thanks."

Brian had scowled and continued. "The alarm's been muted, but it'll vibrate like the clappers if it picks up supernatural activity. These mobile jobs have a much shorter range. So you'll need to get quite close before it clocks anything. Best keep sharp."

The last thing the bodyguard had told her was to stick to the oldest parts of the city. LC's theory was that Guthrum and his undead men would feel most comfortable near familiar surroundings, so the older the better. Scanning the cobbled streets around her, Hayley figured that wouldn't be too hard; she'd never seen so many ancient buildings in one place. She flipped the box open inside her pocket, being careful not to touch the filament. The brass under her fingers seemed to warm up a little as the meter went to work.

A tour guide in a fluorescent yellow jacket, brandishing a closed golfing umbrella in the air, bustled past Hayley, followed by a gaggle of camera-wielding tourists. Stopping at the bottom of the steps that led up on to the old city wall, the guide turned to address her group in a shrill voice.

"The so-called Roman walls which surround York were actually mainly built by the Danes after they occupied the city in the year 867. So those Viking scoundrels weren't all bad!"

The tour guide snorted at her own joke. *I bet she wouldn't say that if she met a real one*, thought Hayley, falling in at the back as they headed off along the wall's walkway. She knew she probably wouldn't find anything, but the change of scene was doing her good – she was going to enjoy this, her first real-life monster hunt.

Alfie, meanwhile, was not having half as much fun. He was face-to-face with an ugly, snarling Viking. Luckily it was only a waxwork figure inside the replica Viking-age village at the Jorvik Centre. He was being shown round by the head curator, a bubbly lady wearing her best lilac pashmina and bright red lipstick that didn't match. They had stopped by a pretend blacksmith's, where the Viking model was waiting for his axe to be sharpened. She had just told Alfie at length how every part of the exhibit was the result of extensive research by a team of archaeologists, and was now staring at him with a rather overexcited smile. Brian arched an eyebrow at Alfie. Apparently he was expected to say something intelligent about what he'd just been told. He wracked his brain, but it was difficult to think, what with the pungent smell that seemed to fill the windowless room.

"Where are his horns then?" Alfie asked. "You know, on his helmet. Are they being sharpened too?"

The curator winced.

"Actually real Vikings did not have horns on their helmets, Your Majesty. That's just, er, in the movies."

Brian chuckled, then coughed to cover it up. Alfie could have kicked himself. He should have remembered Vikings didn't have horns on their helmets seeing as he'd met a bunch of them only the other night. They walked on through the village exhibit, passing actors dressed as peasants doing their best to carry on with their medieval chores and pretend they hadn't noticed the royal visitor.

"We like to think we give our visitors a real flavour

of what life under the Vikings was like," continued the curator. "Even down to the authentic smells."

"Oh, that's deliberate, is it?" said Alfie. "I thought there was a problem with the loos." Awkward laughter rippled through the party. "Although real Vikings smell a bit fishier, if you ask me... Er, that is, I imagine they did. Probably. How would I know, right?" Alfie could feel his face going red.

"Yes, well, we're so honoured that you came, Your Majesty," stuttered the curator. "Especially after the dreadful floods last year."

"I don't expect *they* minded though," laughed Alfie, nodding at a couple of actors dressed as Vikings. "Like a bit of water, don't they?"

The curator's face fell. "The flood damage was terrible. We were closed for six months."

Alfie gulped and shot a glance at Brian that seemed to say, *Help! Get me out of here!*

Meanwhile, Hayley was in real trouble.

"Hey, you're not part of my group!" the guide shouted, pushing her way through the startled tourists as she made a beeline for the shifty-looking girl loitering at the back. Hayley gripped on to the sortilegic meter inside her pocket and ran down the nearest set of steps leading off the high city walls.

"Sorry!" she called back. "Great tour, though!"

Hayley didn't stop running till she'd passed beneath a low archway and found herself on a narrow, cobbled street. A plaque outside a quaint butcher's shop told her that this was the Shambles, a street so old it was mentioned in the Domesday Book of 1086. With its Tudor houses and overhanging timber beams, it certainly didn't look to have changed much since medieval times. The only thing that looked modern about it was the throng of tourists from all corners of the world shuffling along its uneven pavements. As Hayley reached the end of the little street, she could see the royal convoy parked outside the Jorvik Centre at the end of the road. Hayley wondered how Alfie was getting on and wished she had something more exciting than a run-in with an irate tour guide to tell him about on the journey home.

Buzz.

Hayley stopped walking. Was that her phone? Or— *BUZZ!* She shot both hands into her pocket and gripped the meter. It was still, but she was sure she'd felt it move. She turned around on the spot, trying to find whatever might have sparked the meter into life. The faintest flutter passed under her fingers and she froze again. Ahead of her was the dark mouth of a tiny passageway between two shops. She stepped towards it and the meter buzzed ever so slightly once more. Steeling herself, Hayley squeezed into the passageway. The gap between the buildings was so narrow that little light reached the ground and she had to sidle along, her back against one wall, hands locked around the box in her pocket. A little further along, Hayley was relieved as the passage opened out into a small courtyard filled with old wooden crates and leaking bin bags. The meter hadn't vibrated again. It must have been a false alarm, some trace speck of supernatural matter left in the walls of the ancient city.

Disappointed, she closed the meter box and turned back, but from nowhere a giant of a man loomed over her! Hayley just had time to clock the shaggy beard, fur-lined armour and wide sword in his hands before her instincts kicked in. She jammed one leg in front of the Viking's and yanked on his sword arm, using his own weight to topple him over on to his face. The brute's outraged grunt of pain was drowned out by the yells of two more shaggy-haired figures who came tearing out of a dark corner towards her. Hayley grabbed a broken plank hanging from a nearby crate and cracked it into her first attacker's shins, sending him flying. The last man grabbed her sleeve, but she pulled the hoodie over her head and twisted out of it, then delivered a sharp jab to his throat with the heel of her hand, sending him crumpling to the ground next to his friends. Pulse racing, Hayley spun round, checking if there were any more, but that seemed to be the lot. She was proud of herself – that would teach them to mess with Hayley Hicks, Keeper of the King's Arrows!

"I THINK SHE BROKE MY NOSE, STANLEY! IT REALLY HURTS!" yelled one of the figures writhing in pain on the ground.

One of the others was holding his shins and crying. The third was looking aghast at the pieces of a crushed mobile phone cradled in his hands.

Hayley didn't know that much about Vikings, but she was pretty sure they weren't cry-babies. Nor did she think they had mobiles, and she seriously doubted there were many called "Stanley". Hayley caught her breath and focused properly on the courtyard. In the corner where her "attackers" had been lurking, Tupperware boxes had fallen to the floor, scattering ham sandwiches and cheese-and-onion crisps. And now she looked back at the men who were lying in a heap at her feet, she could see that their "armour" was clearly fake and their swords were wooden.

"Who are you?" she asked, fearing she already knew the answer.

"We're ACTORS!" barked one of the two not called Stanley. "We work at the Jorvik Centre! What did you think we were, Vikings?!"

10

DEVIL DOGS

One-hundred-and-thirty miles south, in another city of medieval spires, rain was falling from billowing, putrid purple-black clouds that had gathered with alarming speed. Like York, Cambridge had been an important trading post for the Viking invaders hundreds of years ago. Like York, it was still popular with tourists who flocked to see the grand, ancient buildings of the world-famous university. But unlike York, Cambridge was about to find itself under attack.

Students hurried to park bicycles outside colleges

and libraries as they fled the ferocious downpour. Tour parties grappled against the rising wind to unfold matching waterproof ponchos. Young couples who had thought this was a good day for a punt on the river struggled to control their boats, buffeted by the suddenly choppy waters.

The first scream came from a young woman who spotted the dark shadow of the Viking longship's prow break the surface of the water behind her boyfriend, who abandoned their boat (and her) and swam for it. Thunder bellowed and lightning crackled as Guthrum's rotting boots hit the mud. At first people stared, not comprehending what they were seeing. But as the Viking warlord raised his axe and roared his battle cry, green algae dripping from his tangled beard, they understood. Something foul and dead and evil had come to Cambridge. It was time to run.

Deep below the Tower of London, alarm bells were ringing. The Lord Chamberlain hurried to the ops table.

"Cambridge, sir!" Yeoman Box yelled.

On the east side of the map the city's burgh light was flashing. LC saw that his theory about the Vikings sticking to places they remembered had been right. He'd just picked the wrong city. He turned to the Chief Yeoman Warder, his face lined with worry. "Where is His Majesty?"

In the Jorvik museum, Brian held his finger to his earpiece, his stony face giving away nothing about the urgent message he was receiving from the Keep. Calmly he approached the curator, who was showing Alfie a wall of pictures drawn by young visitors to the centre.

"His Majesty would like to use the facilities," said Brian.

Alfie was confused. He hadn't said anything about needing the loo. "Would I?"

Brian's look told him he should agree.

"Um, yeah, better safe than, er, sorry," said Alfie. "Lead on!"

The curator smiled uncertainly. "Of course," she said.

"Last stall on the left," whispered Brian as he escorted Alfie to the toilets and stood guard outside.

The toilets were empty and spotlessly clean. Someone had even put out a pile of fresh towels in case their royal visitor preferred them to the hand dryers. Pots of lavender were strategically placed on every surface. Unsure what to expect, Alfie eased open the door to the furthest stall and peeked inside. The leather regalia trunk was propped up on the toilet. A note taped to it read: *Fly to Cambridge. W knows the way. Good luck.* A smiley face had been added beneath, which Alfie thought was a nice touch. He rubbed his chin. Suddenly listening to the curator's small talk didn't seem such a bad way to spend the day.

"Oh, well," he said to himself, opening the box and pulling out the Shroud Tunic. "Duty calls."

Getting out of the toilet window wearing his full Defender armour proved quite a squeeze. *Note to self: windows first, armour second*, thought Alfie as he tumbled on to the gravel path outside. Luckily no one was around. No doubt Brian had seen to it that this particular exit was kept well clear of prying eyes. Alfie thought, *Spurs,* and Wyvern materialized beneath him and whinnied.

"Hey, girl, nice to see you too," said Alfie, patting her head. "OK, daylight launch – better make it fast."

Wyvern rocketed straight up, a blur of light too fast for anyone to notice, not levelling out till she hit cloud and turned south. Five minutes later, Alfie felt Wyvern ease her gallop as they began their descent towards Cambridge. The storm was raging now, and it was hard to see much until they were almost touching the college rooftops.

It was clear to Alfie where the Vikings had been. A trail of burning cars and smashed debris snaked through the medieval centre of the city. Terrified screams rose to greet them as they landed on a soggy lawn next to one of the colleges. Choir boys in flowing red cassocks were fleeing from a huge Gothic church, so scared that they barely noticed the white-armoured superhero striding in the opposite direction.

Alfie had never been inside King's College Chapel before, but he had seen its magnificent interior plenty of times on television. Every Christmas Eve his father had insisted on watching the broadcast of the famous carol service and they had all been made to listen in silence to the haunting music of the boys' choir. It was the only time Alfie could ever remember seeing his father's face utterly serene, his eyes closed as he soaked in every angelic note.

Serene was not the word Alfie would use to describe the place today. *Carnage* was a better fit. Choir stalls lay broken and scattered across the black-and-white marble floor. Undead Vikings swarmed across the organ like overgrown apes, wrenching away protesting pipes and throwing them clattering into the aisle below. Guthrum himself ripped a brass candelabra from its mooring and sniffed it, before hurling it through one of the tall stained-glass windows.

Alfie opened his mouth to say something tough and impressive (or the best he could manage at short notice), but a red-faced old man in a black robe and white dog collar beat him to it. "Stop that at once! This is a house of God!"

The Viking horde stopped what they were doing and turned to see who had dared to shout at them. For a moment Alfie thought that the irate chaplain's outburst might have done the trick. But Guthrum reached the man in a couple of mighty strides and lifted him off his feet with a single finger. The Viking growled a few words in his own tongue, green bile splattering over the chaplain's appalled face. Alfie didn't know what Guthrum was saying, but it didn't sound like an apology.

"Go back to whatever hell you came from!" replied the brave man.

None of the Vikings saw Alfie's run up. They were

too eager to see the bone-breaking punishment their leader was about to inflict on the priest. The first Guthrum knew about it was when the Defender's boots collided with the side of his head, making him lose his grip on the chaplain and sending him flying over the high altar.

"What he said," declared Alfie, getting up and unsheathing his sword.

Norse battle cries echoed all around as the draugar charged towards the Defender from every corner of the chapel. Alfie swung his sword in a wide arc, sweeping several of them off their feet, then sidestepped to let the remaining two run into each other with a crack of colliding skulls.

Guthrum swatted the altar aside and charged at Alfie. "*RIDDARI SVIKLIGR!*"* he screamed.

But Alfie lifted a broken pew with his boot and flipped it at him, unbalancing the Viking enough to send his axe blow wide of the mark. Alfie aimed his sword at Guthrum's back, going in for the kill, but the Viking was wise to it. He rolled clear and sprang to his feet, surprisingly fast for such a bulky warrior.

Now it was Alfie's turn to play defence,

---

* "TREACHEROUS KNIGHT!"

summoning his shield from his arm bracelet to parry the blows from Guthrum's axe. Not so long ago, Alfie would have turned and run away by now. But every day since the coronation he had felt a little more at ease with his powers, and more importantly Brian hadn't let him slack off from his training. The other Vikings were getting back to their feet. He needed to keep moving.

The Defender backed off down the aisle, deflecting and dodging Guthrum's axe as he went. As they emerged from the chapel on to the lawns outside, lightning crackled above them as if the sky itself was raging at the unnatural presence of the undead. At least out here the Vikings couldn't corner him so easily, thought Alfie, but he still needed to contain them somehow.

"Spurs!" Alfie said, and riding on Wyvern, he put a little distance between himself and Guthrum.

The Defender pointed his ring finger at a nearby bike rack. Focusing his mind, he commanded a bicycle to break free of its lock and hurl itself at Guthrum. The Viking lord laughed at the puny attempt to hurt him. But then the Defender commanded more bicycles to rise up like a flock of metal birds and slam themselves one after another into his enemy. The Defender turned his hand and the metal frames of the bikes twisted themselves into a tangled cage around the struggling Guthrum. Alfie kicked his heels and Wyvern swooped towards the prone Viking, but he wasn't fast enough. Guthrum tore himself free, scattering tyres, frames and tinkling bike bells across the lawn. Behind him, his men emerged from the chapel. He fixed the Defender with a fearsome glare.

*"Kjǫt ertu hundinum mínum!"** Guthrum said, a grin spreading across his ghoulish face.

Alfie was unnerved. It was the smile of someone who knew something you didn't. Guthrum lifted his war horn from his belt and blew three distinct blasts into it. Not like the summoning call Alfie had heard at Lindisfarne. This was different. Guthrum's raiders started to judder, as if each of them was having some sort of fit. They fell on to all fours as one, their bodies jerking wildly as thick, black fur burst through their armour. Alfie watched in disbelief as their limbs stretched and knee joints bent backwards; their mouths extended into jaws filled with sharp canine teeth; tails appeared behind each of them. Worst

---

* "You are meat for my dogs!"

of all, where the Vikings' eyes had been moments before, there were now only swirling pools of fire. Alfie had seen these monsters before, in the weird dreams he'd had just after he became king. Visions of devil dogs fighting his namesake Alfred the Great a thousand years ago at the Battle of Edington. But this was no dream. Now he was facing the same monsters in the flesh. Wyvern snorted and reared up. Maybe she remembered them too.

"Easy, girl!" shouted Alfie, clinging on.

One of the devil dogs crashed through a KEEP OFF THE GRASS sign and leapt into the air, clamping its jaws over Alfie's leg. He could feel the immense pressure of the bite even through his armour. Alfie tried to grab his sword, but Wyvern panicked and flew in circles kicking her hind legs so hard that he couldn't let go long enough to reach it. As they lost height, the other dogs joined in the attack, jumping and snapping at them, like a pack of hyenas bringing down a buffalo. He couldn't fight them like this.

"Wyvern, retire!" Alfie said, and the horse obediently disappeared back into his spurs.

Alfie fell flat on his back in the mud. The devil dogs stalked in from every side, confident that they had him at their mercy. Through their legs, Alfie could see Guthrum striding away, back towards the river. Snarls filled the air, the hulking shapes of the dogs closing in. Alfie closed his eyes and directed his mind towards the Ring of Command. This one would be tricky and he'd only get one shot at it. He held his hand up towards the chapel. The first devil dog pounced, but as it did so, something long and shiny shot out of the chapel door. The dog looked up just in time to see the organ pipe rocketing towards it. Five more followed, streaking like missiles at their targets, each slamming over a dog's head.

Alfie heaved himself up and watched with satisfaction as the yelping dogs clawed at the pipes that were stuck fast over their heads like giant flea collars. One by one, the groggy devil dogs finally shook them off and turned back into draugar, groaning and rubbing their ugly heads. Alfie raised his sword and was just about to charge the undead warriors, when they suddenly seemed to regain their senses and strike the ground as one with their axes. The earth shook beneath Alfie's feet. Thinking *Spurs*, he summoned Wyvern just in time as a spider's web of wide fissures opened up across the entire lawn.

A startled scream rose up behind him and the

Defender turned to see the old priest, who had just come out of the Chapel, teetering on the edge of a crater that had appeared at his feet. Alfie kicked his heels and Wyvern darted towards the priest, allowing Alfie to scoop him up just as he began to fall.

He set the grateful man down at a safe distance from the battle-scarred green and circled back to deal with the Viking vandals. But they had already beaten a retreat and were nowhere to be seen. By the time the Defender had tracked them back to the river all that was left to see was the stern of the Viking longship disappearing beneath the water.

The unnatural storm evaporated as quickly as it had arrived and the summer sun emerged over Cambridge once more. But Alfie did not feel much relief. He hated to admit it, but LC was right. The Vikings invaders were not going away. They were just getting started.

11

STOWAWAY

"Is he all right in there?" the museum curator asked as she craned her neck to peer over Brian's shoulder into the toilets.

"His Majesty is fine, ma'am," Brian said and shifted to block her view.

Alfie had flown off to Cambridge a good forty minutes ago, and the bodyguard was starting to run out of excuses. A huddle of worried museum staff and dignitaries gossiped nearby, shooting intrigued glances in Brian's direction. He had to tell them something.

"His Majesty is a real stickler for hand hygiene."

CRASH.

Brian winced. He guessed (correctly) that Alfie had just fallen back into the toilets as he climbed through the window.

"Oh my," the curator gasped.

"He likes to get a really good lather going with the soap," said Brian, offering a weak smile.

After a few more bangs, crashes and thumps, Alfie finally emerged from the bathroom, collar askew, his face flushed with exertion from the quick change of clothes.

"Sorry about that," Alfie announced to the worried crowd. "I don't like rushing things. Especially in loos."

The curator turned as bright red as her lipstick and tried not to catch the king's eye as the royal party left the museum. Outside, there was a small crowd of photographers and members of the public waiting behind barriers to see Alfie, but when he waved only a handful waved back. With a sinking feeling, Alfie realized that the prime minister was right; people still didn't seem to like him. Maybe he had been hiding away too much, but that was only because he was so busy being the Defender. He was trying to protect them, and it seemed unfair that he never got any thanks for it. If only he could tell people what he was really doing.

Later, as the royal train sped back to London through the gathering night, Alfie kicked his shoes off and leant back in his seat, relieved to be on the way home. Brian handed him a phone handset. "LC wants a word."

"Since when could Vikings turn into hellhounds?" Alfie said into the phone, without waiting for LC to speak.

On his way out of the carriage, Brian turned on a television. Practically every channel was showing pictures of the "major incident" in Cambridge, including some shaky phone footage of the Defender swatting aside one of the giant dogs as it leapt at him. Scrolling, urgent headlines at the bottom of the screen announced that Britain was under some kind of "supernatural attack", but that people should remain calm as sightings of the Defender were coming in from multiple witnesses.

"It seems even in their undead form, these Vikings retain their berserker abilities," replied the Lord Chamberlain.

"Berserker? Like going berserk?"

"Exactly so, Majesty. Guthrum and his men were said to work themselves up into such a frenzy in battle that they could transform themselves into beasts ... or even worse. The records from King Alfred the Great's time mention them frequently."

"But Alfred the Great ... he took Guthrum down in the end, didn't he?" Alfie asked, hopefully.

"Yes, indeed," LC said, sounding bright before his tone darkened again. "But only after four years of battles, defeats and destruction. Guthrum pushed Alfred the Great into the very fringes of his own land and ushered in a dark age for Britain."

Alfie stared out at the moonlit countryside as it sped by and recalled what LC had told him about the origin of his family's powers. How Alfred the Great hid out in the swamps of Somerset with the remnants of his men, before he prayed to the gods, became the Defender and eventually returned to rout Guthrum and his Vikings.

"So what do we do about it?" Alfie asked.

"If Lock is behind this, as I suspect he is, then we need to do two things: find him *and* put an end to these Viking raids before they get out of hand," LC replied. "You should get some sleep, Majesty. You'll need it. Oh, and read up on Guthrum. Try the abridged *Anglo-Saxon Chronicle*. And with all these raids, we need to get Brian to keep you on top of your swordsmanship. Double drills."

Alfie clicked the phone off, slumped back into the chair and let out a long sigh.

"You need to eat," Hayley announced, giving Alfie a concerned look.

"I wish everyone would stop telling me what to do," Alfie snapped, and then instantly felt bad about it. Fighting the Vikings at Cambridge had exhausted him. He felt like he'd run three cross-country races back to back. "Sorry, Hales. Long day."

Hayley nodded and patted him on the shoulder. "I'll see if they can make us something. And then I'll tell you all about the actors I beat up today."

Alfie opened his mouth to ask what she was talking about, but she had already walked off down the train.

Hayley understood why Alfie was on edge. He looked like the weight of the world was on his shoulders. Well, not the whole world, Hayley corrected herself, just the entire country. But she was annoyed that, once more, Alfie had been in the thick of the action at Cambridge while she had been wasting her time in York. Today was supposed to have been her chance for some excitement. The kitchen carriage was located at the far end of the royal train to keep cooking smells away from the living areas. Hayley paused to steady herself against the padded leather side of the train as it turned a bend. As she did, she could hear Brian on the phone behind the sliding door of his compartment. Thinking he might want to eat something as well, Hayley was just about to knock, when the royal bodyguard's voice boomed from behind the door.

"NO! I've told you before!"

Hayley stopped in her tracks. She had never heard Brian sound that upset. She couldn't see into the compartment because the blind was down. On the other side of the door, Brian continued, furtive now. He was obviously on the phone to someone and trying to keep his voice down.

"I don't like going behind the king's back. If LC ever found out, he'd throw me in the dungeons. All right . . . all right, I get it." Brian sighed. "Look, I'll see what I can do and let you know what happens. Yeah, yeah. I'd better crack on."

Realizing the conversation was coming to an end, Hayley scampered away, disappeared into the kitchen carriage and slid the door closed behind her, just as Brian stuck his head out and looked up and down the corridor. On the other side of the kitchen carriage door, Hayley let out a shaky breath. She didn't know what Brian was up to, but she had to tell Alfie.

But later, back in the royal compartment over a plate of sandwiches Hayley had barely touched, Alfie didn't seem bothered.

"You're being paranoid."

"I'm just telling you what I heard. Something's not right, Alfie. Brian's been acting kind of weird around the Keep too," Hayley said, thinking back to the other night when she saw him sneaking through the tunnel.

"No, he hasn't."

"How would you know? You're never there!"

"I've been kind of busy lately, in case you haven't noticed."

"Yeah, exactly. So you need someone to watch your back and – hello – that someone is me."

Alfie scoffed. "There's nothing going on with Brian. Before he was my bodyguard he was my mum's. He's practically part of the family."

"And I'm not? I see," Hayley said, stalking out of the carriage. "I'm going to get some sleep."

Alfie let her go. Hayley would calm down and he'd apologize. He wasn't sure for what, exactly, but his head was so full of undead Vikings and snarling devil dogs he couldn't deal with anything else tonight. He sat back in the armchair and stared out of the window into the darkness, trying to think of things that would make him feel better. He'd seen off the Vikings twice. *Good*. Maybe they'd just go away. *Don't bank on it*.

"Oh, shush," Alfie said to himself. What else? He was getting better at sword fighting. *True*. Wyvern even seemed to like him more. *Yep*. Brian was not about to betray him. *I mean, seriously?* He was safe and secure on his own personal royal train. *There's someone wearing a red robe and mask sitting on the roof.*

"Whoa!" Alfie stood bolt upright.

The train was passing through a town and in the reflection of a track-side office block he was sure he'd just caught a glimpse of the red-robed figure he'd seen at Glastonbury on the roof of the train! There was no time to tell Brian; if Alfie was going to find out who it was he had to move fast. Red Robe had the habit of disappearing in the blink of an eye.

Above Alfie, concealed in the padded ceiling, was an emergency escape hatch. Brian had pointed it out in his safety briefing that morning. Without thinking, Alfie opened the regalia case and slipped on the Shroud Tunic. For the second time that day, he transformed instantly into the Defender. He popped the ceiling hatch and hauled himself on to the roof.

The train was rattling through dark countryside again, but the view through the visor was always magically clear and pin-sharp. He needed to balance, though, as the train was swaying much more up here. But there was no one on the roof. Maybe he'd imagined it after all. A trick of the light or a—

A faint *POP* sounded from behind him, and someone tapped him on the shoulder. Alfie whipped around. There was no one there, but further down the train was Red Robe, sitting cross-legged on the rocking carriage.

"Who are you?" Alfie shouted, stepping towards him. "Why did you help me get my bag back at Glastonbury?"

With an elegant flourish, Red Robe calmly pulled back his richly embroidered hood to reveal a leering face with bulging white eyes. Alfie took an involuntary step back before realizing it was some kind of mask. At least he hoped it was a mask.

"OK, enough showing off. This is my train, and I need to check your ticket," Alfie said and sprang forward, his armour catapulting him into a super-powered sprint down the train.

But with a shimmer, like the very molecules in the air had parted, Red Robe disappeared, leaving Alfie grabbing at nothing. Red Robe was now at the other end of the train, sitting calmly again as if he was meditating in a temple. *How did he DO that? Some kind of illusion? Teleporting? What?* Red Robe stood up in a smooth, graceful movement and pointed at something behind Alfie.

"Oh yeah, like I'm falling for that old trick," Alfie yelled over the rushing wind.

Red Robe jabbed his finger again, with more urgency this time. Alfie risked a glance behind. The train was heading directly for a road bridge! *Correction*, thought Alfie, *the train is going under a bridge and I've got to—*

JUMP!

Alfie leapt twenty feet into the air. Below him, the train thundered under the bridge as cars and lorries rumbled over it.

"Spurs!" Alfie shouted, and then remembered that in his rush to get out of the carriage he hadn't put the spurs on. His stomach lurched as gravity reclaimed him, forcing him back down towards the train. His momentum had carried him forward and he was going to miss the bridge, at least, and—

CLANG!

With a bone-shaking impact, Alfie landed back on the roof of the train. He was in one piece; the armour had protected him. But as for Red Robe, there was no sign. *Had his fun for the night*, Alfie figured. He decided there and then to keep the strange encounter to himself. Whoever he was, Red Robe didn't appear to mean him any harm – quite the opposite, in fact. It was more like the mysterious figure was watching over him. Alfie promised himself he would find out why.

DRAGON RISING

Richard was desperate to escape. The Vikings had returned from the Cambridge raid to their crypt hideout and were singing. They hadn't actually plundered all that much, but they'd caused some damage and spread a great deal of fear, and that seemed victory enough for them to justify the raucous singalong. Guthrum, on the other hand, still wasn't happy, growling to Professor Lock that he wanted his promised gold, and lots of it. Richard wondered how the professor managed to be so close to the stinking Viking without being sick.

Richard found a quiet spot and leaned against an old tomb, belonging to someone called FRANNY MAY WHITE, DIED 1726, and closed his eyes. The cold of the stone seeped through his coat and into his back, reminding him of last winter. Term had just started again after the Christmas holidays and he was back at Harrow School, sitting in Professor Lock's study. It was two weeks since he had learned the truth about his father. The king. The Defender of the Realm! How could his father keep such a secret from his own family? How could he let them become so ridiculed and even hated by so many in the country when he had such power at his fingertips? His own dad was a superhero, but he acted like he was powerless to do anything! Lock was right: the centuries had turned his family into cowards too scared to use their power.

"Do you want to do something about it?" the professor had asked, leaning across his desk and smiling at Richard.

"What can I do?" asked Richard. "I'm not even the heir. I'm nobody."

"No, that's not true. There is power sleeping in your veins. All we need to do is release it."

That was when Lock revealed his greatest

discoveries to Richard. Two relics, which he said could help them change the course of history. The first was the skeleton of the dragon he had dug up at the White Horse of Uffington. He explained how dragons were real creatures that had once wreaked havoc on the country, until they were hunted to extinction. Their bodies were highly prized, said to contain many incredible properties; men paid fortunes for a single scale. The second was a small fragment of a jewel-encrusted golden crown, which he had found at another chalk-figure site in Westbury. It was part of Alfred the Great's original crown, imbued with immense powers by the ancient gods. Lock said he was working on finding the rest of it, but it already presented them with a unique opportunity, as he explained:

"Even a small part of Alfred's crown has the power to awaken the dragon magic in these bones. But it cannot be used by just anyone. It takes someone special. Someone with royal blood."

Perhaps it wouldn't work and nothing would happen, Lock told him, but there was a chance, if Richard was brave enough to try. Richard knew that what the teacher was proposing was, by any normal measure, insane. But he also knew that he couldn't just go back to his life the way it was before, not after everything he'd learned. He had to do something.

Lock combined the crown fragment with some of the dragon bones to form a rudimentary crown. Every night after lights out, Richard would creep to Lock's study and sit in the darkness wearing the strange creation on his head for an hour or so. Soon it became routine, like doing his homework or going to rugby practice. But aside from the occasional tingling sensation, which could just as easily have been cramp from sitting still too long, he didn't notice any change. Then, one morning, just as he was starting to think Lock's experiments were a waste of time, Richard caught a glimpse of himself in the bathroom mirror. He had always been broad-shouldered and strong for his age, but today the muscles across his chest looked much bigger than before. He flexed his biceps – they were large and rock solid, like he'd been working out for six weeks straight. That night Lock increased the time Richard spent wearing the dragon crown to three hours.

Soon Richard felt fitter than he ever had before. He could run faster, tackle harder, leap further – he actually had to start reining it in so that no one would notice. His skin had become so tough that he couldn't even cut it with a knife. If this was what it was like to be a superhero, like the Defender, then he wanted more. He encouraged Lock to let him spend longer and longer wearing the dragon crown, until he was there almost all night. But even the lack of sleep didn't seem to affect him any more; in fact he'd never felt more alert and quick-witted.

Then, one night, after he had returned to his room for an hour's sleep, he woke in agony. It felt like there was a fire raging inside his throat. He crawled to the mirror and watched in horror as his body mutated, black scales appearing over his skin, his jaw growing and elongating like a lizard's, his eyes turning thin and red. When he woke later that morning he was still on his bedroom floor. He must have passed out from the pain. His body was thankfully back to normal, but he could still feel the remnants of the fire burning deep inside him. That night, for the first time in months, he didn't go to see Professor Lock. When Lock came to find him, Richard explained what had happened, but rather than sharing his shock, Lock seemed excited.

"This is even better than I had dared to hope. The dragon magic is combining with your blood, evolving your body into something new. There's no going back now. The crown will help with the pain; it will only be worse without it."

That night, however, Richard refused to wear the dragon crown. But Lock was right. And soon after, Richard, writhing in agony, was knocking on his door, begging to resume their experiment.

In time, Richard learned to control his lizard transformations, managing his emotions to hold back the symptoms until he was alone, or until he needed them. For as terrifying as it was at first, his monstrous alter-ego did come with certain advantages. The night Lock sent him out on his first mission to the Tower of London, searching for more of Alfred the Great's lost crown, he felt invincible. Even when he killed the Yeoman Warder, he didn't feel bad about it; in that moment, he was the Black Lizard, and he would show no mercy to those who got in his way. His was a noble cause, to make the country he loved great again.

By the time he faced his own father at Stonehenge, Richard was evolving from Black Lizard into Black Dragon. Now when he transformed he had a heavy tail too. Every part of him felt stronger. His heart had hardened so much that he no longer thought of the man inside the Defender's armour as his dad. He was an enemy who clearly had no love for him, so why should he feel anything but hatred back? Later, overwhelmed at the enormity of what he had done, he would have doubts, but in that moment when he killed King Henry, Richard was not himself. The Black Dragon was in control, and the creature had no such qualms; the Defender needed to die.

Afterwards Richard made his feelings clear to Professor Lock about what he wanted to happen next. Alfie and Ellie would not be harmed. None of this was their fault. Lock agreed – the plan was always to encourage the weak-willed Alfie to abdicate, clearing the way for Richard to become the Defender and rule the country as he saw fit, ushering in a new age and a new empire. Richard continued his evolution into the Black Dragon, scaring Alfie just enough in Edinburgh to make him seriously doubt his ability to be the Defender. Lock played his part too, prompting Alfie to think for himself, planting the notion of giving up the throne in his mind. Their plan worked and Alfie abdicated – for a while.

When Alfie came to Richard in the Abbey and told him he had changed his mind – that he did want to be king after all – Richard didn't know what to do. What could he say? He couldn't admit everything he had done to Alfie's face, not yet. So he agreed. But as he stood alone in the ante-room, listening to the organ strike up, hearing the shocked murmurs from the crowd as they saw not him, but his hapless brother processing to the coronation chair, Richard felt a monstrous rage growing inside him. How dare his brother ruin everything? Richard couldn't turn back now; he couldn't be the "spare" again. Worse than that – the ridiculed substitute sent back to the bench. He wouldn't stand aside. Even if it meant killing Alfie.

Placing the restored crown of Alfred the Great on to his head, his transformation into the Black Dragon complete, Richard was filled with immense power unlike anything he had felt before. He would destroy anyone who got in his way. But the surge of strength had made him too confident, and he was blind to his brother's own increased power and cunning. The crown was severed from his head and he was trapped beneath tons of rock. If Lock had not been on hand to pull him clear and take his place, then he would have been captured there and then. Alfie would have known his own brother had betrayed him. But he had been given a second chance. Far from being defeated in the Abbey, his brief contact with Alfred's complete crown had locked the Dragon's power inside him, perhaps for ever.

After he had rested for a while and licked his wounds, Richard returned and rescued Lock from the Tower. His mentor helped him to see what had happened more clearly. It was all Alfie's fault for thinking he deserved the throne more than his brother. But all was not lost. Richard could still have his revenge...

But when?

Richard opened his eyes and looked around. Apart from the deep rumbling of the Vikings' snoring, the crypt was now strangely quiet. Richard stretched and was about to head for the staircase when he heard Lock's hushed voice echoing down the stone corridors. Richard picked his away around the reeking pile of sleeping Vikings, following the sound. Maybe he and Guthrum had taken their argument off somewhere else. But the closer Richard got, the stranger Lock's voice sounded. He wasn't speaking Old Norse, and there was something else to his tone Richard couldn't quite place. He crept through the cold chambers towards a small chapel that glowed with sputtering candles.

"Everything is going according to plan. . ."

Was he imagining it, or was Lock's voice shaking? And if there was someone else involved in the conversation, Richard couldn't hear them. But there *was* something else – not a voice, but a low-level droning, like a million flies buzzing their wings.

"The way will soon be clear. I promise." Lock's voice was tight and dry with fear.

Richard peeked around the corner to see Lock kneeling in front of a stone plinth, upon which stood his seeing mirror. He was staring at it like he was hypnotized, the fly-wing droning sound rising and falling. Desperate to see who Lock was speaking to, Richard slipped inside the chapel, trying to get an angle over the professor's shoulder. The closer he got, the louder the drone became. He was so close to being able to see what was on the other side of the mirror, the edges of the glass were black and yellow, streaked with red, like something pulsing, alive and—

"Richard!" Lock sprang to his feet and whipped the velvet cloth over the mirror. The buzzing sound disappeared.

"Who was that?" Richard said.

"No one," the professor snapped, his voice back to its commanding best.

"Didn't sound like no one to me," said Richard, pulling the cloth from the mirror. But all he saw in the glass was his own face staring back at him.

"I mean, no one that need concern you." Lock sounded calmer. "Just know that we are not alone in this struggle. We have friends who also want to help you win the throne, Richard. Powerful friends."

Richard stared at Lock for a moment. "What's in all this for you?"

The professor seemed taken aback, as if he were insulted by the question. "Nothing. To serve the rightful king and true Defender, Richard the Fourth."

"Spare me the sales pitch," said Richard. He was tired of Lock talking to him as if he were still just one of his pupils back at school. "What do you really want from me?"

Lock leaned against a stone arch and smiled. "All right. I suppose you are old enough to understand these things. You know what they called me at university? Loony Lock. People laughed at my theories. How history as we are taught it is a lie. How magic exists. How dragons once soared in our skies. How kings once wielded power beyond imagination before they became too afraid. I learned soon enough to keep my mouth shut and play along, pretended I'd come round. But I could still see them sniggering at me, talking behind my back. I want to prove those people wrong."

Richard met Lock's defiant stare. He had a feeling there was still something the professor wasn't telling him. But then what did it matter, if he got the throne?

"*GULL!*"* Guthrum's voice boomed through the crypt, coming towards them.

All at once, the huge, smelly Viking was filling the chapel door, stamping his feet like a toddler having a meltdown.

"*GULL! GULL! GULL!*"

"You'll get your gold, you stupid, dead Norseman!" Lock said.

"*GULL!*" Guthrum yelled again, filling the small chapel with his dead breath.

"This is NOT the same Britain you and your men knew a thousand years ago!" Lock shouted back.

He'd either forgotten Guthrum spoke no English, or he'd given up on explaining in Old Norse.

_____

* "GOLD!"

"If you just listen to me, I will tell you about somewhere really worth raiding!"

"Another raid?! Why?" shouted Richard, flabbergasted. "So they can wreck more of the country before I even take the throne?"

Lock held his hands up. "Patience, Richard. It's all part of my plan."

Richard laughed bitterly. "So you keep saying. What plan? Do anything to keep Captain Dead and his zombie morons happy? I'm out of here."

Richard tried to shoulder-barge his way past Guthrum but the vast Viking wouldn't budge and grabbed Richard by the neck, lifting him off his feet.

"NO! PUT HIM DOWN!" yelled Lock.

But it was too late. Richard's eyes flashed red and with a terrific cracking of bones he transformed into the Black Dragon and turned the tables on Guthrum, pinning the Viking lord against the crypt's vaulted ceiling with *his* clawed hand. The rest of the draugar rushed into the chapel and surrounded the Dragon, snarling and cursing, but he simply flexed his wings to keep them at bay. None was brave enough to charge him first. Fire glowed hot in the Dragon's throat as he flicked his tongue over Guthrum's face.

"Tell me why I shouldn't burn this stinking corpse?" hissed the Dragon.

Guthrum went for his axe, but the Black Dragon swatted it with his tail, sending it clattering away.

"Because if you do, you will never be king," said Lock, his voice like ice.

The Dragon paused, then tossed Guthrum to the ground. The rattled Viking chief got up, spat a wad of green bile at their feet, and returned to his men, grumbling at them for their cowardice. The Dragon returned to his corner, slowing his breathing, and transformed back into Richard. He pulled on his spare clothes and made for the exit.

"Where are you going?" asked Lock.

"I have somewhere better to be," Richard shot back and stormed out.

"If you see your brother, just remember this: we need him alive, for now," Lock called after him. "Richard!"

But Richard was gone.

PARTY TIME

Alfie was still sitting in the car. They were parked at the end of the long approach to the majestic Windsor Castle, which had been hung with lanterns for his sister's birthday party. He was late, but Alfie needed to collect his thoughts first. It was always so hard talking to Ellie when he couldn't tell her anything about the whole Defender half of his life. He felt like the secret had put an invisible wall between them.

"Not in the party mood, then?" asked Brian, drumming his fingers on the steering wheel.

"Have you seen Ellie's friends when they get excited?" Alfie replied.

"Fair enough. Did you invite Hayley?"

"Hayley?" The thought hadn't even occurred to Alfie.

"She seems a bit down in the dumps, that's all. Might have cheered her up."

"She wouldn't have wanted to come... Would she?"

"Maybe not, boss. But a girl likes to be asked all the same."

Great. Now on top of everything else, Alfie was worried that Hayley was sitting back at the Keep fuming that he hadn't invited her to the party.

Brian continued, "Well, *I'm* not going to be your date, so are you going, or...?"

Alfie took the hint, grabbed Ellie's present and got out of the car. He had not spent much time at Windsor since that dreadful autumn several years ago when his parents were splitting up. His mother had brought them here to try to shield them from the fallout. It was far enough out of London to avoid the crowds, and Alfie used to love staying for the weekend. He, his brother and his sister had the run of the lavish State Apartments and the acres of grounds. The "castle" was actually more like a small town, and there was always some undiscovered tower or hidden room to explore. But that holiday the royal divorce story was in the news every single day, so even here there was no hiding from it. Then, before Alfie knew it, his mum was gone, they were back living with their dad at the palace and he soon realized the only people he could really depend on were his brother and sister. He wondered if even that was true any more.

At the entrance Alfie greeted the staff, some of whom had known him since he was a baby, then made his way past the colourful flags of the Knights of the Garter – the mysterious order who had used Windsor as their base during the reign of Edward the Third, seven hundred years ago. As he approached the Upper Ward, he could already hear music thumping somewhere inside. A depressed-looking butler was hiding outside, playing on his phone. When he saw the young king approaching, he scrambled to attention. "Sorry, Majesty!"

Alfie waved as he went in. "Don't worry, I'd rather stay out here too!"

Princess Eleanor's party was being held in the Grand Reception Hall, a venue so festooned with gold – from the finely sculpted Rococo ceiling to the glittering chandeliers and elegant, priceless furniture – that you really needed a good pair of shades to take it all in without getting a headache. More used to hosting ambassadors and foreign royalty clad in bow ties and ballgowns, tonight it would be stuffed with hundreds of dancing young teenagers. Alfie had braced himself for that, but what he hadn't expected to see the second he walked in was the hideous face of the Black Dragon bearing down on him.

"WHOA!"

Alfie stumbled backwards, knocking a tray of pink lemonades out of a footman's hand with an almighty crash. Everyone in the ballroom turned to look. Which is when Alfie realized that there were in fact about ten Black Dragons there, along with a half dozen Defenders and many other famous heroes and villains. Fancy dress. He'd forgotten, naturally. Because remembering something crucial that could help avoid public humiliation was just not something Alfie was any good at.

"Nice entrance, Alf. What are you going to do for an encore, stick your face in my birthday cake?" Ellie scowled at him, arms folded. She was wearing sports whites with a golden foil trophy plate pinned to her chest.

Alfie took a breath and composed himself. "Sorry. But if you're giving out prizes, that Black Dragon costume over there is seriously good. Who are you supposed to be?"

"Kate Robertson, of course," she tutted. "The tennis player? She just made it to the quarter-finals at Wimbledon. Wow, what do you *do* all day?"

"Search me," Alfie shrugged. "Oh, yeah, happy birthday."

He retrieved the present from the sticky debris on the floor and handed it over. Ellie hefted it, smiling.

"No. Way." She ripped the wrapping paper off and eagerly inspected the top-of-the-range Bianca Chandon skateboard. "Alfie, just when I think you'll always be a complete idiot, you go and impress me— Oh."

She stopped, looking at something on the underside of the skateboard. She flipped it over to show Alfie the engraved gold plaque stuck to the underside.

"Presented to His Majesty, King Alfred II by the Government of the United States of America, on the occasion of his coronation," read Alfie, his heart sinking. "Didn't notice that. The thing is, I kept falling off, so I figured it might be more your sort of thing."

"It is. But you're still an idiot," said Ellie, hopping on to the board and weaving her way off through the crowd. "Have a great party!"

A gaggle of girls was looking over at Alfie and giggling. *Typical*, thought Alfie, *no one fancied me before I was king, but now—*

Then he realized what they were actually laughing at was the "God Save The King" ringtone coming from his pocket. Hayley liked to programme it into his phone as a joke whenever his back was turned. Embarrassed, he retreated to a quiet corner and hurried to answer it. "Hello?"

"Hi, honey! Sounds like you're at the party already?" said Queen Tamara's voice at the other end of the line.

"Mum! You just missed Ellie. I'll see if I can find her," said Alfie, scanning the crowded room for his sister in vain.

"Don't sweat it, Alf, she's having fun. I just wanted to check you've been taking care of yourself. Saw some crazy stuff happening over there on the news."

Alfie knew what she meant. Last time he had seen her, just after the coronation, she had made it clear that she thought her phone was bugged. He was pretty sure she knew he was the Defender now too. This was her way of asking how his fight against the Vikings was going.

"Yeah, I'm fine, thanks. The new job's keeping me busy. You know, meeting new people, shaking a lot of hands, the usual." *Beating up undead Vikings, wrestling devil dogs. . .*

"Good. I'm so proud of you, Alfie. And I'm sorry I couldn't stay longer. The ranch takes up so much of my time. But I'd love to see you soon and catch up properly."

His mum had flown straight back to the United States after the coronation. She wasn't the sort of woman who was easily intimidated, but Alfie sensed she was scared to spend any more time on British soil.

"I'll talk to LC, see if I can arrange a trip," said Alfie.

"That would be awesome. I'll make up the spare bed. Hey, tell that brother of yours to answer his phone when you see him, OK?"

As it happened, Alfie saw Richard much sooner

than he expected. Alfie had spent an awkward hour at the party, trying to talk to Ellie's friends and not make a prat of himself again. Now he was relieved to be outside, waiting for Brian to bring the car round, when Richard stepped out of the shadows.

"Evening, Alfie."

"Rich!"

Alfie went to hug his brother, but Richard backed off. He looked pale and sweaty.

"What's wrong? I've been calling you."

"Flu," rasped Richard.

That explained how ill he looked. But Alfie could tell there was more to it. There was something his brother wasn't telling him.

"Listen, I don't know what's been going on with us," said Alfie, "but I'm your brother, you can talk to me. If it's something I've done—"

Richard laughed a hoarse laugh. "You still have no idea, do you?"

Alfie was confused. This wasn't the Richard he knew, there was a darkness hanging over his face that he'd never seen before. "No idea about what?"

Richard's shook his head and turned away from Alfie, towards the house. "I'm just here to see Ellie."

But Alfie chased after him and grabbed his shoulder. "Tell me!"

Richard lashed out an arm, cracking Alfie hard on the side of the face. He fell down, stunned. His brother stood over him, angrier than Alfie had ever seen him before. "Why did you have to change your mind? Why didn't you just stay away like you were supposed to? This is your fault! Everything that's going to happen. It's all on YOU, Alfie!"

Alfie was confused. What did he mean? What was going to happen? But before he could catch his breath, Richard had stalked off into the castle. Alfie was still in a daze when the car arrived and Brian jumped out. He helped Alfie back to his feet and inspected the bruise on his cheek.

"Who did this to you?" Brian asked, scanning the area on high alert.

"I honestly don't know," replied Alfie.

14

KEEP SECRETS

Hayley made herself a cup of tea, keeping one eye on the huddle of Yeoman Warders talking at the table. The Keep's Mess Hall was at the other end of a long, stone corridor from the Map Room and consisted of a rickety old kitchen that hadn't been updated since 1942 and always smelled of soup, and several large oak tables, stained black with age. Generations of Yeoman Warders had scratched their names into them: J Algar, 1972; Herbert Wyatt, 1921; S Theobald, 1878. The tables were so crisscrossed with signatures it would take you a year to read them all. Hayley liked to hunt for the oldest date she could find while she ate her dinner, tracing her fingers over the names and wondering who they were and what they were like. The oldest she had found so far was the elaborate signature of some guy called JOSIAH MOTT, 1702. But that was before one of the beefeaters had pointed out that the underside of the tables were also carved with names. They'd just flipped over the table tops when they had run out of room all those years ago.

But tonight Hayley didn't want to play hunt the ancient name. Tonight she was waiting for the Yeoman Warders' shift to change so she could sneak into Brian's room. Ever since she had seen him creeping out through the sally port tunnel and then overheard him talking on the royal train – *"I don't like going behind the king's back!"* – Hayley had become more and more convinced he was up to something. She didn't like the idea of their friend being untrustworthy any more than Alfie had when she'd made the mistake of raising it without any evidence, but she just knew something was off about Brian at the moment. Weirdly, it reminded her of when her gran was in the early stages of her illness back at their old flat. At first it was small things Hayley noticed: Gran forgetting what she'd come into a room for or mixing up her words. Then gradually it all added up to something terrible. She didn't think Brian was sick, but something was going on and she was going to find out what.

"Didn't fancy the shindig at Windsor tonight, Hales?" Brenda deposited her plate next to Hayley and took a seat.

Oh no, she must be part of the new shift, ready to take over when the old one comes in, thought Hayley. Slipping away unnoticed was going to be much harder now.

She smiled at the beefeater, trying to act normal. "Ellie's party? Nah. Not sure how I'd explain what I was doing there with all those posh kids."

"No need," said Brenda, with her mouth full. "Fancy dress. You could've worn a superhero mask, incognito like."

"Oh. Not really my sort of thing, anyway," Hayley lied.

She would have loved to have gone, just to see Alfie try to dance again. His moves at Glastonbury were so bad they were almost good.

"Besides, Alfie didn't invite me," she added.

"Would've been nice if he'd asked though, eh?"

Brenda's eyes twinkled. She liked to tease Hayley

about her and Alfie getting together one day. Hayley wondered if Alfie hadn't invited her on purpose. Was he still angry with her about suspecting Brian?

The old shift of Yeoman Warders bustled in from the Map Room, all guffaws and yawns. They'd been busy for the past two hours monitoring the giant map and dealing with nervous Burgh Keepers from all over the country phoning in reports about Vikings. Most of them were false alarms, but it was taking its toll on everyone.

As the beefeaters joined the dinner queue, Hayley told Brenda she was going to have an early night, and slipped out. As soon as she was out of sight, Hayley sprinted down the corridor into the deserted Map Room. She knew that there was always a short gap between shifts – the beefeaters hated to leave any food on their plates – and she would have just enough time to search Brian's room for any evidence of what he was up to. She probably wouldn't find anything, but she had to try.

A growl from the sofa made her jump, but it was just Herne chasing a footman in his sleep. The shaggy dog opened an eye, yawned and went back to his dream. Crossing her fingers that there wouldn't be a general alarm that would bring everyone running back into the Map Room, Hayley checked her watch. She would give herself three minutes.

GO!

She twisted the door handle to Brian's room and pushed. Locked. Hayley's heart sank. Of course it was. But as she removed her hand the door opened – it had just been a bit stiff. Hayley slipped inside.

Brian's room was sparse and well-ordered. Hayley didn't know which army regiment Brian used to serve in, but he'd clearly had tidiness drilled into him. There was a desk and pair of ancient swords crossed over on one wall above a neatly made bed. A medieval suit of armour stood in one corner. Brian's official title was the King's Armourer, after all, Hayley reminded herself. But it was kind of creepy having the metal figure looming over her and Hayley was suddenly paranoid that there could be a little spy camera monitoring the room from the helmet's eye slits. Panicked, she flipped up the visor. Nothing inside. Just dust and cobwebs. Brian's cleaning regime clearly didn't extend in here. A phone suddenly started ringing in the Map Room and Hayley froze, her breath shortening. Would someone come in and answer it? She strained her ears. No voices. After a while it stopped.

What am I doing? Hayley thought as she swept her eyes across the desk. *This is crazy.* Still, she had to know. One minute left. The drawers of Brian's desk were full of alphabetized files and folders and even the pencils were standing to attention in little rows. There was nothing out of the ordinary here. But then she saw it, a scrap of paper with a long phone number on it. It stood out because it so obviously didn't belong in the neat drawer; it was crumpled, like someone had been folding and refolding it, checking they still had it on them. Maybe this was the number of the person Brian had been talking to on the train. Hayley took a deep breath and started to memorize the number, but before she could finish it, she heard voices in the Map Room.

Busted.

Shame washed over her. There was no way out of Brian's quarters back into the Map Room without the Yeoman Warders seeing her. And there was no chance she could talk her way out of it either. They'd see her disloyalty plain as day and, in one stupid second, the months spent gaining their trust would vanish. What would the Lord Chamberlain say? What would Brenda think of her? She felt sick imagining what it would be like.

I'm just looking out for Alfie, Hayley thought, miserable, when something caught her eye. Behind the suit of armour there was a door. Old, studded with black nails and strapped with bands of iron. It was worth a try. Hayley squeezed behind the armour and prayed the door wasn't locked. With a whine of hinges that made Hayley wince, it opened, and a blast of cold, stale air bellowed out like it had been trapped there for centuries, waiting to escape. Stone steps led down, lit by dim, old-fashioned bulbs. She had no idea where the steps led, but she had no choice. Hayley stepped through and closed the door as softly as she could behind her.

The further she descended, the colder it became. And there was something else here: magic. Hayley could sense it, the same prickle of electricity that she got standing near Alfie when he transformed into the Defender. A goosebumpy, hairs-on-the-back-of-your-neck-standing-up feeling. Just as she was beginning to wonder if this was a shortcut to the centre of the earth, the steps ended and she found herself in a huge, circular room with heavy oak doors spaced evenly around it. How many doors Hayley couldn't say. A hundred? More? But what really got her attention was something in the middle of the room. Hanging down from the ceiling was a thick silver chain and at the end of it, the biggest bunch of keys she'd ever seen, as large as a beach ball. The keys were glowing faintly with swirling blue, magical light that radiated out in transparent beams to each of the doors.

"Mistress! What cheer?"

Hayley jumped. The voice had come from behind the door closest to her. Hayley noticed that the door had a tiny barred window set into it.

"How do you do, pretty lady? Methinks you are lost, no?" The voice was sing-song, airy. "Come hither. Come, come! I shall not bite."

Wary, Hayley approached the door the voice was coming from, trying to peer inside through the small window, but it was pitch black beyond. "Are you a beefeater?"

A high chuckle rattled from the dark. "Nay, but I did serve my gracious sovereign in times past."

Hayley looked around, nervous. "What is this place?"

"A gathering of the great and good. Or rather the great and not-so-good." Another light chuckle, like a songbird twittering. "Pray thee my rare beauty, find my key and unlock my door?"

Hayley felt light-headed. She looked at the beam

of swirling light stretching from the door back to the great bunch of keys. Somehow she could tell which key the beguiling voice meant, a rusted iron one. She could probably reach up and get it—

A hand fell on Hayley's shoulder and she cried out, spinning around. "No, no, no!"

An old Yeoman Warder – one she had never seen before – was directly behind her. His uniform was tattered and dirty, and his long face was creased like leather. His grey hair was straggly and long. All in all he looked like a tramp who'd put on a beefeater's uniform by mistake. He pulled Hayley away from the keys.

"Unhand her!" the voice on the other side of the door tittered.

"Put a sock in it, Blood," the beefeater said and thumped on the door before turning back to Hayley. "Sweet talk you into anything, that one." He looked her up and down. "You're that girl, ain't ya?"

"I'm Hayley," she said, her mind starting to clear.

The old Yeoman sneered. "You might be His Majesty's special little friend, but you can't just wander around the dungeons willy-nilly."

Dungeons. Of course, that's where she was. And the beefeater in charge down here was the Yeoman Jailer. Hayley shook off his hand. "I got lost. Sorry."

"As I foretold," Blood, whoever he was, twittered from his cell.

"Shut your cakehole, traitor!" the Jailer barked, kicking the door again and grabbing Hayley's wrist. He led her away from the cells towards another staircase. "You shouldn't be down here."

"Fine, all right, I'm going," Hayley snapped back.

Relieved, she headed for the new staircase. But despite her wish to get back before someone wondered where she was, Hayley couldn't help being curious. "Who was that talking to me?"

"Colonel Blood. Stole the Crown Jewels in 1671. The real ones," said the Jailer. "Tried to melt them down, make a potion of them and turn himself into a super-villain. Almost worked too. Except for what it did to his body."

Hayley decided she'd rather not know what he meant by that. She scanned the rest of the prison doors. "Are they all full?"

"Not every cell, but near enough. Only the worst of the worst wind up as my guests. We used to behead traitors in the good old days, but now if the Defender can catch them, they get banged up here at His Majesty's pleasure. Let's see..."

The Jailer ran his hand over a row of doors, eliciting a series of muffled yells, grunts and monstrous howls from the other sides that made Hayley's skin crawl.

"We got Spring-Heeled Jack in here – terrorized London ever since the nineteenth century. Triple-locked his cell, just in case. Bloomin' demons, you can't trust 'em. . . And next door to him you'll find the dastardly Robyn Hood."

"Robin Hood? I thought he was one of the good guys?"

"Fell for that old steal-from-the-rich-give-to-the-poor story, did you? What kind of hero wears a hood? I mean, I ask you. Anyway, this is Robyn with a 'Y'. She's a descendant of the original, but no less a villain."

The Jailer moved on to the next door. He reminded Hayley of a market trader, proudly displaying his wares, although she thought he seemed to like his gruesome job a little too much.

"This here contains our latest resident. The Beast of Bodmin. Cor, King Henry had quite a time catching this one, God rest him."

"The Beast of Bodmin? That's just, like, a big cat, isn't it?"

"CAT?! I'd love to see you call him that to his faces!" laughed the Jailer.

"Face," Hayley corrected him.

"You heard right the first time. Want to have a look-see?" the Jailer asked, snapping open an iron viewing window.

Hayley shook her head and he closed it again. From some of the inhuman grunts and wails the inmates were making, Hayley dreaded to think what would happen if any of them ever broke out.

"Now then, how exactly did you say you'd got down here?" the Jailer asked, staring at her.

Hayley was just about to start spinning a story about losing her way when the shrill bell of the general alarm rang from the Map Room above. It had to be another Viking raid.

"Sorry, it's been fun, see ya!" Hayley said, dashing up the new set of steps.

"Up there, left then right, then left again. But you knew that anyway, didn't you?" the Jailer called after her cheerfully, but his smile was thin and knowing. "We'll talk again."

Hayley ran up the steps as fast as she could, pleased to be out of the hellish place.

GOLD RUSH

Inside the Bank of England's dimly lit marble front hall, Gordon Frimley sat watching the tennis highlights on a small TV. His black top hat was perched on his desk, but he was still wearing the long, colourful tailcoat that gave the old bank's security guards their nickname: the Pink Coats. Gordon had always thought the colour suited him – that's what his wife said anyway, and he secretly liked to catch a glimpse of his own reflection whenever he was on duty.

Gordon winced as the British player Kate Robertson put another return wide of the line. Outside the bank, thunder crashed and boomed, but Gordon was totally engrossed in the match. He groaned as Robertson swatted yet another shot into the net. She was struggling against her statuesque Swedish opponent. *They don't half make 'em strong up there,* Gordon thought.

BANG!

Gordon jumped as something heavy thumped against the bank's main doors, the sound echoing around the marble chamber. *Probably some drunk looking to get out of this filthy weather.* Grumbling about missing the match, Gordon got up and crossed the entrance hall, past the large mosaic of two lions standing guard over a map of England, and put his ear to the cold bronze doors.

"We're closed!" he yelled.

He was just about to get back to the tennis when the heavy doors exploded off their hinges and flew inwards, knocking Gordon out and sending him skidding across the floor on his backside. He came round just in time to see a dozen shaggy-furred boots stomp past his face towards the stairs. The smell of dead fish and seaweed filled the air.

Gordon did the smart thing: he closed his eyes and played dead.

"*SEM SKJÓTAST, ÞIÐ ROTTUR!*"* Guthrum yelled at his men, impatient.

The steps of the wrought-iron spiral staircase that led down to the bank vaults were too narrow for huge Viking feet, and his men were stumbling into each other like rush-hour commuters on the Tube. With a grunt, the massive Viking picked up the warrior nearest to him and heaved him over the bannisters. The Viking dropped the remaining five floors and landed on his back with a groan. Guthrum leapt over the rail and plummeted after him, bouncing off the crash-mat Viking and back on to his feet at the bottom. The rest of his men followed his shortcut, and moments later they were standing at the vault door.

Guthrum ran his fat, death-blackened fingers over the enormous circle of thick steel and frowned. Issuing a guttural command to his warriors, he stepped back and closed his eyes. One of the Vikings began to sing. A low, mysterious ballad in their ancient tongue:

---

* "HURRY UP, YOU RATS!"

"Tegit beinina á honum!
Óttazk øxina!
*Guthrum gnæfir yfir allir!"**

The others joined in until the bank vault rang with the Viking voices. Guthrum's body started to shake. Strange convulsions like those that had overtaken his men when they went berserker in Cambridge and turned into devil dogs. Except that Guthrum was not transforming into an animal.

He was growing.

The muscles on his arms and legs expanded at a startling rate, every part of his body swelling as if inflated from inside, until his head was touching the ceiling. He gripped the handle on the vault door and began to pull. Plaster fell from the wall either side of the door and ugly cracks appeared all around them. With a roar louder than an express train, he tore the massive door off its hinges, and dropped it on to the smashed floor. As the dust began to clear, the giant Guthrum squeezed himself through the opening into the vault, followed by his men.

Shelves stretched before them in all directions

---

* Stretch his bones! Fear his axe! Guthrum towers over all men!

as far as the eye could see. Every one of them was stacked high with gold bars. Four hundred thousand of them – the entire gold reserve of the United Kingdom. Guthrum's mouth dropped open in wonder.

"Valhǫll!"* he gasped, invoking the name of the Vikings' mythical paradise.

The next Viking into the vault took one look and fainted. The rest fell on the vast treasure hoard, hollering with glee as they hugged and stroked the gold bars as if they were puppies.

Alfie plunged through the storm astride Wyvern and circled over the Bank of England. An armed police team had thrown up a cordon around the grand old building and a man in a dishevelled pink tailcoat and crumpled top hat was yelling at the commanding officer, waving his arms about and gesticulating towards the building.

"How does it look, Majesty?"

It was LC's voice in his ear. He was monitoring the Defender's approach via his helmet-cam from back in the Keep. Next to him, Hayley was sneaking

---

* "Valhalla!"

suspicious glances at Brian, who was busy briefing the Yeoman Warders.

"Looks like our Viking friend might have kicked it up a gear," replied Alfie, scanning the ground to give them all a better view.

"Keep your distance until we know what we're dealing with," advised Brian.

The front of the Bank of England erupted in a shower of pulverized stone, and the gargantuan figure of the berserker Guthrum stepped out into the rain.

"WHOA!" Alfie blurted, taking in Guthrum's new, giant form. "Somebody's been hitting the gym."

Alfie was instantly taken back to his final "Succession" vision: the bloody end of the Battle of Edington as seen through the eyes of his ancestor Alfred the Great; the giant Viking lord smashing his way out of a wood and confronting him on the battlefield. It was scary enough when it was just a bad dream, but here he was in the rotting flesh. Alfie was starting to miss the devil dogs. Talking of which, Guthrum's undead Viking mates followed him out of the wrecked bank, pulling a string of trollies piled high with gold bars.

"Armed police! Drop what you are carrying and

lie on the ground!" shouted the police commander in a shaky voice through a loudhailer.

"*VÉR ÓTTUMZT EKKI DAUÐLEGRA MANNA!*"* Guthrum roared back and pounded his chest as the armed police unit readied their weapons.

The meaning was clear: *Bring it on.*

Alfie was so intent on the bizarre scene unfolding below him that he almost didn't see the police helicopter descending towards him. Wyvern banked out of its path at the last second, close enough that Alfie made eye contact with the startled pilot. The Vikings advanced into the road junction outside the bank, snarling and growling at the police snipers.

"THIS IS YOUR FINAL WARNING!"

Alfie scoped out the area – large buildings boxed them in on all sides. Cars were still passing by the end of the road, oblivious to the danger.

"Looks like the police want to pick a fight. This could get messy," Alfie said into his helmet mic, but his words were drowned out by the sound of gunfire.

One of the police marksmen had let loose a nervous shot at the nearest Viking. The undead

---

* "WE FEAR NO MORTAL MAN!"

brute shook with the impact of the bullet, but didn't fall. Instead he looked down at his chest irritably and hurled a gold bar at the policeman who'd shot him, barely missing his head. Guthrum slapped the Viking who'd thrown the gold and gestured for him to fetch it back.

The Defender landed between the Vikings and the police, Wyvern withdrawing into his spurs in the blink of an eye. He unsheathed his sword with a flash, and some of the police, unsure what to do, trained their weapons on him too. The police commander wiped his brow and spoke into the loudhailer again. "You there, in the white armour! Get out of the way! We're handling this."

"Trust me, you could do with the help!" the Defender shouted back.

Guthrum flexed his tree-trunk-sized arms and pointed his axe down at the white knight. *"Beinin þín í brauðit mitt skal ék mala!"** he shouted.

Whatever that meant, Alfie had a feeling it wasn't nice.

Guthrum charged at the Defender, who met his swinging axe with his sword in a shower of sparks.

_____

* "I will grind your bones into my bread!"

The force behind the giant's strike rocked Alfie back on his heels. This berserker magic was almost a match for his Defender powers. Another blow from the axe sent Alfie somersaulting backwards into the road.

Laughing with satisfaction, Guthrum kicked the first police car on to its side, clearing a path for his men.

"OPEN FIRE!" yelled the police commander.

Bullets thumped into the undead Vikings, but Guthrum's men hardly flinched as they barrelled through the police line, pulling their convoy of stolen gold as they went.

By the time the Defender had picked himself up, the raiding party had turned the corner, heading for the river. Alfie scooted past the dazed policemen and summoned Wyvern from his spurs. The sight that greeted them as they swooped round on to the main road was one of pandemonium. Pedestrians ran screaming in all directions as the Viking raiders stampeded down the middle of the road with their loot. Drivers abandoned their vehicles in panic as the giant Guthrum thundered through, stamping an empty car flat under one mighty foot. A sleek, classic Jaguar E-type sat stranded in Guthrum's path. Alfie could see the old man at the wheel struggling to undo his seat belt, eyes wide with fear at the sight of the approaching monster. Urging Wyvern on, Alfie gained height and extended his ring finger towards the car, focusing his mind. The old man in the Jaguar covered his eyes as Guthrum's shadow fell over him. But at the last second, the car lurched backwards, spinning in the air and landed softly out of harm's way. The driver looked up to see the white knight superhero standing next to the car. The Defender patted the bonnet.

"Always buy British!" he said, and resumed chasing the Viking bank robbers.

Guthrum curled his lip at the sight of the Defender still pursuing them and bellowed at his men to quicken their pace. On the river, a tourist ferry veered off course, sounding its horn as the Vikings' longship rose from the waters in its path. Sludge dripped from its pitted black timbers as it steered itself to the shore to await its crew. Bounding on to the wharf, Guthrum ordered his men onboard. The giant tipped the contents of the trollies one by one into the boat until his men were all knee deep in gold bars. On the road nearby, the Defender was boarding a double-decker bus and checking it was empty.

"Majesty? What are you doing? They're getting away with the gold!" shouted LC in his ear.

"Yes, thanks, LC. I've got an idea."

Happy that there were no passengers left cowering upstairs, Alfie drew his sword and thrust it into the side of the bus just above the windows. He sliced along the length of it, the metal screeching in protest. Watching from the Keep, the others were confused.

"What the dickens is he doing?!" bleated LC.

"Maybe he prefers open-topped buses," shrugged Hayley.

Alfie was surprised how quickly his sword had finished the task. He sheathed it and pushed up against the roof with all his strength. The roof of the bus popped off and slid to the ground with a loud *clang*. The Defender stepped off the bus and looked to the river. Guthrum was shrinking back to his normal size. The Viking lord cracked a smug smile at Alfie and stepped on to the mound of gold that filled his boat. Alfie cast his eyes along the riverbank. At the water's edge he could see a line of sleeping swans, their heads tucked under their wings, apparently not at all interested in the supernatural events unfolding close by.

"LC," said Alfie, "does my command power work on animals too?"

"Animals, Majesty?"

"Yes, yes. Birds, you know. Swans?"

"But of course, sir! The monarch owns all the swans on the Thames. Ever since the royal charter of 1482 under Edward the Fourth—"

"Give me the history lesson later!" Alfie said and raised his hand at the sleeping birds, which flapped their great wings as they woke up.

Meanwhile the Vikings were struggling to gain speed as they rowed their heavily laden boat out on to the river. Guthrum was just giving one of his men some constructive feedback about his laziness (by pounding him with his fist), when something big and white whacked him on the side of his head. Swans flocked around the boat, dive-bombing the Vikings and pecking at their bloated faces. Startled, the men abandoned their oars and took to swatting in vain at their feathered attackers.

The Defender, happy that the swans were obeying his silent command, turned his attention to the severed roof of the bus lying on the road. He pointed his hand and commanded it to skim over the water until it was hovering alongside the beleaguered longship. He took a running jump off the wharf and summoned Wyvern, who flew him out to within reach of the boat's stern.

Guthrum, perhaps sensing what the Defender was about to do, tried to get to him. But between his panicking men, the tumbling piles of gold bars and the psychotic swans, there was no way through. The Defender speared his sword hard into the longship's hull and tipped it with all his might to the side. Gold bars poured overboard, landing on the upturned bus roof that still hovered alongside. The Vikings that hadn't clung to the boat in time tumbled out too, skidding on the tide of gold and splashing into the river. The more that fell out, the easier it was for Alfie to lift and within seconds there was hardly a gold bar left in the longship. Seeing their bounty desert them, the remaining Vikings forgot the swans and desperately tried to grab any gold they could. But the Defender had them at his mercy now. He rocked the boat back the other way, throwing the entire crew into the water.

Spotlights danced across the bobbing heads of the foiled robbers as police boats surrounded them. Through a mouthful of water Guthrum spat a curse at the Defender, and dived beneath the waves, along with his men and boat.

As the storm retreated and the air grew still, Alfie directed the roof of rescued gold back to shore and deposited it on the ground in front of the bemused police commander. Officers aimed their guns at the Defender, who hovered above them on Wyvern.

"Get off the ... the flying horse!" croaked the commander, sounding like he'd had easier days at work.

"All right, relax," the Defender called down. "Just returning some lost property. You're welcome, by the way."

And with that, he shot into the sky. He may not have vanquished the Vikings for good, thought Alfie, but surely after his slick moves recovering the gold, people would give the Defender some credit for once.

16

THE RAVEN BANNER

"This so-called 'Defender' is a problem. A big problem. As much a threat to this country as the Vikings!"

Prime Minister Thorn glared at the assembled press corps from over her lectern outside Number Ten, Downing Street, as if daring them to contradict her.

"You've all seen the footage. Whoever this interfering 'superhero' is, he is potentially sabotaging the fine work of our police and security services, as well as putting the public at even graver risk."

Hands shot up from the fevered throng of journalists as they shouted questions like a class of unruly kids. *Didn't the Defender stop the Vikings? Wasn't it the Defender who saved the Bank of England's gold reserve from being stolen? Why is the Defender the only one standing up to the Vikings? What about the army? Is your government failing to keep Britain safe?*

Thorn sighed inwardly. These newsroom vultures were probably right; the chances were the Defender wasn't a threat. But since when did telling the truth get her anywhere? What she did know for sure was that if anyone was going to get the credit for solving this crisis it was HER, not some jumped-up vigilante in a silly costume. Fighting the Vikings head-on, however, was a non-starter. A war was only good for prime ministerial popularity ratings if it was a war you knew you would win. An enemy which was immune to bullets and which could turn itself into devil dogs and giants was not what she had in mind.

The prime minister held up her hands and hushed the journalists.

"After much consideration and due consultation with my cabinet, it has been decided that the best way to safeguard the British people is to reach a peaceful truce with these Vikings. A little gold is a small price to pay to guarantee our security and the safety of our children."

A cacophony of questions exploded from the press once more, but the prime minister merely smiled, waved and went inside. She had regained the spotlight. No one would be talking about the Defender on the news tonight.

"WHAT UTTER TOSH!" LC shouted as he thumped the off switch on the Map Room television. Or tried to. In fact he only managed to turn the sound up, then accidentally turn it to MTV at high volume. "Oh for goodness' sake. HAYLEY!"

Hayley smirked and flipped the TV off with the remote. "Red button, LC – remember?"

But the Lord Chamberlain was in no laughing mood. He was fuming, pacing up and down in front of her, Alfie and Brian. "The problem with these politicians is that none of them paid close enough attention in their history lessons. The Vikings will keep raiding and ransacking until they've plundered the entire country if we don't find a way to stop them for good."

The old man slumped down at a desk, exasperated. All eyes in the Map Room turned to

Alfie. He sensed they wanted him to say something, to give them a rousing "fight them on the beaches" type speech, but he felt pretty defeated himself.

"Maybe the prime minister is right. If we pay them they'll go away." Alfie shrugged.

"There's a word for that, Majesty. Appeasement," LC barked, going red in the face. "And when it comes to dealing with pure evil, appeasement never works. Alfred the Great himself tried to pay off the Vikings with something called the 'danegeld'. But where did that get him? Hiding in a Somerset swamp getting bitten to death by midges!"

"Well, I don't know what else I can do," Alfie said, frustrated. He couldn't stand it when LC flipped into full-on lecture mode. "You're not the one going out there putting your butt on the line fighting smelly zombies every other day. And by the way, no one in here or outside has even said a word of thanks. If people don't want me to help, then why should I?"

"Because you are Defender of the Realm!" LC shouted, for once forgetting to add *Your Majesty*. "You should not expect fan mail just for doing your job. Loyalty from your subjects is something you *earn*. Furthermore—"

"SHHH!" Hayley said and stood bolt upright.

"I beg your pardon?" LC spluttered. "The Keeper of the King's Arrows will remember her place—"

"Just zip it!" Hayley shouted. "LISTEN!"

Everyone did as they were told. A grating, staccato screech was heading towards them down one of the Keep's passageways, getting louder by the second.

"BEHIND ME!" Brian yelled, throwing himself in front of Alfie just as six *kraa*-ing ravens burst into the Map Room, flapping around their heads in a mass of black feathers and noisy beaks, knocking books and pens off the beefeaters' desks.

"Look out!" hollered Yeoman Eshelby the Ravenmaster, too late, as he huffed after his birds, waving his arms. "Edgar! Gwenn! Stop it! No, bad birds, bad! I don't know what's got into them, sir!"

The ravens flocked around Alfie, their raw-throated croaks ringing in his ears.

"Get them off me! Hey!" Alfie yelled as the frenzied ravens forced him to retreat across the Map Room.

Brian punched at thin air, while Herne snarled and snapped, but even he wasn't quick enough to catch a raven in full flight.

Alfie was obscured from view by a cloud of black

wings until suddenly he was gone! Dumbfounded silence descended over the others, broken only by Herne's whining. "Majesty?" gasped LC, gazing around in vain.

"The Archives!" Hayley shouted, pointing.

The great wooden hatch in the stone floor had somehow been wrenched opened by the birds in all the excitement, and Alfie must have fallen down it. Gwenn stood proudly by the bolt she had managed to slide open with her beak, and *gronk*ed at them, defiant.

"Gwenn! You naughty old girl!" said Yeoman Eshelby.

"Never mind that – the king, the king!" LC yelled, pushing past the Ravenmaster and peering into the chasm-like library below. "Majesty! Are you down there?"

A cough rose out of the darkness. "Yes! Do you want to give me a hand?" Alfie called from far below, his voice echoing around.

"Let's get some lights in there!" ordered Brian and several lanterns on ropes were lowered down to Alfie.

He was hanging from one of the old wooden ladders that extended right down into the inky blackness of the Archives. Around him, the ravens circled, calling madly.

LC watched them, intrigued. "Hold still, Your Majesty, and let's see what they're up to."

"What?! Oh sure, don't mind me!" Alfie said and sneezed in the dusty air.

He hoped the rickety ladder wouldn't suddenly snap in half. He didn't dare look down. In the soft glow of the lantern light, the ravens alighted on a shelf near Alfie and began pecking at one of the old books, pulling it out.

"What is that, Majesty? Can you read the title?" LC called down.

Alfie clung on to the ladder (which creaked alarmingly) and leant across, straining to read the Gothic-style font on the old book. "*Prose... Edda*?" he said and the ravens *kraa*-ed as one, making everyone jump. Alfie almost lost his grip again. "Can I come up now? Please!"

"Yes, of course, Majesty," LC said. "But I think you'd better bring that book with you."

A few minutes later, everyone was crowded around LC, who was studying the old book, making lots of happy-sounding sighs. Hayley thought if he was a cat, he'd be purring.

"Of course!" LC declared. "*Prose Edda*! Thirteenth century! Old Norse history written by Snorri Sturluson! Don't you see?"

"Not really," Alfie said, straining to see over LC's shoulder as he tried to find the page he was looking for.

"The Raven Banner!" LC shouted, triumphantly holding the book open at a page showing a medieval woodcut of a triangular flag with tassels depicting two ravens in flight. "The magical flag of the Norse god Odin himself. Flown by the first Vikings on their longships and said to be able to command all those of Norse blood. This could be the key to defeating Guthrum!"

"Who's a clever girl then?" said the Ravenmaster, tickling Gwenn under her beak.

The raven croaked proudly and preened her glossy wings. Alfie could feel hope rising in the room; everyone was looking at each other and smiling. Everyone that is, except Hayley.

"So, what ... we wave this old book in front of Guthrum and his dead mates and hope he goes home?" she said, puzzled. "It's not much of a plan, is it?"

"No, Miss Hicks. We find the flag and bring it

back here!" LC said, his eyes blazing. "The Raven Banner is said to be one of the crown jewels of the Norwegian royal family!"

"And what... They'll just give it to us?" Alfie asked.

"We'll cross that bridge when we come to it. Brian, we need a jet. ASAP," LC commanded, before turning to Alfie. "It's time for your first state visit. I suggest you wash your hair." Alfie ran his fingers through his hair and found that he was covered in black raven feathers ... and not a small amount of bird poo.

"I think I read somewhere that it's good luck," Hayley said, grinning.

"Excellent," replied Alfie. "I have a funny feeling I might need it."

17

THE NORWEGIAN QUEEN

"I would like my hand back now, if you don't mind, Majesty."

Queen Freya of Norway was the most beautiful young woman Alfie had ever seen. She was taller than him, with skin like fresh mountain snow and green eyes that were as dazzling as they were large. Her intricately plaited hair was so fair it was almost white. She wore an elegant silver satin gown, and he suspected that she did not need the diamond tiara, exquisite emerald earrings and necklace to look regal. She was royalty itself, and Alfie couldn't take his eyes off her.

"Are you feeling all right?" she added, arching an eyebrow.

Alfie realized he was still holding the hand she had offered him in greeting as he got out of the car at the steps of the Royal Palace in Oslo. How long had he been standing there while the TV cameras recorded him staring at her like an idiot? Alfie let go of her hand and willed his voice to say something, but the noise that came out sounded more like a cat stuck in a drainpipe than one monarch addressing another.

"Nice you meet to. . ." his voice crackled. "I mean, nice to meet you."

She smiled, though more at the cameras than at Alfie, and ushered the royal party inside. Alfie hoped his face didn't look as red as it felt. Though seeing how Brian also couldn't take his eyes off the queen made him feel a little better.

"Honestly, you two," muttered LC as they proceeded inside. "One would think you'd never seen a young lady before."

Alfie was surprised how similar the palace was in layout to Buckingham Palace, although it was a fraction of the size.

"I hope you will feel at home while you are here, King Alfred," said Queen Freya, as if reading his mind.

"Yes, it's just like my place," said Alfie, desperate to sound normal after his shaky start. "Except, you know, smaller."

Freya stopped and turned to him, frowning. "We'll be sure to build a new wing in time for your next visit."

"What? No! That's not what I meant!"

But Freya had already turned on her heel and continued down the long hallway. Alfie hurried after her, trying (and failing) to look dignified while jogging.

"I am sorry that we have not had time to organize more interesting events for your stay," said Queen Freya. "We normally receive more notice for state visits. About six months more."

"Yeah, sorry about that," winced Alfie. "I'm terrible at planning holidays!"

Note to self, thought Alfie, *STOP TRYING TO MAKE JOKES WHEN YOU'RE NERVOUS.*

"I must say, though, I could never leave my own kingdom unattended when it faced such dire peril," the queen added.

Alfie wasn't sure what to say; he thought talking to the prime minister back home was hard, but with Freya he was completely out of his depth. She was only six years older than him, but he had never felt more intimidated.

"Our American friends were keen to host the first royal overseas visit, Your Majesty," said the Lord Chamberlain, coming to his rescue, "but King Alfred was insistent that he wanted to visit the great Kingdom of Norway before any other."

Queen Freya nodded her thanks, but Alfie could tell she didn't believe a word of it. "Won't you join us in the Bird Room?" she said.

It was like walking into a forest. A mountain scene stretched across every inch of the walls. Painted trees, vines and birds so realistic that Alfie felt that if he reached out he could touch them. The ceiling was painted like the sky, with a majestic sea eagle hovering above them at its centre. It was like standing inside a fairy tale. The queen seemed amused at Alfie's wonder.

"You like it? A reminder of how we used to live," she said.

Alfie had no time to ask her what she meant, as they were invited to join other members of the royal family who were already gathered in two neat lines for the official photograph.

"Well, that was a disaster," said Alfie a few hours later, collapsing on the grand four-poster bed of the guest suite, while Brian checked the room for bugs. LC looked on, impatient.

"No matter," said LC once Brian gave him the "all clear" nod. "We are not here to further diplomatic relations. We must find the banner and return with it to England at the earliest opportunity."

"Great, because stealing from the queen is going to make her like me even more, isn't it?"

"I hardly think it matters if she likes you, Majesty," said LC.

"Bet he wouldn't mind, though, eh?" Brian chuckled.

Alfie felt himself going red again. "Fine. Focus on the mission. I get it. I just hope we can find this stupid flag before I make a complete fool of myself."

"He's making a complete fool of himself there, ain't he?" said one of the beefeaters back at the Keep.

They were watching the TV news replaying the

205

footage of Alfie's eighteen-second handshake with the ravishing Queen Freya.

"Not half. Don't blame him, though," smirked another.

They knew it was eighteen seconds because the reporter had actually used a stopwatch to time King Alfie's "Handshake Hiccup".

Hayley had missed all the coverage as she busied herself with archery practice in the Training Arena. She was trying to pretend that she didn't care about not being included on the trip, but deep down she felt upset about being left out again. She knew it was silly; sneaking her on-board the royal train was one thing, but an international flight was another matter. And yet every time Alfie, Brian and LC went off without her, the old feelings of being an outsider, of not being wanted, started to dent her confidence all over again. The fact that she had bugged Brian's phone before he left wasn't helping her feel much like a team player either.

Once Hayley had looked into how to do it, she couldn't believe how easy it was. There were loads of websites offering apps that could secretly record someone's phone conversations and all you needed was their mobile number. She simply had to call Brian's phone using the software she had downloaded. The call would never appear at his end, but would plant a remote recording device that would send back any calls he made direct to her phone. And to think, she had actually risked breaking into his room when she could spy on him this easily without being anywhere near him! Hayley knew that Alfie wouldn't like what she was doing, but she wouldn't tell him, not unless she found something bad. She really hoped there was an innocent explanation for Brian's recent behaviour, then no one would have to know what she had done.

Herne was lounging on the Arena floor watching Hayley fire arrow after arrow into the targets at the far end. It was unusual for him to hang out with her this much. *He must be missing Alfie too*, she thought. Although her shoulders were aching, she was getting better at using the longbow; her last arrow was only an inch off hitting the bullseye.

The sound of laughter drew her to the Map Room, where she found the Yeoman Warders gathered round the television. The news was showing pictures of the royal photocall in Norway. Everyone was looking at the camera, apart from Alfie, who seemed unable to take his eyes off his glamorous hostess, Queen Freya.

"Over here, Your Majesty!" called one of the beefeaters, laughing. "Watch the birdie!"

"I think that's what he's doing!" said another and they all descended into gales of laughter again.

"Sexist!" Hayley shouted.

But when the beefeaters turned round she was surprised to see Brenda was there too, laughing alongside the others.

"Come on, Hales, it's just a bit of fun," said Brenda. "No need to be jealous."

"I am NOT jealous!" Hayley said, and then she pulled back the bow's string and shot an arrow clean into the television, exploding it with a dull pop, like a wet firework going off.

In Oslo the state banquet was not going much better for Alfie. As guest of honour, he had been seated at the head of the hundred-strong table of VIPs, next to Queen Freya. She had changed into a sleek black evening gown for dinner, but was still wearing the same emerald necklace. Alfie's first mistake came with the starter, when he failed to recognize the curious, cold, salty white meat presented in a finely arranged salad.

"Mmm, this is, er, unusual. Is it a local delicacy?" he asked.

"Klippfisk," replied Queen Freya, evidently not inclined to give him any more help.

"Does it have an English name?" Alfie persisted. "Maybe our chef could try to get hold of some."

"Why, yes, King Alfred, I believe it is known in your country as cod. You're probably more used to eating it with chips. Out of a newspaper."

His second foul-up came as Alfie tried to compliment the queen when he noticed her wolfing down a third helping of the roasted pork belly main course.

"I'm surprised you're not enormous with an appetite like that!"

After that she turned to talk to the British ambassador who was seated on her other side. Alfie was left for the rest of the meal trying to make conversation with an elderly lady who may or may not have been something to do with shipping, or perhaps shopping, it was hard to tell as she didn't speak much English. At the end of the evening Alfie managed to make a speech of thanks without messing up too much, until he toasted Queen Freya not with his glass but with the pepper pot sitting next to it. By the time he got back to his room again he was ready to make a run for the airport and never come back. But, as LC reminded him, that was out of the question. His real night's work was only just beginning.

Alfie checked that the corridor was empty then slipped past the security desk and into the long gallery where the Norwegian Crown Jewels were on display for the summer. A few minutes earlier Brian had distracted the guard by claiming he had spotted an intruder outside. If the plan worked, it would give Alfie time to find the Raven Banner and take it back to the room before the guard returned. In theory.

Past kings and queens of Norway gazed down disapprovingly at Alfie from the huge portraits lining the gallery walls. He tried not to look at them and focus instead on the regalia in the cabinets before him. It was a familiar collection, much like his own, back in the Keep – crowns, sceptres, orbs – except for the small golden anointing horn, used, he assumed, during coronations to pour sacred oil on the monarch's head, much like the spoon used in his own crowning ceremony. It reminded him of Guthrum's hunting horn, and he wondered with a shudder whether Queen Freya, sleeping upstairs, had any Viking blood in her. It might explain her frosty attitude.

Then he saw it – a tall flag, faded with age, but bearing the image of Odin's black birds: the Raven Banner. Alfie tried to prise open the glass case, but it was locked, of course. He pulled out the razor-sharp glass cutter that Brian had given him. He hoped that it would not set off the alarm. If it did, the plan was to blame the "intruder" Brian had said he'd seen, evacuate Alfie due to the "inadequate security" at the palace, and head home with the banner. Alfie placed the tip of the glass cutter against the display case.

"You must be a history buff, Your Majesty."

Alfie stuffed the glass cutter back in his pocket and spun round to see a tall, severe-looking elderly lady in an old-fashioned tunic with long grey hair tied in a neat ponytail. She reminded him of someone, but he couldn't think who.

"I was just ... um, that is ... yes," said Alfie.

"If your Majesty wishes for a tour of the regalia, he need merely ask."

"Oh, you know, didn't want to make a fuss. Thanks, though. Terrific. Sorry, who are you?"

"I am the Lord Chamberlain."

Alfie burst out laughing. "Yes, that's who you reminded me of! I mean, *my* Lord Chamberlain. Er, not being funny, but shouldn't you be called the *Lady* Chamberlain?"

"That wouldn't really work," the Norwegian Lord Chamberlain said, a hint of an amused smile playing on her lips.

"No, I knew it didn't sound right as soon as I said it. You two should really meet though. You'd get on like a house on fire."

She nodded politely and stared at him. Was she waiting for him to say something? Alfie thought he might as well try to salvage something from the situation.

"I was just admiring your Raven Banner. Do you ever get it out to clean, or..."

"Alas, Majesty, that is not the real banner of Odin," replied the Norwegian Lord Chamberlain. "It is only a replica. The original is long since lost."

"Lost?"

Alfie couldn't believe it. Had he come all this way, made a fool out of himself and quite possibly permanently damaged international relations with Norway for nothing?

"Yes. Centuries ago."

"OK, well, nice to meet you. Goodnight."

Alfie sloped away, but as he reached the gallery door, the old woman spoke again. "There is the legend, of course..."

"Legend?" asked Alfie.

"That the banner was hidden away somewhere in the North, near Geirangerfjord."

"Geiranger-what?"

"Fjord," she repeated. "It is what we call our large lakes that are fed from the sea. I am surprised that your staff did not brief you on this."

"It was all a bit last minute," shrugged Alfie. "Does this banner legend say anything else?"

The elderly lady thought for a moment. "There is an old poem. I will try to translate... 'In northern lands, beyond Troll's Path, where Geiranger meets the sea, and seven sisters dance for their suitor, that's where in eternal sleep, Odin's banner black shall be.'"

"Wow, that's, um... You couldn't write it down for me, could you?" Alfie asked with a grin.

18

HOLGATROLL

As the lights of Oslo faded from view below them, Alfie couldn't help feeling uneasy. This wasn't like any normal Defender outing. This time he would not be able to rely on Wyvern to chart a course. Rather he would have to rely on his memory of the map LC had briefed him with, as they headed north and followed the fractured coastline – a thousand islands and inlets scattered like jigsaw pieces waiting to be assembled. Even if they found Geirangerfjord, he would need to be careful. As LC had said to him (at least five times):

"Remember, Majesty, you are on foreign soil, so there is very little your command powers will work on here."

Kind of obvious, thought Alfie. Unless this fjord was stuffed with British trees, iron and stone, he would be relying on his sword and his horse to get him out of any trouble. After twenty minutes flying, Alfie noticed the white dots of snow-covered peaks far below them and a large three-pronged claw of inlets that looked familiar.

"What do you think, Hayley?" said Alfie, directing his gaze downwards to give her a clearer view on her monitor back at the Keep.

"Not that you care what I think," she replied, "but yeah, that could be Geir-whatchamacallit-fjord."

"Somebody's in a mood she weren't invited," quipped Brian to LC back in Oslo, loud enough for Hayley to hear.

"Hey, Brian, why don't you stuff your—"

Alfie coughed loudly, drowning out what remained of Hayley's outburst.

"Thanks, team. Maybe the arguments can wait till I'm safely tucked up in bed again?" said Alfie. "I'll find somewhere to land, see if we're in the right place."

Moments later, the Defender was standing on a quiet mountain road looking at a sign and trying to decide whether or not it was a joke. It was a red warning triangle, at the centre of which was the silhouette of a dumpy humanoid creature that Alfie had already seen on T-shirts and posters in every tourist shop window on the drive through Oslo. A troll.

"Um. . ."

Below it was another road sign that read: TROLLSTIGEN.

"That's it!" said Hayley in his ear. "Trollstigen means Troll's Path. The fjord should be right over the next hill."

The Defender summoned Wyvern and she carried him over the tall pine trees that lined the dark road, startling the biggest owl Alfie had ever seen in his life, and emerged over the calm, icy waters of Geirangerfjord. Even at night-time it was a spectacular sight. Moonlight shimmered off the huge lake, which snaked out of sight towards snow-peaked mountains. Immense wooded cliffs rose straight out of the water on both sides. Alfie thought it was the most beautiful place he had ever been. The problem was that it was also vast. Alfie had the mobile sortilegic meter strapped to his belt, but he would have to get close to the banner to pick up a signal. Wyvern buzzed past the trees down one side of the fjord. In his excitement at finding the right place, Alfie had forgotten that he would still be faced with the task of pinpointing a hidden relic the size of a flag. A couple of miles later and he still couldn't see an end to the water.

"This is impossible," said Alfie. "It could be anywhere."

"What was it the poem said about seven sisters?" asked LC.

"It's just some stupid old poem," said Alfie. "It probably doesn't mean anything."

"And yet somebody chose those words for a reason; do not be so quick to dismiss them."

Alfie sighed. "Fine. It was, er ... seven sisters dance for their suitor, that's where in eternal sleep, Odin's banner black shall be."

"Good. Now look for any sign of habitation, perhaps these sisters used to live there."

"Believe me," said Alfie, "the only things living here are fish and maybe the odd mountain goat."

"You're such a bunch of dummies," said Hayley, cutting in from the Keep. "The seven sisters and their suitor aren't people. They're waterfalls."

"Waterfalls?" said LC. "Where did you find that, in the Archives?"

"No, I have my own really-secret ancient source," replied Hayley. "It's called Google."

Alfie stifled a laugh and steered Wyvern out over the water. A minute later they had found it. Seven waterfalls – the "sisters" – dancing over the cliff face on one side of the fjord, while another – their lonely "suitor", he supposed – watched from the other shore. There was just enough ground for him to land at the foot of the waterfalls, but looking around he couldn't imagine where you might hide a flag. There was nowhere to bury it and there were no obvious hiding places in the bare crags above him. Nevertheless he took out the meter and started to scan for activity. Nothing. No hint of a vibration from the brass instrument in his hand.

"Not a sausage," he said. "Looks like the Raven Banner was just a story after all."

Disappointed, he turned back to the cliff and sat on a rock with his feet in the water. What a waste of time. The sun would be up in a couple of hours and he didn't fancy trying to sneak back into the palace in broad daylight. He stood up, accidentally knocking the meter into the water.

"Oops. Are these things waterproof?" he asked as he stooped to pick it up.

Buzz. Alfie looked at the dripping meter as it buzzed eagerly. Alfie waded out until he was standing knee-deep in the fjord. "Whoa. I've got something here."

"What is it, sir?" asked LC.

"Not sure yet. But it looks like I'll be out of touch for a while. I'm going for a swim."

Alfie was not a strong swimmer. Along with football, rugby, cricket – OK, let's just say sport in general – he'd just never been that good at it. By the end of one swimming gala at Harrow there was genuine debate among the spectators about whether the future king was attempting the butterfly stroke or simply drowning. But in his Defender armour it was another story. Aside from the rather handy fact that it allowed him to breath underwater, the slightest kick of his legs propelled him through the water like a dolphin. In his hand, the meter was going crazy.

Buzz. Buzz. BUUUUUUUUZZ.

Alfie pulled his sword halfway out of its hilt, sending a powerful glow all around him as he swam on into the murky depths of the fjord. He was just wondering whether you got dangerous eels in Norwegian waters when he saw a strange light coming from a jagged fissure in a vast underwater cliff. He arrowed towards it, the vibration of the meter growing stronger with every stroke. The fissure was just large enough to squeeze through.

If he'd felt nervous being so deep underwater, then being underwater AND in a narrow tunnel was even worse. He had to force himself not to hold his breath, it was making him dizzy. *Trust in the armour – it's got you this far.* The rough tunnel seemed to go on for ever, deeper and deeper, but still the meter rattled like a bell against his belt and the warm glow he had spotted was getting brighter and brighter, like daylight ahead. Suddenly the tunnel opened up into a pool and he found himself bobbing to the surface inside a cave.

The glow wasn't coming from daylight. Phosphorescent algae on the dripping walls reflected off piles and piles of gold. Coins, jewellery, caskets and crucifixes – the floor of the cave was awash with treasure. It rattled and slipped beneath Alfie's feet like pebbles on a beach as he walked over it. He wondered who it all belonged to, or whether its owner had died long ago, leaving it here, forgotten.

But he wasn't here for gold; he couldn't afford to get distracted. Ahead of him the clinking golden blanket came to an end, plunging the cave into darkness once more. Stalactites hung from the roof of the cave like jagged teeth in a giant monster's mouth. As he walked on, a smell of decaying seaweed filled his nostrils.

And then Alfie saw it, standing on a raised patch of rock on the far side of the cavern. It wasn't much to look at – a tattered triangular piece of cloth depicting a crude image of a raven, worn tassels hanging off it, all attached to a simple wooden pole. Was this really the great Raven Banner? The sacred Norse relic so powerful it had to be hidden deep beneath a remote fjord? The buzzing meter on his belt said yes.

As he edged through the darkness towards the banner, he felt the ground underfoot become soft and uneven. He hated to think how many dead fish had washed in here over the centuries; he just knew he didn't want to end up falling into it all. The seaweed underfoot squeaked as he walked on it – air pockets being released, he figured. Squeak. . . squeak. . . snoooooore.

Wait. . . SNORE?!?

Alfie unsheathed his sword as quietly as he could. Light flooded the corner of the cave, confirming his worst fears. Seaweed, of course, doesn't snore. But sleeping Viking draugar do. There must have been a thousand of the ugly, stinking, farting-in-their-sleep undead warriors, piled on top of each other like they'd dropped unconscious at the end of an epic party. Celebrating their latest treasure pillaging expedition, no doubt. Alfie didn't know how many centuries this ghoulish sleepover had been going on and he didn't want to know. He just wanted to grab the banner and get out of there before anyone's alarm clock went off. He thought about summoning Wyvern and flying over them, but the roof was low in here and if he knocked a stalactite down it was sure to wake them.

Dulling the light from his blade, Alfie tiptoed as best he could across the carpet of bodies, trying not to tread on any of the Vikings' more tender parts. As luck would have it, this lot seemed to be seriously deep sleepers. Even after he had retrieved the Raven Banner and accidentally poked the end of it quite far up a snoozing draugar's nostril, the Viking had merely grumbled in his sleep and swatted it away.

Not hanging around long enough to even think

about taking any other souvenirs from the treasure trove, the Defender dived into the entrance pool and made his way back through the tunnel with the flag. Breaking free of the cave, he kicked hard for the surface of the fjord.

Alfie was just congratulating himself on another narrow escape and a mission accomplished when he was hit by the lake monster. He cartwheeled through the water, struggling to catch his breath, but the creature was already coming at him again. *That can't be real*, he thought, gasping inside his suit. At least fifty feet long, with four enormous flippers and a long, snake-like neck, the monster opened its gargantuan jaws, wide enough to swallow him whole. The Defender summoned his shield and kicked away, turning what would have been a fatal strike into a glancing blow. Still, Alfie knew this was one fight he could not win, at least not underwater.

SPURS!

Wyvern spiralled out beneath him and, seeing the hulking shadow of the lake monster rising fast towards them, needed no prompting to head topside. They exploded from the lake and banked hard for the trees. If they could just clear the top of the cliffs... But the lake monster was right behind them, its long neck shooting up like a torpedo, its whole body clearing the surface. *THHHWACK!* The beast sideswiped them with its huge head, sending them smashing into the rocks. Wyvern disappeared with the impact, leaving Alfie hanging from the cliff face. Somehow Alfie still had the Raven Banner gripped in one hand. The lake monster splashed down into the shallows with a tremendous *SMACK*, then wasted no time in gliding back to the cliff and raising her neck towards him. If he hadn't been about to die, Alfie would have marvelled at the prehistoric grace of the creature and the smoothness of her grey-green skin. His communications system crackled back into life. It was Brian.

"You there, boss? We were about to dispatch the Navy to find you. How's it going?"

"BADLY!"

He could hear their shocked gasps as his helmet-cam came back online giving them a close-up view of the incoming monster's jaws! From the position in which he was dangling, Alfie was having trouble reaching his sword. He estimated he had about a second to do something before he was eaten.

A skull-shuddering yell unlike any he had ever

heard before came from above him. Tree trunks snapped like matchsticks as something huge and green leapt from the top of the cliff straight at the lake monster and punched it on top of its vast head. The lake monster howled like a kicked dog and retreated into the water, leaving its attacker to jump off into the shallows with a triumphant roar. By the time Alfie realized he was falling it was too late to call on his spurs, so instead he opted for landing flat on his face. His helmet communications crackled and went offline again.

Shaking the stones from his armour, the Defender sat up to see the huge *troll* that had scared off the lake monster stride out of the water. He *assumed* it was a troll, anyway. It certainly matched the picture on the sign he'd seen earlier, except this one had real green flesh and bulging muscles and warts and tussocks of wiry black hair. The troll, all ten feet of it, squared up to him. It was close enough for him to get a whiff of the drool falling like a black waterfall from its hideous mouth. Oof. And he thought dead Vikings smelled bad!

Alfie was grateful for being saved from the lake monster, but he also wished that Norway would just hurry up and decide which mythological monster was going to kill him, because this was getting silly. Without thinking, the Defender reached out his ring finger towards a boulder and hurled it at the troll. Except that he didn't, because the boulder stayed precisely where it was.

"Oh right, foreign soil. That's annoying," he said to himself.

The troll started to guffaw, burping between laughs like a helpless child. Alfie considered taking this chance to summon Wyvern back and fly away over the fjord, but he could see the dark shadow of the lake monster patrolling just under the surface.

"Nice try, but you're on my patch now, remember?" said the troll.

For some reason Alfie had not been expecting the troll to speak. Probably because it didn't look smart enough. "Who are you?" he asked.

"I am Holgatroll. But you know me by another name..."

The troll began to shrink, its skin turning from green to pink as it transformed from the ugly monster into a graceful young woman. Queen Freya. She was still wearing the same dress she'd had on at dinner, and the emerald necklace, which shone with a dazzling green light as she transformed back into her human form.

"No. Way," Alfie stammered.

His head was spinning. Lake Monsters, and now trolls who were queens. His legs buckled and he had to steady himself on a boulder.

"What?" asked the queen, enjoying his surprise. "Did you think you were the only one with unusual gifts?"

Alfie removed his armour. The king and queen stood unmasked before each other on the shore. "No, but, a *troll*? I mean you did NOT smell good. No offence."

"My family did not exactly choose our curse. But it has had its uses over the centuries." Freya took the Raven Banner from Alfie's hand and inspected it for damage. "Stopping people stealing from us, for example."

"You knew I was going to try and take it, didn't you?" said Alfie. "You might have warned me about your lake monster."

"Selma? Oh, she's not so bad if you know how to keep her in line. Besides, I wanted to see how you handled it. Better than some, I must say. Although I give your horse most of the credit."

"I'm sorry I tried to steal your flag," said Alfie. "But we have a bit of a Viking problem back home, as you know."

"Indeed you do," she said. "Nobody wants a band of draugar on the loose. That is why we try to keep ours underground. They flock to the banner, and it lulls them into an endless sleep. Without it they would wake eventually. Then where would we be?"

Alfie was annoyed. If she had known all along what he was up to, then why put him through so much only to snatch away his prize at the last second? He prepared to put his armour back on.

"You could have told me all this at dinner. If you'd bothered to talk to me. Now if you don't mind, I need to get home. I've wasted too much time on this wild goose chase."

Freya stepped over and put her hand on his arm. She smiled sweetly – the first sincere smile she'd given him since he arrived. Alfie reminded himself that no matter how drop-dead gorgeous she was, he was still supposed to be very cross with her.

"I'm sorry, Alfie. Really. I would have told you sooner, but my Lord Chamberlain advised caution. She said we could not be sure of your true intentions until we had tested you. She's rather strict like that."

"Yeah, well, I can relate," said Alfie.

Freya handed Alfie the banner.

"What?" said Alfie. "But I thought you said. . .?"

"I said our draugar would wake *eventually*. Now take it before I change my mind. But I want it back as soon as it's over, or else there'll be trouble."

She wasn't smiling now.

"I believe you. Thanks."

"One thing. The banner has never left its native land. How it will behave somewhere else I cannot say. . . Well, then – race you back?"

Without warning, Freya transformed back into Holgatroll. Alfie backed away from the fresh stink and whipped his Defender armour back on.

"I need to get home before sunrise or I turn to stone," grunted Holgatroll.

"Seriously?" asked the Defender.

"Yeah. That boulder you tried to chuck at me? Great Uncle Magnus."

Selma stretched her neck out of the water and let out a mournful cry that echoed across the fjord.

"She is saying goodbye," said Holgatroll. "By the way, why did you not try your command powers on her?"

"She's Norwegian, isn't she?" said Alfie, confused.

"No," laughed Holgatroll. "She only summers here. In winter she goes home to Scotland. You have a different name for her there, I think. What is it? Oh yeah – Nessie."

And, with that, the royal troll bounded up the cliff face in a single leap.

"I wish I could tell when you're joking," yelled Alfie as he recalled Wyvern and took chase, pursuing the speeding troll through the countryside back towards Oslo.

The next morning on the flight home Alfie waited till the stewardess had left the cabin, then leaned over to the Lord Chamberlain.

"Queen Freya – you knew she had … *another side* to her, didn't you?" Alfie was still getting over the surprise. It was huge news. It meant there were others out there like him. It meant he wasn't alone.

"I confess I did, Majesty," replied LC. "Many of the world's royal families are known to have heroic, or not-so-heroic, alter-egos. Great Britain has enjoyed good relations with some, not-so-good with others. You will come to know more about all that in time. For now we need to concentrate on issues at home."

"But then why didn't we just ask her for the Raven Banner in the first place?"

"We could not risk her saying no. In any case, all's well that end's well, sir."

Across the aisle, Brian opened the luggage compartment and placed a long wrapped parcel inside. The Raven Banner was on its way to England.

LC smiled at Alfie, proud. "Very well played, Majesty. Now we can really take the fight to those Vikings."

Half an hour later, as Alfie enjoyed a well-earned nap, Brian walked to the toilet at the back of the plane. Inside he took out his mobile phone. He gazed at his reflection in the mirror for a moment, the expression on his face impassive, then dialled a number.

19

THE WHISPERING GALLERY

Oranges and Lemons say the bells of St Clement's.
The tune of the famous nursery rhyme pealed out
from the bells of the neat little white church every
day at noon. St Clement Danes, which now stood
on a traffic island between the Strand and Aldwych
in London, got its name from the Vikings who
originally built it after Alfred the Great had expelled
them from the centre of the capital. Regular visitors
always knew it had a crypt at the west end, which was
used nowadays for prayer meetings. But none knew
about the secret crypt deep beneath the eastern end.

Professor Lock had discovered its entrance years before while exploring the long-forgotten world of subterranean London – just the latest of countless ancient secrets revealed to him by his shadowy accomplice. This was the place that he had chosen as his final hideout for Guthrum and his men. Its central position in the city, with discreet access to the River Thames, was perfect for executing their stealth raids on the country. But above all, the historical irony amused him: after more than a thousand years, he had brought Vikings back to the heart of London.

"What people forget about this little ditty," said Lock, leading Guthrum and his axe-wielding men out of the crypt and past a handful of startled tourists in the church, "is that as nice as it sounds – 'oranges and lemons', la-di-dah – it has quite a sting in the tail. 'Here comes a chopper to chop off your head, chip chop chip chop – the last man's dead.'"

Lock stood aside as the Vikings marched outside. Within seconds he heard screams mingled with the boom of thunder rolling in and the crackle of lightning hitting the bell tower, silencing its tolls.

The police had erected barriers along every road to Trafalgar Square. All traffic in central London, including the river, was banned as the nation waited to see if the Vikings would turn up to collect their ransom. "Danegeld" had become a household term over the last couple of days, and the debate about whether a Viking pay-off was a good idea was still raging. In the latest poll, most people had agreed with the prime minister's argument – if it was a choice between paying the ransom or risking further violence at the hands of the Vikings, then Britain should cough up. There was no guarantee it would work, but these were desperate times.

Heavy rain washed over the Strand as Guthrum and his men passed by Charing Cross train station, watched by the astonished crowds packed behind the barriers. People couldn't decide whether to hold their noses against the deathly stench or cover their ears from the loud blasts of the Viking lord's war horn.

"Leave us alone! Get out of here!" a brave soul shouted as the Vikings passed by.

Guthrum's head snapped around and stared at the crowd, daring them to hold his gaze. "ÞEGIT, ÞRÆLAR!"* he screamed.

---

* "SILENCE, SLAVES!"

The crowd fell silent, huddling beneath umbrellas and hoods. Guthrum roared with laughter and gave the biggest blast on his horn yet to announce his war band's arrival at Trafalgar Square.

"Look at them, marching around as if they own the place," Prime Minister Thorn muttered as she gazed down from her position overlooking the square, watching the undead Vikings parade, swinging their great axes and thumping their shields. *Problem is,* she thought, *with the amount of gold we're about to give them, they kind of do.*

Lightning forked across the bruised purple sky. Three large armoured vans from the Bank of England stood ready at the base of Nelson's column, each filled to the brim with bars of precious gold. Squads of nervous riot police with shields and truncheons stood to attention on the steps like a waiting army. But there would be no battle today; this was all about peace. A senior police chief stepped forward and fumbled with the plastic visor of his riot helmet as he tried to raise it.

"On behalf of the population of Great Britain and Northern Ireland I hereby offer this tribute in gold," he said.

Guthrum towered over him, his fierce eyes

glowing and the smell of rotting fish cascading off him in thick waves. Bravely, the police chief went on, his voice shaking as much as his legs.

"In return, you and your men as well as any other undead creatures in your service, shall agree to leave this great nation in peace and—"

"*GULL!*" Guthrum yelled, shoving the police chief aside and ripping the back door of the armoured van clean off its hinges with a screech of metal.

Like wasps attacking a pot of jam, the Vikings swarmed over the gold.

"*GULL! GULL! GULL!*"

They grabbed armfuls of gold bars and danced around with them, tossing them back and forth as if they were playing catch with tennis balls. With an effortless leap, Guthrum sprang up on to the roof of the second van and peeled off the roof like he was opening a tin of sardines.

"*GUUUUUUUULL!*" he screamed to the square, holding up a gold bar, triumphant.

From her viewpoint, the prime minister watched, impassive. It was far from the dignified handover she was hoping for, but what could you expect with such primitive creatures? As least they seemed happy, as they began to drag the gold-laden vans away. It had never occurred to her that the Vikings wouldn't know how to drive. Around Thorn, her advisors and ministers were all shaking hands and patting each other on the back, relieved it was over. The Viking threat to Britain was at an end. With any luck, they might even take these thunderstorms with them.

"LOOK!" an advisor shouted.

Everyone rushed back to the window to see the Defender fly out of the dark sky on his shimmering horse and land in the square, blocking the Vikings' escape. The crowds below let out a roar of delight. But the prime minister was furious.

"What's HE doing here?" she screamed. "He'll mess everything up!"

Alfie held tight on to Wyvern's reins as her front hooves pounded the pavement, keeping the Vikings at bay. "You really don't look very well, Guthrum," he said.

Guthrum dropped the van he was dragging along with a heavy *clang* and strode forward, shoving his men out of the way to get to the Defender. But before he reached axe-swinging distance, Wyvern kicked her front legs and whinnied defiantly. The great Viking lord retreated and circled Alfie, bellowing his annoyance.

"Seriously, you're really pale – big bags under your eyes," Alfie went on. "And is that part of your skull showing through your cheek? Eww. What you need is a really good night's *sleep*."

The Defender lifted the flagpole and unfurled the Raven Banner. Guthrum and his Vikings gasped in awe and stepped back, shielding their eyes like the banner was the hot summer sun.

"Yeah, that's right, recognize this? It's time for a nap. A long one. Years. Or eternity even. Any second now. . ."

Alfie was drying up. Whatever the Raven Banner was supposed to do, it wasn't working very fast. The Vikings were peeking out from behind their shields, losing whatever fear they had.

"Does this banner have an on button?" Alfie hissed under his breath. "Help me out, LC."

LC's voice crackled in Alfie's earpiece. "Perhaps you could try waving it about, Majesty?"

Alfie did just that, waving the ragged Raven Banner above his head but instead of falling asleep, Guthrum was chuckling.

"He's laughing, guys. Why's he laughing? Something's not right here," said Alfie.

Guthrum and his very much awake Vikings were

surrounding Alfie, brandishing their axes, while behind him armed police were levelling their guns at his back. *Hey, I'm on your side!* Alfie wanted to shout as Wyvern spun around, unsure which direction to face first.

"I'm out of here," Alfie said and kicked his spurs.

Wyvern shot up into the stormy sky. The crestfallen crowd gasped in dismay as they watched the Defender fly off. The jeering Vikings picked up their gold and moved off, the police making way for them.

"Well, that was embarrassing," said Alfie, rain spattering against his visor as Wyvern charted a course between the towering thunderheads that had gathered over London. "I thought the banner was supposed to command all those of Viking blood? I didn't see much commanding going on!"

"Majesty, I can't explain it either," LC said. Alfie could hear the disappointment in the old man's voice. "But Queen Freya did warn you that it might behave differently outside Norway—"

BOOM! Something collided with Alfie and sent him and Wyvern spinning out of control. For a moment Alfie thought a plane had hit them. But as he strained to catch his breath and pull out of the spin, he scanned the storm clouds and caught sight of a large, dark shadow, wheeling round for another attack.

"I'm not alone up here!" gasped Alfie.

But if there was a reply from the Keep, it was drowned out by the ear-piercing shriek of the Black Dragon as it streaked towards him once more, scraping its claws across his armour, sending sparks flying. Wyvern screamed in fear as the Dragon's thick, scaly tail wrapped itself around her, squeezing like a python. Alfie's arms were pinned to his side; he couldn't move. All he could see was a chaotic collage of scales, yellow fangs the size of milk bottles and the Dragon's fiery eyes—

Lightning flashed all around them, blinding Alfie for a moment. But, suddenly, much to his surprise, he found they were free of the Dragon's tight grasp. His enemy had disappeared as fast as it arrived.

"Majesty? Majesty?" LC's voice was frantic in his ear.

"The Black Dragon!" panted Alfie. "It was here! It's back. Lock is back!"

"It was flying?" interjected Brian.

"Yes. Its wing's regrown. It had me. I don't understand. Why did it let me go?"

Alfie's stomach lurched as he realized what was missing from his hand. "The banner!" he managed to splutter. "It took the Raven Banner!"

"WHAT?" shrieked LC.

"Wyvern, track it!" commanded Alfie.

He could tell his horse was reluctant to follow the Dragon, but he had to retrieve the banner.

"NOW, WYVERN!"

Wyvern whinnied fiercely and galloped east into an enormous canyon of yellow-stained dark clouds, following the Black Dragon's trail. Soon Alfie could see it up ahead, flitting in and out of sight, clutching the Raven Banner in its talons as it plunged through the broiling storm that raged over London.

Alfie urged Wyvern on, but the Black Dragon was fast, and it had a head start. Losing the race, Alfie felt frustrated and angry. The Vikings had humiliated him in front of the entire country, and now the Black Dragon had ambushed him and stolen the one thing that might stop them. How dare they run riot in his kingdom? It was time to put an end to this. Alfie pulled Wyvern to a halt and raised his hand. The Ring of Command glowed. He didn't know if his idea would work, but it was worth a try. The way he looked at it, these were the Defender's clouds, made of good old British rain. Maybe they would respond to his commands too? Alfie swished his hand and the nearest storm clouds seemed to react, moving from side to side. He gestured again, this time focusing on the distant cloudbank where he could still just make out the figure of the Dragon flying. The clouds swirled at his command – it was difficult to control, but Alfie could feel them, as if they were a silk cloth draped across his hand. He turned his fingers and the dense blanket of clouds spun around the Dragon, trapping him inside their funnel. Alfie closed his fist and lightning exploded through the clouds. Stunned, the Dragon dropped like a stone.

"Yes!" Alfie shouted in triumph. He kicked his heels, and Wyvern dived after their target.

A ragged, dragon-sized hole had been punctured in the great lead dome of St Paul's Cathedral. Alfie flew through and landed, Wyvern disappearing back into his spurs. He was standing on a high, narrow walkway bordered by an iron railing that circled the circumference of the dome. It was eerily quiet and gloomy, as if the storm outside had sucked up all the daylight. Far below, Alfie could see debris from the roof scattered across the black-and-white tiles of the nave, but fortunately it looked like the church was empty of visitors. No doubt most people were still out on the streets watching the danegeld handover. There was no sign of the Black Dragon.

A whisper in his ear. *"Alfie?"*

The Defender spun around and drew his sword, but there was no one there. Distant thunder rumbled, echoing dimly inside the vast cathedral.

"Alfie!"

The voice again, like someone was standing right next to him, but again there was no one there.

A plaque on the wall told him that this was called the "Whispering Gallery", said to be built in such a way that the softest of voices could carry all the way round the dome.

"Bit old for games aren't you, Professor Lock?" Alfie said in hushed voice, figuring it too would reach his enemy's ears.

Alfie drew his sword and crept around the walkway.

"Did you raise Guthrum and his men, professor? What do you want with the banner?"

But as Alfie rounded the far side of the gallery, what he saw next made him stop dead. A naked figure was crouched in the corner, his skin grey and glistening with sweat.

"You're better at hide and seek than you used to be, Alfie."

The figure turned his face into the light. Gaunt, with wild eyes, but still unmistakable. It was his brother. It was Richard.

Alfie's mind whirred. *What was Richard doing here? How did he know who he was?* He patted his armour, making sure the visor was still over his face.

"Don't worry, big brother, your little secret's safe with me," Richard giggled, but there was no joy in it.

He moved his hand and now Alfie saw that he was holding something on the ground. The Raven Banner.

"Oh, and thanks for saving me a trip to get this. I promise I won't lose it like you did."

Alfie reached up with a shaking hand and removed his armour. He took a step closer to his brother.

"Richard, are you all right? What are you doing here? What's going on?"

"Let's call it a little ... revolution," Richard said, and then jumped over the iron railings and plunged towards the floor.

"RICHARD!" Alfie screamed.

He ran to the railings, just in time to see his

brother transform into the Black Dragon, his bones elongating and cracking, leathery wings unfolding and scales growing in an instant, covering his monstrous head and jaws. With one powerful pump of his wings, the Dragon pulled up from the dive, circled the interior of the church, then swooped back over Alfie's head and smashed back out through the hole in the dome, flying into the storm.

Alfie fell to his knees, trembling, almost unable to take in what he had just seen with his own eyes.

IT'S RICHARD. THE BLACK DRAGON IS MY BROTHER.

20

SPLIT LOYALTIES

Alfie had been crying.

He was sitting on the lead roof at the top of the White Tower, the central fortress of the Tower of London, and thinking about the first time he had ever set foot here. He and Richard were nine years old, and they couldn't have been more excited. The Tower had been closed to the public for the princes' visit, not that they realized that, of course. This was back when they were yet to learn not everyone gets to be escorted by the police through traffic, and to be greeted by a waiting crowd of well-wishers and beefeaters standing to attention. They had the run of the place, chasing each other through the courtyards and exhibits, wrestling on the grass next to the chopping block, running, screaming, from the ravens after one of them pecked Richard's finger. Alfie hadn't even slowed down to look at the Crown Jewels – growing up in the palace, he'd seen plenty of dusty old gems and swords before. But he remembered that his brother had stopped, fixing the display behind the glass with a serious stare, as if he was in a trance. In the end Alfie had grown bored of waiting and left him there to go and check out the toys in the gift shop.

Now, as he gazed south over the river, Alfie wondered if Richard had already started to resent him back then. He had always thought his brother didn't care about being the "spare", but what if he had been wrong? What if Richard had always hated him?

Alfie couldn't get the image of his brother changing into the Black Dragon out of his head – the twisting limbs, the rage etched across his monstrous face. He closed his eyes and gripped the railing that ran around the battlements. This was worse than the feeling he'd had when his father died. Worse than the turmoil of the Succession when he'd been sure he was losing his mind. Worse than when he had found out – *thought* he'd found out – that his trusted teacher Professor Lock was really a monster and his family were in terrible danger. How could he not have seen what was there right in front of him all this time? Richard had killed their father. He had tried to kill Alfie too, at the coronation. What had happened to Richard? How could the loving twin he had known his whole life have become so evil?

A whistle drew Alfie's attention to the courtyard below. Yeoman Eshelby was letting his birds out of their cages for the day, patting them on their shiny black heads as they hopped past him. Perhaps sensing someone watching, the Ravenmaster looked up and saw the young king standing on the tower. He gave a formal nod and carried on tending to the ravens. Alfie wiped his eyes. *Everyone in the Keep must know by now,* he thought miserably.

Car horns blared from the traffic jam on Tower Bridge as if it were just another normal summer's day. The Vikings hadn't been seen since they were paid off, and the prime minister was basking in the nation's praise. "THE DEAD REST IN PEACE!" the headlines shouted in glee as the country heaved a huge collective sigh of relief. The storms had disappeared, the sun was shining again and the only worry on the horizon seemed to be whether Kate Robertson could win her first Wimbledon title. Alfie could only imagine their panic if they knew what he knew. The Black Dragon was still out there, dreaming up dark schemes with Professor Lock, cooking up the next phase of their plan. Something terrible was coming and—

"I'm so sorry."

Alfie had not heard the Lord Chamberlain come out on to the rooftop. He looked even older than normal. Deep worry-lines fanned across his brow like a crinkled road map.

"He tried to tell me, you know. At Ellie's party," said Alfie. "He said it was all my fault. Did I do this to him?"

LC moved closer, placing a hand on Alfie's shoulder. "None of this is your fault. If it is anyone's, it is mine. I should have seen this sooner. It makes perfect sense now."

"Sense?" Alfie brushed his hand away. "None of this makes any sense!"

"I understand, Majesty. All I mean is the Black Dragon – how it came to be. It was Richard's blood, the royal blood that Lock needed to combine the power of King Alfred's crown with the dragon bones and create a new creature. That was what I was missing. It's so obvious now."

"But why hide who he was after the coronation? Richard could have killed me any time he wanted!"

"I don't know, Majesty. But they went to great lengths to make sure we obtained the Raven Banner for them."

"What do they want with that stupid flag? It doesn't even work."

"Not in the way *we* intended. But perhaps Lock knows something we don't. Whatever it is, we must hunt them down before they have time to execute their plan. Defeat them once and for all. Lock and the Black Dragon."

"You mean Richard?" Alfie said. There was something in LC's troubled expression he didn't like at all. "What is it?"

"Majesty, I have known you and your brother since the day you were born. I may not be the best at showing it, but I care for you both, very much. Perhaps if this had come to light earlier, but now. . ."

"What are you saying, LC?"

The old man stiffened and raised his head, as if addressing the audience at a state banquet. "Prince

Richard has made his choice. He is a traitor and must be dealt with as such. The Defender must kill the Black Dragon."

Alfie felt his legs wobble beneath him. Did LC really just say that to him? "You want me to. . ." Alfie could hardly bring himself to say it. "To kill my own brother?!"

"He is no longer your brother, sir. He is your enemy. And make no mistake, this is war."

Alfie pushed past him, towards the door. "I can't listen to any more of this."

"Majesty, we must all stand firm and face this battle together!" LC pleaded.

Alfie swung open the door, only to march straight into Hayley. She burst on to the roof, out of breath after running up the staircase.

"Miss Hicks, now is not the time," began LC.

But she held up her phone, silencing him. "You'd better make time. 'Cos you need to hear this. Both of you."

She pressed play. At first all they could hear was a low rumble, like engines turning. But then an automated voice spoke:

"Leave your message after the beep."

Alfie and LC recognized the next voice

immediately, even though he was talking in an uncharacteristic whisper.

"It's me," said Brian's voice on the tape. *"We have the banner. We're on the way back from Oslo now. They're planning to use it at the handover. But keep your distance. I think the girl suspects something. I'll call again when I can."*

The recording ended. LC and Alfie looked at each other in stunned silence.

Minutes later they sat opposite Brian in the Keep as the message played again. LC had commanded the Yeoman Warders to vacate the room, though he told two of them to guard the doors and listen out in case he summoned them. Alfie was disturbed by what he had heard, but he was sure Brian would have a good explanation. The phone message came to an end once more, and LC fixed Brian with a penetrating stare.

"Well? Explain yourself, King's Armourer. For whom were you leaving this message?"

Brian hadn't stopped looking at Hayley, a cold, hard expression Alfie had not seen before on his bodyguard's face. Only now did Brian turn to the Lord Chamberlain.

"Sorry, guv, but I can't tell you that," he replied.

LC sprung forward. "WHAT DID YOU SAY?!" Alfie actually thought the old man was going to hit Brian. "YOU HAVE PASSED SECRET INFORMATION TO PARTIES UNKNOWN, AND YOU WILL EXPLAIN YOURSELF!"

Brian barely flinched and kept his stony silence. Nearby, Herne got up and paced back and forth, restless. The hair on his back stood up and he growled at Brian, low and deep. Alfie, his head spinning, stepped in between them.

"Please, Brian, just tell us what's going on and we can forget it."

Brian leant back in his chair and sighed. "Sorry, kid, no can do."

"YOU ARE ADDRESSING YOUR SOVEREIGN!"

LC was purple with rage and he coughed and stumbled for a moment. Alfie helped him back to his chair. Hayley kept her eyes on the floor.

All were quiet for a few moments. The Yeoman Warders who had been guarding the doors had rushed in when they heard the shouting and now they stood, pikes at the ready, unsure what to do.

"Is there nothing you wish to say in your defence?" LC croaked.

Brian stared at the wall, unmoved. "No."

LC wiped sweat from his brow with a handkerchief, his hand shaking. "Yeoman Warders, take the Armourer to the cells," he commanded. "Inform the Jailer."

The startled beefeaters exchanged a glance, then walked over to Brian and pulled him to his feet. Alfie looked to LC and Hayley in disbelief, but neither met his gaze.

"Wait!" Alfie shouted. "This is wrong, you can't do this! If Brian says he had his reasons, then that's good enough for me."

But Brian smiled at him. "It's OK, chief." And then he allowed the beefeaters to escort him from the Map Room.

Alfie felt numb. First he had lost his brother. And now Brian? It felt like the cornerstones of his world were crumbling into dust, one by one. Unable to hold his tongue, he turned on Hayley.

"What have you done?" he snapped.

"What are you having a go at me for?" said Hayley, shocked. "How about 'thanks, Hayley, for watching my back'?"

"I told you to drop it, and look what's happened now."

"You ungrateful little—"

Yells interrupted them from outside the Map Room. At first Alfie thought maybe it was just somebody else joining in the screaming match, but then he realized it was coming from the direction in which the Yeoman Warders had taken Brian. They rushed into the corridor to see one beefeater lying unconscious on the floor and the other doubled-up in the corner, holding his stomach and groaning.

"What happened? Where is the prisoner?" shouted LC.

A secret passageway was open in one wall, pumping out cold draughts of air. Alfie ran over to it and looked inside. It snaked away into darkness.

Brian was gone.

21

MOUNTAIN OF LIGHT

"And how about the recent supernatural events here in London? Has it been a distraction?"

Kate Robertson smiled at the interviewer and leant in to the microphone. "The only thing that scares me is not playing my best out there today. It'll take more than a few mangy old Vikings to stop me trying to win this title."

The spectators watching the replay of the interview on the big screen inside Wimbledon's Centre Court erupted into raucous cheers. A chant echoed around the arena: "Ka-tie, Ka-tie, Ka-tie."

The Women's Singles finalists were not due on court for another half hour, but already the atmosphere was electric. Robertson was the first British woman to get this far since Virginia Wade way back in 1977, and no one with a ticket was going to miss this. The sun was shining, the Vikings were history (again) and life was returning to normal.

Princess Eleanor took her seat in the royal box and scanned the rows around her. She was surrounded by familiar faces – movie stars, celebrities and aristocrats – but she wasn't here to spot famous people. Ellie was all about the sport. She still hoped to compete in gymnastics at the Olympics one day. Superheroes like the Defender were one thing – and he *had* saved her from the Black Dragon at the coronation – but she couldn't help feeling that having all those superpowers and gadgets was cheating. Sports stars like Kate Robertson, who got to the top through sheer hard work and determination, were her real heroes.

Ellie's phone buzzed and she took it out to see the word "Twerp" on the screen. It was her current nickname for Alfie, ever since he'd left her party early and not even bothered to say sorry. She didn't want to ruin her good mood by talking to him right now, so she let the call go to voicemail and settled back to enjoy the build-up to the big match. Robertson's opponent was three-time champion Svetlana Volkov, "the Russian Wolf". Win or lose, this was going to be brutal.

Alfie hung up, frustrated. Why wouldn't Ellie answer his call? The Keep had been on high alert all night, but Alfie had never felt so alone. He had to see Ellie and warn her about what had happened to their brother. He didn't know how he could begin to tell her, or how he could even make her believe him, but he had decided that he couldn't leave her in the dark any longer. Normally he would have talked to Hayley about what had happened with Richard, but Alfie was still too angry with her. The Lord Chamberlain, meanwhile, was busy marshalling the beefeaters as they attempted to relocate Lock and the Black Dragon, to get some sense of when and from where the next strike would come. Every time Alfie tried to bring up the issue of his brother, LC only said the same thing: "Nothing is more important than loyalty, Majesty. Nothing."

That's the problem, thought Alfie. *Who am I supposed to be loyal to – my country, or my brother?* True, Richard had done something terrible, but Alfie wanted to understand why. Was it his fault? Or was Richard sick? What had Lock done to him? How could LC condemn Richard when they still had no idea how he had turned into the Black Dragon?

Hayley walked into the Mess and a hush descended over the Yeoman Warders in the breakfast queue. She could tell they had been talking about her. She took a plate of bacon and eggs that she didn't really feel like eating and sat down at one of the long tables. But the beefeaters who had been sitting there got up and moved. Only Brenda remained, but even she looked uncomfortable.

"What did I do wrong?" Hayley pleaded.

"Brian's one of us, Hayley."

"And I'm not?"

"That's not what I said. I can't explain what Brian's been up to, but I know one thing – he's no traitor. I just wish you'd talked to me about it first."

Brenda drained her tea and left. Hayley was devastated. She'd only tried to protect Alfie, but now it felt like she was losing her family all over again.

LC stormed into the Map Room, arguing with the Ravenmaster. "The ravens can look after themselves for once. I need every hand at their post!"

"My birds haven't even had their breakfast yet," protested the beefeater. "Don't blame me when they start pecking the tourists!"

"We have bigger problems than unhappy tourists, Yeoman Ravenmaster. We must track down the Black Dragon!"

Alfie noticed how LC didn't use the name "Richard" when he talked about his brother. It was like he didn't exist any more. Easier to order his death that way, Alfie supposed. For him it wasn't that easy. Richard was still his brother, no matter what he had done. If he could just talk to him...

"What do you think you're doing?!"

LC had just discovered another beefeater hiding in a corner watching the Wimbledon tennis TV coverage and scoffing chocolate bourbons.

"Our enemies are out there somewhere plotting heaven-knows-what and you are watching television! All tea breaks are cancelled until further notice!"

The Yeoman Warders grumbled with indignation and returned to their desks. *Of course*, thought Alfie, *Wimbledon – that's where Ellie is!* He made for the door, but LC headed him off.

"Majesty, please wait. I have an important mission for you."

"Sorry, LC, I've got my own mission. I have to warn Ellie about Richard. If he tries anything, she needs to be ready."

"But, Majesty," spluttered LC, "that would mean telling her your secret, telling her you are the Defender. You can't—"

"Ellie lost her dad too, and she doesn't even know why. And if she's about to lose her brother as well. . . She deserves to know the truth."

The Lord Chamberlain sighed. He could see that Alfie's mind was made up. "Very well. But I implore you, let us bring her here first, for her own safety. I'll send Chief Yeoman Seabrook to fetch her himself. But in the meantime, I need the Defender's help."

Alfie didn't want to fight LC any more than he had to. At least he was trying to compromise. He turned back from the door with a sigh. "What's the mission?"

"The prime minister. She is a fool if she thinks the Viking threat has passed. The armed forces should be on high alert, but she has buried her head in the sand. Someone needs to make her see sense."

"And by someone, you mean. . ."

"If the Defender were to talk to her one-on-one,

to show that his intentions were good, perhaps she would listen."

"Talking to Thorn is not my idea of fun, LC. But say I went along with this. Where exactly am I supposed to have this meeting with her?"

LC cleared his throat. Clearly Alfie wasn't going to like the sound of what came next. "Number Ten, Downing Street, Majesty."

"TEN, DOWNING STREET? You mean, the house where the prime minister lives? The most secure building in Britain apart from this place?"

"If you would just hear me out, sir. We have a plan. Yeoman Gillam!"

A rosy-cheeked beefeater hurried over carrying a leather box. Alfie recognized him as Brian's apprentice, who spent most of his time polishing the regalia. He was timid for a beefeater, with no hint of a beard, which made him unique among the tower guard, aside from the women Yeomen. Well, most of them.

"Yeoman Gillam has taken on the Armourer's responsibilities, just until we are able to appoint a successor. He has a rather interesting idea about how we might get you inside without raising the alarm."

LC nodded to Gillam, who blushed and eased back the lid of the box to reveal a small crown. Alfie had never seen it before. He was sure he would have remembered if he had, because along with its lush purple velvet and shiny platinum arches it was topped by the most enormous diamond he had ever seen.

"Wow, talk about bling," said Alfie, lifting out the crown.

The immense gem was almost see-through. As he turned it, light refracted through its countless edges, dancing across his face.

"The Koh-i-Nur Diamond, Majesty," said LC. "It means 'Mountain of Light'. Rather apt, don't you think? Believed to have been discovered in India some time in the thirteenth century, though its exact origins are something of a mystery. Try it on."

Alfie felt silly putting the tiny crown on top of his head. There was no way it would fit. But the moment it touched his hair it seemed to press down on him as if he were trying to carry a gallon bucket of water on his head.

"It's heavy!' he cried.

"Take a look at yourself," said LC, turning a long mirror to face him.

Alfie blinked. He was standing right in front of the mirror and yet he could not see himself. Instead all he saw were the rows of Yeoman Warders busy at their desks behind him. He spun round, then looked down at his hand. It wasn't there.

"WHOA!"

Alfie heaved the crown off his head and tossed it back into the box. He checked the mirror and patted his body. Sure enough he could see himself again.

"Don't ask me how it works, sir," said LC. "Nobody knows."

"Wait a minute," said Alfie. "Are you telling me that all this time I've had a crown that can make me INVISIBLE and you're only telling me now? Don't you think that might have been useful, like when I was fighting for my life against those Vikings?"

"No doubt, Majesty," said LC. "But Brian was in charge of weaponry, and he didn't approve of using it."

"Why not?" asked Alfie.

Yeoman Gillam finally piped up. "Probably a bit worried about the curse."

Alfie couldn't speak for a moment. Both LC and the beefeater were avoiding eye contact.

"Um. . . what curse?"

DOWNING STREET RAID

Twenty minutes later, the Defender was walking down Whitehall wearing a small crown topped with a cursed diamond, his only consolation being that he was at least entirely invisible. He loitered by the tall iron gates of Downing Street, within touching distance of three armed policemen, breathing as quietly as he could. The curse of the Koh-i-Nur Diamond was purely a legend, according to the Lord Chamberlain. Supposedly, it only affected men who wore the crown, a number of whom were said to have died rather sooner than they might have wished. While the women who wore it, such as Queen Victoria, didn't turn invisible, they seemed to suffer no ill effects either, which felt a little unfair to Alfie. LC assured him there was no proof the curse was real, but perhaps to be on the safe side not to wear it for any longer than absolutely necessary and to be sure to take it off if he started to feel faint or sick or like he might die suddenly.

At last a civil servant trotted up to the gates waving her security pass at the policeman, and Alfie was able to scurry through behind her like a Tube fare dodger, being careful not to bump into her back. He followed the official as she hurried along the pavement and up to the grand black door with the famous number ten on it. The police constable standing guard wished her a good morning and knocked. Alfie heard the heavy clunk of a bolt being released from the other side and it swung open, letting the woman and her invisible hanger-on through. Alfie had done it; he was inside the prime minister's house! He hurried up the wide, curving staircase past the oil portraits of prime ministers, from the very first, Sir Robert Walpole, all the way to the formidable Vanessa Thorn herself, complete with her black hair in a bun.

LC's voice crackled in Alfie's ear. "No time for sightseeing, Majesty. You must find the prime minister and persuade her to help us."

Alfie wanted to snap back at LC, something about not needing a reminder of the mission, thanks very much, but he couldn't risk talking out loud. The first and second floors were bustling with officials and house staff, so there was no taking the invisibility crown off here.

Alfie turned a corner and knocked the elbow of a young man in a suit who was hurrying past him.

"Sorry!" Alfie blurted, and immediately clamped his hand over his mouth. Oops.

The staffer looked around for a moment, puzzled, before quickening his pace and disappearing into an office. Another ghost story to be added to the legends associated with the old residence.

Alfie took a deep breath, turned another corner and found himself standing right in front of the hulking figure of Agent Fulcher.

"Oh no," said Hayley, watching the video feed.

Alfie froze. Fulcher was sitting down, resting her hand on a large silver box, while her partner Agent Turpin was arguing with a prim-looking secretary nearby.

"We've been waiting for an hour!"

"I know, sir, but as I told you, the prime minister's last meeting is running late. I will let you know as soon as she is able to see you."

Turpin grunted and returned to the waiting area. As he passed by Alfie, he stopped for a moment and sniffed the air, like a rat catching a scent. Alfie held his breath. But Turpin shrugged it off and slumped on to the chair next to his partner.

"The cheek of it, making us wait like this," he grumbled. "She's the one who wanted the demonstration."

"She is the prime minister, I suppose," muttered Fulcher.

Turpin blew out air between his teeth and folded his arms. Alfie padded to the nearest staircase.

The third floor residence was much quieter. Alfie knew that Thorn didn't have a husband or family, so with any luck she would be alone. It might have been his imagination, but he was starting to get a headache around his temples. Was this what an ancient curse taking hold felt like? *Stuff it* – he removed the crown and clipped it on to his belt.

LC's voice came in over the radio, sounding alarmed. "Majesty, I'm not sure that is wise."

"Says the guy who gave me a cursed crown," Alfie whispered back.

Alfie unclipped a scout orb and sent it hovering ahead of him through the maze of corridors. He followed at a safe distance, seeing in his mind's eye what the orb was seeing, waiting for any sign of the prime minister. A security guard crossed the corridor ahead of the orb. Thinking fast, Alfie commanded the orb to set itself down on the nearest side table. The guard, catching the movement out of the corner of his eye, doubled back and approached the table. Alfie watched the guard's curious face in extreme close-up as he picked up the orb and frowned at it. Dismissing it, he put it back on the table and ambled away. Alfie waited for him to disappear before rounding the corner and retrieving the orb.

Suddenly Alfie heard a strange grunting sound coming from the other side of a door. He eased it open and poked his head in to see the prime minister, her back to him, wearing gym kit and boxing gloves, whacking a punch-bag with surprising force. His first instinct was to laugh – it was so unlike his mental image of her – but in that second she caught sight of his reflection in the window. Thorn gasped and dived for her desk – Alfie guessed she had

269

some sort of panic button there, which would bring armed guards running. Gambling that the desk was made from British oak, he whipped his hand up and commanded it to move. The desk shot across to the other side of the room, leaving the prime minister spreadeagled on the carpet in its wake.

Alfie tried to help her up, but Thorn shook his hand away.

"Don't touch me, you freak!" she snapped.

"I just want to talk, Prime Minister," Alfie said in his best low superhero voice.

He knew he had to be careful what he said. Any hint that beneath the Defender armour was just the boy king she loved to look down her nose at, and Thorn would never listen to him. She sat in her chair and waved a hand at the leather armchair opposite. "Fine, let's talk. You have two minutes before I scream for help."

Alfie sat. "The threat to the country is not over," he said. "The Black Dragon has returned. We know who he is."

"Who?" asked Thorn.

"I. . . I can't tell you that."

"Ha! You know nothing."

Alfie kept his cool and continued. "The Dragon

and the man who created him are the ones who raised the Vikings from the dead. They plan to use them; we're not sure how, but we know it's going to be ... well ... um ... bad."

Behind the visor, Alfie winced. He was messing this up. He could imagine LC and Hayley back in the Keep rolling their eyes as he fluffed his pitch to the PM.

"You can't tell me *this*, you don't know *that*..." said Thorn. "Not the most convincing argument for, what, a full deployment of the army? Nation on red alert?"

"Yes. Please."

"I'll tell you what I think," she said, apparently not phased by having a superhero sitting in her office, "I think the Vikings are long gone, back to whatever hole they crawled out from, along with our entire gold reserve. And rather than letting me get back to the business of running the country, you would have me plunge us into another full-scale panic! No, I'm more interested in who you really are. The almighty Defender. I wonder..."

Hayley screamed through the radio at Alfie: "IT'S A TRAP! MOVE!"

But before Alfie could react, the door crashed open and Fulcher burst in, carrying what looked like a ray-gun from a science-fiction movie. She pointed it at the Defender and pulled the trigger. A spiral of blue light shot out, coiling round Alfie like a serpent, pinning him to the leather armchair.

The prime minister took the portable panic alarm from her pocket and tossed it on to her desk. "Always have a back-up plan," she said.

Alfie tried to reach his sword, but his arms were pinned to his sides. He tried to command the strange, pulsating lasers to release him, but they didn't respond. Turpin strolled in, looking very pleased with himself.

"You wanted a demonstration, Prime Minister," smirked Turpin. "I'd say money well spent, wouldn't you?"

"What is this?" gasped the Defender.

"Cyclotron Particle Accelerator. Most powerful energy there is, state of the art," boasted Turpin. "The army's been developing them for years, but they let us borrow one after Fulcher had a word with them."

"This is a mistake," said Alfie. "We're on the same side!"

He could hear shouting from the Keep over his radio, the Lord Chamberlain issuing orders.

"Hang tight, Alfie – LC is scrambling the Yeoman," said Hayley.

Thorn circled the Defender, revelling in having him at her mercy. "We'll see whose side you're on," she said. "Agent Turpin, can it remove his armour?"

Turpin nodded to Fulcher who turned a dial on the apparatus. The laser coils tightened on the Defender's armour, twisting and gripping it with immense power. Alfie groaned in pain – it felt like someone was pulling his arms and legs from their sockets. A coil slid round his neck, squeezing till he was choking. The armour might not break, but if this carried on much longer he would have to remove it himself.

POP!

A sudden rush of warm air swept through the room and Red Robe appeared next to the Defender. Before anyone had time to react, Red Robe punched a hand through a gap in the laser ropes and touched the Defender. Both of them disappeared into thin air and the lasers, cut loose, whipped around the room for a few moments like severed power lines, sending Turpin, Fulcher and the prime minister diving for cover.

RED ROBE
REVEALED

Alfie landed on his backside right outside Number Ten. Red Robe appeared beside him at the exact same moment with his hand still on his shoulder. The policeman standing guard at the door opened and closed his mouth like a goldfish, then snapped out of it and scrambled to grab his radio.

"CODE ONE! INTRUDERS INSIDE EXCLUSION ZONE!"

Two other officers were already running in their direction from the black iron gates that blocked off one end of Downing Street.

"DON'T MOVE! ARMED POLICE!" they screamed, raising machine guns.

Red Robe pulled Alfie to his feet.

"I don't know how you just did that," said Alfie, "but I wish you'd landed us further away!"

Red Robe took his hand and gripped it tight. "Don't let go. This might make you a little dizzy."

Gunfire erupted, but in the same split-second they disappeared again. Alfie gasped as they reappeared slap bang in in the middle of the busy road on the other side of the iron gates. An open-topped bus was bearing down on them, the driver leaning on the horn, and waving in panic behind the windscreen as the brakes screamed. Alfie screwed his eyes shut and braced for impact. But the next thing he knew he had landed with Red Robe on a quiet rooftop overlooking the road they had been standing in a moment before.

"Sorry about that," said his saviour as he pulled Alfie away from the edge and, gliding ahead of him like a ghost, led him through a maze of air ducts, gutters and flagpoles. Across the rooftops of Whitehall, Big Ben chimed the hour. "I can only blink-shift to a place I can see."

"Blink-shift?" asked Alfie, wary.

The leering, bug-eyed mask Red Robe was wearing was kind of freaking him out. Now that Alfie was up close, he could see it was carved out of some kind of wood and painted in faded silver and gold.

"Yeah, blink-shift. I made it up. Easier than saying 'teleportation spell'. But it's more like stepping stones than one giant leap," Red Robe replied. They'd reached a fire escape on the other side of the building. "You'll be all right from here, won't you?"

Alfie grabbed Red Robe's arm before he could disappear again. "Wait. Why have you been watching me? Why did you help me?"

Red Robe stroked the chin of his carved, monstrous mask. "Look, I'm supposed to be somewhere else. . ."

"Come on, it's not like it'll take you long to get there, is it?"

Red Robe laughed. "Fair enough. Well, the reason I helped you is easy. Anything for a friend, Alfie-bet!"

He removed the grinning mask to reveal a face that was very familiar to Alfie. *"TONY?!"* Alfie whipped off his own armour and gaped at his friend in shock.

"Surprise!" laughed Tony.

"But, how did you—? When did you—? You're so tall!"

"Yeah, I have a little help with that."

Tony pulled back his embroidered red cloak to reveal that he was in fact hovering two feet in the air on a curious-looking ornate green disc with a hole in the middle. On its outer edge was carved a dense pattern of Chinese characters.

"You have a hoverboard. Cool," Alfie said.

"Ha, you're funny, Alfie. It's the chuán guó xǐ. The Heirloom Seal of the Realm. Been in my family for centuries."

They sat down together on top of an air-conditioning unit, listening to the sirens of the police cars that were flooding the streets below. Alfie looked at his friend, amazed.

"So you didn't know I was a blue blood too, huh?" Tony said.

"Are you kidding? I thought your dad was a banker."

"He is. But a hundred years ago his great-great-grandfather was Emperor of China. After they ditched the monarchy our family changed its name and moved away. But our family's powers must have stuck around." Tony shrugged. "I've been blink-shifting since I was three years old. We got through so many nannies."

Alfie smiled, amazed. "You knew all along that I was a superhero, but you didn't say anything?"

"It's kind of complicated."

"Yeah, tell me about it. Tony, there's something else you should know. Richard – he's not who he seems to be, he's. . ." Alfie's voice faltered.

"The Black Dragon, I know. Bummer or what?" Tony surprised Alfie with a fierce hug. "I'm sorry I can't tell you everything. But it's classified."

"Classified?" Alfie smiled, half laughing, half-annoyed. "I am the king, you know."

"I made a promise to someone super important that I wouldn't tell you anything. Sorry, Alfa-betty spaghetti." Tony pulled his staring-eye mask back on, gathered his red cloak around him and drifted to the edge of the roof. "But don't worry, I'll never be far away."

"Hey, what do I call you now? You know, the other you?" Alfie asked.

"They call me Qilin. Like 'Kill-in' but with a Q. See you around, Mr Shiny-White-Armour-Man-on-a-Ghost-Horse."

"Defender."

"Yeah, that's easier."

Qilin gazed to the horizon, and with a pop, disappeared into thin air. Alfie thought he saw him rematerialize on a distant rooftop for a moment and wave back, before vanishing again.

LC's voice crackled in Alfie's ears – his radio and helmet-cam were coming back online.

"Majesty! Thank goodness! How did you escape?"

"I had a little help, actually."

"Help? From whom?"

"A new friend. Well, old friend really, I'll fill you in later. Has Yeoman Seabrook fetched Ellie yet?"

"He encountered some heavy traffic on the way to Wimbledon, Majesty. But he'll be with her soon."

"Alfie, if it's all about to kick off," Hayley interrupted. "You should really get back here."

Alfie knew he should be putting the country first right now, but it felt like his family was falling apart again, just like it did when his parents split up. He had to cling on to what was left.

"No. I'm going to get Ellie myself. I won't be long."

Alfie summoned Wyvern and rocketed off the rooftop.

THE ENEMY
WITHIN

Back in the Keep, Hayley put down the radio. She could hear the coldness in Alfie's voice and it burned her up. It was like someone had taken a pair of scissors and snipped the bond of friendship between them clean in half. He just didn't trust her any more. *Join the club, Your Stupid Majesty, no one here does either,* Hayley thought, gazing around at the busy Map Room. Having learned about the underhanded way in which Hayley discovered Brian's secret phone conversations, most of the beefeaters wouldn't make eye contact with her.

Even Herne seemed to have changed his mind about hanging out with her, as he gave her a wide berth, growling.

"What am I doing here?" Hayley said out loud.

If London really was still in danger, then she needed to get to her gran. Not stay hiding out somewhere no one wanted her anyway. If Alfie was putting his family first, then why shouldn't she do the same?

"I'm out of here. Good luck with the war and everything," Hayley said to LC and headed out of the Map Room.

LC blinked like he'd just been slapped. "Miss Hicks? You cannot abandon your post! You are the Keeper of the King's Arrows!"

"Oh purlease, old man. I'm Hayley Hicks, from Watford," she said defiantly, taking one last look around.

None of the beefeaters, not even Brenda, said a word as she stalked off to the sally port tunnel.

"Wait! Miss Hicks!" LC pleaded and hurried after her.

But Hayley disappeared into the tunnel, slamming the door behind her. The old man stood facing it for a moment, stiff as a post, aware that every beefeater in the room was staring at him. LC whirled around to face them.

"Get back to work!" he shouted, his voice booming off the walls.

At Wimbledon the crowd was on its feet.

"Advantage, Miss Robertson," said the umpire.

Ellie was ecstatic. She had watched the British girl battle back from one set and five games down to level the match. Now, deep into the deciding set, she just needed one more point and she would be serving for the match.

"Wait, please," said the umpire.

Confused, the players looked up at the royal box. Ellie realized that there was some sort of commotion going on behind her. She turned round to see Alfie edging his way along the row in her direction. A murmur went up around the court as people realized who had just interrupted the match. Alfie caught Ellie's eye and waved, but then he stepped on a poor lady's foot and stopped to apologize. Sniggers rippled through the crowd. The players did their best to ignore the fuss and keep their concentration. Ellie put her hand to her face and looked at her shoes.

"Sorry," said Alfie, reaching the seat next to her.

"Sit still and shut up," hissed Ellie.

On court, play resumed. The Russian served hard down the centre line. Robertson reached it easily, but hit the return well wide of the line.

"Deuce," said the umpire.

"That was your fault," whispered Ellie.

"Sorry, but I need to talk to you. Can we get out of here?"

People were frowning at them.

"Seriously, Alfie," whispered Ellie, "if you want to get beaten up by your little sister on live TV, then keep talking."

Alfie bit his tongue and settled into his seat. The things he needed to tell her – about the Defender, about the Black Dragon, about their brother – were not things he could tell her here, surrounded by all these people. But he had to tell her soon. Because Alfie had a terrible feeling that time was running out.

Lord Mortimer slapped a chubby hand against the horn of his classic Bentley and swerved into the bus lane as he negotiated the heavy traffic round Parliament Square. "Out of the way, you oiks! Some of us actually work here, you know!"

There was a time when Lord Mortimer ("Call me Morty, old bean.") had been as sporty as his son Sebastian and, like him, had made a clean sweep of the captaincy of the big three sports teams at Harrow: rugby, football and cricket. But he had evidently spent most of his career in the House of Lords shoving as much food as he could into his wet, red mouth. *He was a revolting man, selfish and scheming,* thought Professor Lock, who was sitting in the passenger seat gazing up at the clock face of Big Ben. *Which makes him the perfect collaborator for the final part of my plan.*

"Did you know that the correct name for the Houses of Parliament is actually the Palace of Westminster? It's still owned by the Crown," said Lock.

"Hear that, Sebastian?" asked Lord Mortimer, looking in the rear-view mirror at his lug-headed son, who was sitting on the back seat alongside Prince Richard. "You should listen, you might learn something for once."

"Shut up, dad," sneered Sebastian. Then he leant over to Richard and added, "We'll take the place back for the king, won't we, Rich? The new king. Ha, I can't wait to see your brother's stupid face when he finds out what we've got in store for him!"

Richard pulled the cap he was wearing down tighter and ignored him. He'd had no time for the dimwitted bully Mortimer when they were at school; he didn't see why he should treat him any differently now just because they were technically on the same side. Anyway, he needed to mentally prepare himself for what was to come.

"Now, you're sure this outlandish plan of yours is going to work, Lock?" Lord Mortimer asked for the thousandth time that morning, smoothing back his thin, oily patch of dyed black hair.

"Just get us inside and I'll do the rest," said Professor Lock.

"And don't forget our little deal," Lord Mortimer said with a wink. "I'll scratch your back if you scratch mine. If there really is a new order on the way like you chaps promise, my family is first in the queue when you're handing out the spoils."

"Don't you worry," replied Lock, shuddering at the thought of scratching any part of the slob's hideous body. "You'll get what's due to you. And you'll make your ancestors proud."

Lord Mortimer frowned. It sounded like Lock was making a dig about his ancestor, Sir Roger Mortimer, who famously betrayed King Edward the Second. And he was right. The professor knew the whole story: how Mortimer had seized control of the country with the help of the king's own wife, Queen Isabella of France, who also happened to be a werewolf. It was a grim period of British history known as the Age of Treason. Today a new dark age was beginning and soon nothing would be able to stop it.

The car pulled up outside Old Palace Yard, and once Lord Mortimer had levered himself out of the front seat, he escorted his guests to the members' entrance. A quick pat-down by the police found no concealed weapons or explosives. Lock was faking a limp and using a long metal walking stick, but the police barely glanced at it.

For a man who was about to watch the "mother of all parliaments" crumble, Lord Mortimer was very keen to show it off as they wandered through. Westminster Hall, the House of Lords Library, the Royal Gallery – Mortimer would have given them the whole guided tour if they'd let him. Richard hung at the back with his cap pulled low to conceal his face from prying eyes. He found nothing about the place impressive. Every inch of the "great" building may have seemed to be painted in rich golds and blues and encased in red leather and fussy, ornamental architecture, but if you looked closer, the carpets were threadbare, every other stone was crumbling and mouldy damp patches stained the walls. Lock was right: this once-noble place, just like the country, had fallen into a state of decay. It was time for a new beginning and something truly glorious.

As Mortimer droned on, Lock nodded at Richard, who slipped away unseen into a side room to prepare himself. Alone now with Lord Mortimer, Lock continued his tour, leaning on his walking stick.

"The Central Lobby!" Mortimer announced as they entered a grand octagonal hall with a black-and-white tiled floor and an enormous, two-tiered chandelier glowing above them.

Marble statues of great politicians faced into the lobby, watching them silently.

"The epicentre of the British Empire, or what's left of it," Lord Mortimer continued. "From here you can see the throne in the House of Lords at one end and the Speaker's Chair in the House of Commons at the other. Kings at one end, plebs at the other."

"I know which I prefer," Lock said, pushing Mortimer out of the way.

"Steady on!" said the surprised lord, wobbling off

balance and bumping into one of the statues.

Lock barged past the surprised doorman into the House of Commons, marched across the floor of the chamber and leapt up on to a heavy oak table. Outraged MPs stood up from their benches and shouted for security. The Sergeant-at-Arms sprinted in, drawing his sword. The sergeant was the only person allowed to carry a weapon in here and he looked like he knew how to use it, but Lock was ready for him. With a deft flick of his wrist his walking stick smacked the sword from the sergeant's hand, and he followed it up with a crack over his head. Everyone in the chamber gasped as the sergeant collapsed.

"This parliament is at an end!" Lock yelled at the top of his voice. "Your pathetic democracy is over!"

"Rubbish!" shouted an old MP with a shaggy white moustache sitting on the front bench. "Clear off!"

"I don't think so," Lock muttered.

With a sudden roar, the Black Dragon crashed through the doors and flew down the length of the chamber. Politicians ducked under the creature's scaly tail and ran screaming for the exits, colliding with police coming the other way. The Dragon sprayed a searing jet of flames over the top of the fleeing politicians' heads, forcing the police to fall back, then landed and kicked the door closed, trapping the members inside.

"Order, order!" Lock smiled as he surveyed the chamber.

A stunned, fearful silence descended over the House of Commons as all eyes turned back to Lock. The Black Dragon perched on the Speaker's Chair behind him like a giant, glaring gargoyle.

"Now that I have your attention, I hereby disband this parliament. There will be a new order, administered by me. Pure, incorruptible and enforced with my Viking army."

"This is an outrage!" the old MP bellowed.

Lock could only admire his bravery.

"And if you think the great British public are scared by your little band of dead savages, you've got another thing coming!"

The Black Dragon shot a thin jet of flame at the old MP, and he sat down immediately, smoke wafting from his singed moustache.

"The time for debating is over. But the honourable gentlemen is right, of course," Lock conceded. "It would indeed take a force greater than I have currently at my disposal. Which is why I have this."

Lock twisted the end of his walking stick and pulled out a long extension tipped with a sharp spike at the bottom. He then unscrewed the top, retrieved a folded triangle of material – the Raven Banner – and attached it to the top of the pole. Unfurling it fully, he waved it in the air for all to see.

"The Vikings may have retreated from our country long ago, but they left their mark. In our language, in the founding of our great cities . . . and in our bloodlines."

Lock threw the flag across the chamber like a javelin. The Black Dragon took off, caught it and hovered over the petrified MPs.

"Ancient Northman blood runs deep in countless British veins," continued the professor. "It has lain dormant for centuries, just waiting for the day when it would be called upon again. Legend says that whoever controls the banner of Odin controls all those who carry his blood."

The Dragon dropped to the floor and speared the Raven Banner deep into the stone with a deafening CRRRRACK! The MPs cowered on their benches.

"But it is not enough to merely know the legend.

A proper historian does his research." Lock pulled his small, ancient book of Old Norse sorcery from his pocket. "They say knowledge is power. In this case, that is the literal truth. Without the right words, the banner is nothing but an old flag. With them, however ... well, you'll see. There are going to be some changes around here."

Lock stepped forward and gripped the banner with one hand, holding open the book with the other and reciting in a booming voice:

> *"Hart er í komandi ǫld,*
> *Brœðr munu berjazk*
> *ok at bǫnum verðazk,*
> *skeggǫld, skalmǫld,*
> *vindǫld, vargǫld.*
> *Mun engi maðr*
> *ǫðrum þyrma."**

---

* "In the harsh age that follows
Brothers will fight
And kill each other,
An axe age, a sword age,
A wind age, a wolf age.
No man will have
Mercy on another."

As he spoke, the air around the professor crackled and sparked with static electricity. The men and women on the benches trembled in fear as a swirling red cloud began to form over Lock's head. As he reached the end of his incantation, the cloud seemed to be sucked into the top of the banner with a crash of thunder. Lock stepped back, eyes wide with wonder, as the banner glowed red and an explosion of energy blew out from it through the whole chamber, shaking its foundations and throwing people off their feet.

Cracks appeared where the banner was planted, glowing crimson red, spreading out in all directions, zigzagging like angry, swollen veins. As they passed beneath the benches, one in every thirty MPs began to shake with convulsions. Those affected groaned in agony. Eyes bulged, limbs stiffened, heads shook violently from side to side. The old MP with the singed moustache staggered to his feet, but he no longer looked as he had moments before. His face was harder, reddened, his eyes keen and full of madness. His wizened body grew as bulging muscles burst through his suit, crisscrossed with blue tattoos that materialized on his skin. Thick, knotted hair sprouted from his face like a horrible time-lapse movie, until a shaggy beard hung from his chin. In every corner of the chamber, people cowered from the grunting, drooling Viking berserkers that had appeared in their midst. They were the fresh-born, living, breathing cousins to Guthrum and his undead draugar. Lock looked on with satisfaction as the Raven Banner broadcast its dark magic.

"It seems we have a few Norse descendants with us, even here," he chuckled. "Together we shall bring this kingdom its Ragnarök – death and rebirth. And from the chaos we will begin a new reign."

25

RAGNARÖK

Big Ben pulsed like an evil heart as the Raven Banner's magical energy wrapped around it in a shimmering red haze. At the tower's base, red cracks ripped open the pavement, radiating out along ancient ley lines like a spider's web. Soon they would spread the berserker spell across the whole of Britain, waking the blood of every Viking ancestor.

On Westminster Bridge, Declan Appleby, a mild-mannered bus driver from Catford, transformed into a Viking berserker and deliberately crashed his open-topped bus into the back of a taxi. The bald-headed taxi driver got out of his car, up for a good old-fashioned London road-rage argument. That was until he saw Declan's bulging muscles, foaming mouth and burning red eyes.

In her Lambeth primary school, Sarah Axelsen was teaching fractions to Year Four when she suddenly went full berserker as the spell hit, let out a roar, kicked her desk over and jumped through a window. Her class sat in stunned silence, until two of their classmates also transformed, bellowing Old Norse oaths as they ripped their maths textbooks to shreds with their sharp, yellow teeth.

Everywhere the red cracks in the earth appeared, someone turned into one of the Viking monsters. Berserker chefs abandoned their kitchens, but not before noisily feasting on the raw meat they were preparing. Metamorphosed plumbers smashed toilets and sinks, screaming in rage. Transformed traffic wardens tipped over the cars they were giving tickets to moments earlier. London was fast finding itself in the grip of berserker mayhem.

At Ten, Downing Street, Prime Minister Thorn, still recovering from her encounter with the Defender and Qilin, found herself hauled from her office by two security agents.

"Ma'am, there is an emergency. We have to get you to the safe room."

As they ran her along the corridor and down the stairs, Thorn caught a glimpse of the chaos outside. A bus was on fire and what looked like a crazed giant in a ripped policeman's uniform was tearing up paving slabs with his bare hands.

"What's happening?" she shrieked as they reached the basement.

"We'll brief you inside COBRA, ma'am," said the agent as they pushed confused staffers aside and stampeded through.

COBRA stood for "Cabinet Office Briefing Room A", which didn't sound very exciting, but it was the specially equipped room from which the prime minister could deal with any crisis, even a war. Thorn knew that if they were going there, then this was serious. Behind them a crack ripped through the floor, carrying its glowing red magical payload. They reached a heavy metal door. One of the agents keyed in a code and opened it. Ignoring the screams and yells coming from the rest of the building, the agents pushed the prime minister inside, followed her in and secured the door.

The COBRA room contained a long desk and a bank of screens that were already being monitored by those senior military figures lucky to be have been close enough to Downing Street when the disaster began. Here, in the secure bunker, they were completely safe. The senior agent wiped the sweat from his brow and spoke into his radio.

"The prime minister is secure. Repeat, the prime minister is. . ."

A low growl filled the room. Everyone looked around for the source of the noise. The prime minister was hunched over the desk, her body shaking with violent jerks. As the assembled staff watched in horror, her shoulders burst through her suit, her hair turned blonde, growing thick and long, and her face became purple with Norse tattoos. She roared and punched the desk in half with a mighty, gnarled fist, as the agents scrambled too late for their guns.

At Wimbledon, Kate Robertson was about to serve for the title. A few people in the crowd had suddenly become engrossed in something on their phones and a couple had even left, but most were still enthralled by the game. A chorus of "Come on, Kate!" echoed around the arena.

"Quiet please!" said the umpire.

In the royal box, Ellie leaned forward, excited, while Alfie kept a concerned eye on the darkening sky. Was that thunder he heard rumbling in the distance?

"Alfie, just watch," Ellie hissed. "This is going to be historic."

Kate Robertson bounced the ball patiently and waited for complete silence. She tossed it high in the air to serve. Around the country, several million pairs of eyes watched the ball reach the top of its trajectory and fall back to Robertson's waiting racquet. *WHACK!* She sent the ball high over the net ... and clean out of the arena! The crowd's gasp was as loud as a jumbo jet. Britain's number-one tennis player had transformed, her berserker face stained with bright blue tattoos, her hair suddenly blonde and bushy. Brandishing her racquet like a club she pounded the ground. With a ripping sound, a glowing red crack appeared in the famous grass as if a knife had been drawn across the court.

"Racquet violation, Miss Robertson!" the umpire yelled.

But no one in the crowd was listening. They were too busy scrambling for the exits away from some of the spectators who, as the magic took hold, were also turning into Viking berserkers, tearing up their seats and throwing their picnics into the air.

"Alfie, what's going on?" said Ellie, looking to her brother.

But Alfie wasn't in his seat. He was already disappearing through the exit to the private VIP area behind the royal box. Ellie was aghast – he had deserted her at the first sign of trouble.

"ALFIE!"

What Alfie was really doing was looking for somewhere quiet where he could put on his Defender armour without being seen. Because whatever was happening out there, he knew what this was – this was Lock and his brother and the Vikings – this was their plan. He just hoped it wasn't too late to stop them.

Meanwhile, a few miles north of London, Hayley had finally reached the Whisper Grove Care Home and burst into her gran's room.

"Ah, nurse, good, I need some help," said Gran, not recognizing her as she glanced up from the television she was watching. "The tennis has gone all funny."

Hayley just clocked a snippet of the panic on Centre Court before the broadcast abruptly ended. She took the brakes off her gran's wheelchair and helped her into it. Whatever was going down at Wimbledon, she hoped Alfie could handle it. Right now, she needed to get Gran out of here.

"Gran, it's me. I thought we'd go on a little trip – the countryside, maybe," said Hayley, as she weaved the wheelchair towards the exit.

She thought she would have trouble getting past the home's staff, but everyone seemed glued to the TV news.

"That sounds nice, dear," said Gran, seeming to understand who she was again.

Outside, a strong wind buffeted the trees. A storm was blowing in. Hayley ran quicker, looking for a car she could take.

"What's the rush, child?" Gran said, gripping the wheelchair's armrests.

"Just want to beat the traffic, Gran," Hayley said.

"Can we offer you a lift?" said Agent Turpin, leering as he stepped out from behind a bus stop.

Agent Fulcher appeared and grabbed Hayley, lifting her off the ground. They must have been staking the place out all along.

"Thought we'd given up on you, didn't ya?" Fulcher shouted, triumphant.

"Get off!" Hayley cried, struggling.

But Fulcher had her in an iron grip. Turpin was holding a pair of handcuffs. They'd obviously learned their lesson since last time.

"Hurry up and cuff her, she's as slippery as a bag of eels!" Fulcher said as Hayley squirmed.

With an ominous click, the handcuffs locked themselves tight around Hayley's wrists.

"Hey, you're the man who wants to stop bingo!" Gran said to Fulcher.

"No, I'm not. And I'm not a man, either," Fulcher complained.

"DON'T TOUCH HER!" yelled Hayley.

Turpin, smiling like a piranha, helped Gran out of the wheelchair and into the back of their car.

"Now, then, Mrs Hicks. How about that day trip, then? We've got a lovely place we can take you while we have a little word with your granddaughter."

Gran looked doubtful, her eyes clouded. "I want to see Lawrence."

"Don't listen to them, Gran!" Hayley shouted, glaring at the agents. She couldn't believe they would stoop so low as to tease a fragile old woman. "Gran might be sick, but she's not as sick as you two!"

"You know, I almost hope you resist spilling the beans about who your Defender friend is," Turpin said. "That way I can let Agent Fulcher do what she does best."

Fulcher grunted her approval and threw Hayley into the back seat next to her gran.

As the car sped back into the city, Hayley stroked Gran's hand, comforting her, and plotted her next move. She couldn't make a run for it and leave Gran with these two thugs. But maybe she could get someone's attention and scream for help. However, as she scanned the streets for the police, she noticed cars abandoned everywhere and people running around in a panic.

"Something's happening out there," she said.

Turpin turned round and sneered. "Nice try. But you're not getting out of it this time, missy."

Suddenly the car jumped as a red crack split open the road beneath them. Hayley flung herself in front of her gran as they skidded to a halt. She sat up to see Fulcher with her nose to the window, watching a group of berserkers rampage past, pulling down road signs and terrorizing screaming pedestrians.

"The girl's right. Something's wrong, Turpin."

She looked over to see Turpin's head touching the roof of the car, his face bulging and wild-eyed, his shoulders and arms expanding till they were bigger than hers.

"RAAAAAAAARGH!" berserker Turpin bellowed, wrenching off the steering wheel and punching it through the windscreen.

Fulcher screamed a surprisingly girly scream and tumbled out of the car.

"WAIT! HELP US!" shouted Hayley.

A cab slammed into the back of them with a *crunch*, sending their car spinning again. When it came to a rest, the door next to Gran was hanging off its hinges. Relieved to find they were unhurt, Hayley leant against her gran, pushing her out.

"GRAN, WE NEED TO GO!"

Hayley rolled out to see berserker Turpin leap on top of Fulcher, clawing and biting like a rabid dog. Fulcher was punching back, giving as good as she got, but for once they were evenly matched. As they rolled past grappling with each other, Hayley saw the key to the handcuffs fall from Turpin's torn trousers. "The key!"

"I'll fetch it, dear," said Gran breezily, not seeming to grasp how perilous their situation was.

"No, Gran!"

But before Hayley could stop her, Gran had shuffled over, picked up the key and brought it back – just in time as Fulcher staggered past again, carrying a flailing Turpin on her shoulders like he was an unruly toddler.

"GET OFF ME!" pleaded Fulcher.

Gran released the handcuffs and Hayley rubbed her sore wrists. She pulled Gran away from the havoc on the road, looking for somewhere – anywhere – they might be safe from this outbreak of . . . of whatever it was.

Meanwhile, in the Map Room, LC and Yeoman Box stared, dumbfounded, at the ops table alarm lights. Every single one of them, the length and breadth of the kingdom, was flashing. As the Raven Banner's magic travelled along the ley lines of Britain, Burgh Keepers were sending in frantic reports of sortilegic meters ringing off the scale. In the Keep, grim-faced Yeoman Warders rushed around, answering the phones and plotting the dark magic's unstoppable advance.

"The Wandle ley has gone past Wimbledon now, sir!" shouted Brenda.

"Greenwich Burgh Keeper says his meter's just exploded!" yelled another beefeater.

LC stared at the map in despair. Nowhere was safe from the magical infection. Transformed berserkers would soon be in every city, every county, every village. A ready-made army of lunatics to do Lock's bidding.

"Ragnarök," muttered LC, darkly.

"I think I've got one of their albums," said Brenda.

"It means the Viking apocalypse. Chaos. Fear. The end of the world as we know it. We MUST find His Majesty!"

"No word from the Defender!" shouted the beefeater manning the radio link.

The last they'd seen of Alfie he'd been at Wimbledon before the screens went down. The powerful magic sweeping the land must have been interfering with mobile communications, as only the old-fashioned landline telephones seemed to be working.

"What are your orders, Lord Chamberlain?"

asked Yeoman Warder Gillam, not quite managing to control the tremble of fear in his voice. "What should we do?"

LC gazed around the Map Room. With Alfie missing, Brian on the run and Hayley also absent, panic was starting to creep in. Even Herne was behaving oddly, turning in circles, barking and whining.

"Keep calm and defend the realm!" LC barked, striding up and down. The beefeaters stopped what they were doing and watched him. "The Tower of London has stood impregnable for nearly a millennium. It has faced down every enemy ever sent against it. The Black Death Rat Men of 1348. The Dragon Storm of 1666. Even Hitler's Abominable Snow-Nazis could not crack its walls. It shall not fall—"

The Keep shook as a powerful earth tremor struck. Plaster fell from the ceiling and a grand tapestry depicting a past Defender's victory over the giant bats of Wookey Hole fluttered to the floor. A wide, red crack snaked under the main doors and through the Map Room, sending Yeoman Warders diving for cover and splitting the Tudor Rose on the floor in half. The ravens called in alarm and flew to the battlements. Next to LC, who was gripping the ops table, there was something wrong with Brenda. Her body spasmed as the banner magic woke the Viking blood sleeping in her veins, transforming her into a snarling berserker. In moments, her uniform hung in tatters, drool fell from her mouth like a river and her eyes were red and wild.

The enemy was inside the Keep.

2G

BERSERKER BRITAIN

Ellie swung the Venus Rosewater Dish – the large silver plate that was the trophy for the Wimbledon Women's Champion – and smacked it hard into Kate Robertson's face. It wasn't exactly how she'd imagined presenting it to her hero, but then she hadn't expected the tennis player to turn into a berserk Viking monster either. Seeing as her worse-than-useless brother had chosen to save himself, Ellie figured it was up to her to set a better example. So she was doing her best to guide panicking spectators away from the marauding berserkers and towards the exits. It had been bad enough knowing that there was a gang of zombie Vikings out there causing mayhem, but seeing normal everyday people all around her transform into these hideous, mad creatures was much more terrifying. What was going on?

A loud crash and renewed screaming drew Ellie's attention to the far entrance, as Guthrum and several of his draugar warriors burst on to Centre Court. Lightning coursed across the blackening sky and torrential rain fell, turning the grass into a quagmire. The stench of rotting flesh and dead fish filled the air as the corpse Vikings stamped into the arena. Guthrum scanned the crowd, and his cruel, dead eyes locked on to his quarry.

"ELEANOR!" he thundered.

Guthrum pointed at her with a finger that was more bone than flesh, and his men pounded towards her, shoving bystanders out of the way. The Viking lord was following Lock's instructions to the letter.

"Bring me Princess Eleanor," Lock had told him. "She is not to be harmed, or you'll have the Black Dragon to answer to."

Ellie vaulted the net, skidding through the mud and rolling off the court as a hollow-eyed Viking lunged for her. Tangled in the net, the Viking roared with anger and ripped himself free as two more of Guthrum's men closed in on her from either side. Ellie picked up a broken racquet handle and threw it at one of them, impaling him in the neck. But the beast plucked it out and tossed it aside as if it were nothing but a splinter. Ellie backed off and heaved the umpire's chair over in front of her pursuers, but they crushed it underfoot and kept coming. Just as Ellie had resigned herself to being grabbed by the foul-smelling Viking dead, the sodden turf beneath their feet rose out of the ground of its own accord and carried the confused savages back the way they had come, clattering them into the scoreboard. Ellie looked up to the sky to see the Defender astride Wyvern. He landed in front of her, reaching out his hand.

"Get on!" he shouted.

Ellie wiped the rain from her face and looked around at the terrified faces of the spectators still cowering inside the arena. "What about everyone else?" she called back.

"The Vikings are here for you!" yelled the Defender.

As if to prove Alfie's point, Guthrum himself

began to stomp the length of the court towards Ellie. As he approached, his Viking followers stood still and started to sing their strange song. Their leader's body shook and expanded at incredible speed, so that within two more strides he had become a giant. Ellie fell on to her back in shock, while the Defender drew his sword and spun Wyvern round to face Guthrum. The giant Viking chief roared, sending ropes of green drool flying out of his mouth, and heaved his axe down at the Defender. Ellie fully expected to see the superhero cut in half, but somehow his glowing sword withstood the blow. Guthrum bellowed with rage as he circled, attempting to reach the princess, but the Defender blocked him each time, hovering just out of range of his swinging blade. Seeming to tire of the stalemate, the giant stepped back and glanced around the court.

"Time to go!" shouted the Defender, holding out his hand for Ellie once more.

But before she could take it, Guthrum hurled his huge axe across the court into a large steel buttress that supported one side of the arena. The impact shook panels loose from the roof and they tumbled down like boulders in an avalanche. Alfie looked with horror at the dozens of scared people trapped in the stands below the beam – if the wall came down they would be crushed.

"What are you waiting for?" Ellie screamed at him. "HELP THEM!"

Alfie twitched Wyvern's reins and she shot across the court towards the stands. The Defender reached the damaged buttress just as it was toppling over and used all his strength to prop it up. But not before he had whipped out his nunchuck sceptres and hurled them at the giant. He glanced back just in time to see one of Guthrum's draugar leap into their path and take the strike intended for his master, the magical thread which joined the sceptres severing his head in an instant. Not that it stopped the disembodied draugar's head from spitting curses at the Defender from its resting place on the front row of seats. Guthrum guffawed with laughter and scooped up Ellie with one mighty hand. She screamed and squirmed, but to no avail.

"NO!" yelled Alfie.

But below him spectators were still running clear of the stands. He couldn't risk letting go of the wall yet. All Alfie could do was watch as the giant undead Viking clambered up and over the lip of the arena and carried his sister away.

"Ooh, that's a nice hat," said Hayley's gran as she gazed into the shop window. "Do you think they've got my size?"

Hayley pulled her clear, just as a stone bollard whizzed past their heads and shattered the window. Oxford Street looked like a war zone. Even more so than usual. A bus lay on its side while its berserker former driver jumped up and down on top of it, chewing a snapped windscreen wiper. The berserker who had just lobbed the bollard through Topshop's window had now turned her attention to a black cab and was heaving the bumper off, cackling with delight. What looked like a nurse's uniform hung in rags off her now blue-tattooed, muscle-bound body. Hayley shuddered to think how many other people had woken up and gone to work that morning as normal, unaware that, hours later, they would become hulking, grunting maniacs. A shrieking teacher ran past them, pursued by a group of blonde, bug-eyed child-berserkers, who were spitting with rage and tearing off what was left of their school uniforms.

"Tsch, no manners, today's youngsters," said Gran.

Hayley pulled her into a doorway as half a motorbike skidded past on fire. "This is serious, Gran. We need to get off the street."

"Why don't we take the Tube then? Where are we going?"

Hayley realized there was only one place she knew which was likely still to be safe. If they could get there – which right now was a big "if". "The Keep."

"Where, love?"

"Sorry, the Tower of London. I have, um, friends there."

"Simple," said Gran, "Central Line east to Bank, then change on to the District line at Monument, one stop to Tower Hill. We'll be there in a jiffy."

"Can you walk that far? We don't have your wheelchair."

"Wheelchair? What wheelchair? Never used one of them in my life!"

And with that she hobbled off towards the Tube entrance, pausing only to take a free newspaper from the hands of a vendor who had just turned into a gibbering berserker. Hayley pulled her away

314

before the crazed Viking had a chance to grab her. This was one day when her gran's failing mind had its advantages, she figured.

The situation underground, however, was not much better than on the streets. Hayley and her gran squeezed their way on to the crowded eastbound platform just as a Tube train pulled in. But the moment the doors opened, terrified passengers poured out, pursued by yet more berserkers – berserker commuters, berserker tourists – every carriage seemed to have one. Hayley even caught a glimpse of a berserker policeman inside the train, ripping up seats and smashing handrails.

"What's the matter, dear?" asked Gran. "Why aren't we getting on?"

"Out of service," replied Hayley. "We'll have to find another way."

"Oh, blow it, why don't we just hike it through the service tunnels? We used to do it all the time at the end of our shifts."

Decades before, when she first moved to London, Hayley's gran had been a Tube driver. She had always boasted that there wasn't a corner of the city she couldn't find her way to using the subterranean network. She led Hayley to a small staircase which spiralled down to a door marked: DO NOT ENTER. AUTHORIZED PERSONNEL ONLY. Hayley stopped – she had no doubt that once upon a time her gran knew the Underground like the back of her hand. But the way she was now, Hayley feared they might get lost down here in the dark for ever.

"Are you sure you know the way, Gran? Your memory's not what it was, you know."

"Ye of little faith! Trust me, child. Come on now, chop chop."

Somewhere not far behind them, people screamed as a berserker's roar echoed through the tunnels. Hayley smiled at her gran and opened the door.

"You're the boss. Let's go."

Inside the Tube's central control room, it was pandemonium. Drivers were reporting outbreaks of random violence on every train. Station controllers were calling in with panicked reports of sudden rioting. Everyone was glued to the CCTV feeds trying to make sense of the chaos that had erupted. By the time they had noticed what was happening in the pump room it was already too late. Because what most people who ride the Tube every day don't realize is that if it were not for a series of powerful pumps that never turn off, much of the network would be underwater. The ancient underground tributaries of the River Thames are only kept at bay by the constant work of the pumps. Pumps that were, at that very moment, being smashed to pieces by one of Guthrum's Viking draugar.

"Pump failure, sector nine! Water levels rising!" yelled one of the operatives, finally noticing the panel of flashing alarms in front of her.

Everyone in the control room looked to their chief supervisor. Surely he would know how to handle this. Unfortunately for them, their supervisor was hunched over a nice, juicy dead rat that he had just decided to eat. He looked up at them, eyes wild, neck muscles bulging, blue tattoos popping up all over his new berserker face.

Minutes later, on a District Line train, scared passengers were standing on their seats to get out of the water which was rising through the floor. And if that was a nasty surprise, it was nothing compared to their shock at seeing a Viking longship overtake them, sailing through the tunnel!

Hayley was kicking herself. It was cold and dark down here, and they had already crossed and then recrossed several tracks as her gran kept changing her mind about the right way to go. She knew that if they touched the wrong rail with their feet they would be electrocuted. What had she been thinking, letting her gran lead the way? This was a big mistake. "Do you know where we are, Gran? Maybe we should go back."

"Stuff and nonsense! We're almost there, girl!"

But Hayley couldn't see any sign of daylight, or even an obvious exit. And there was something else now. A strange rushing sound was coming from somewhere far behind them. "Shh, Gran, listen. Is that a train?"

"No, that's no train, dear," said her gran cheerily. "Sounds more like someone left the tap on."

Hayley strained to see back down the long, dark tunnel. Something white was moving their way. Shifting side to side, growing. . . WATER!

"It's this way," piped up Gran, pointing at a nearby service door. "I'd stake my life on it!"

Hayley tightened her grip on her gran's arm and pulled her as fast as she could towards the door and away from the approaching wave. "MOVE!"

Above ground, at the entrance to Tower Hill Tube station, staff were just pulling down the shutters when they heard Hayley yelling, out of breath, from the escalators.

"WAIT!"

Hayley sprinted for the exit. She was giving her gran a piggyback ride, which was slowing her down. But the giant wave thundering at her heels was more than enough motivation to keep moving. They barrelled out of the station exit and dived clear as an immense wall of water crashed out behind them. Seconds later the front of the station exploded as the Viking longship smashed its way through, carried on the flood, over the main road and straight into the Tower of London's moat, which was filling with water for the first time in nearly two hundred years.

Meanwhile Hayley, nursing her aching limbs, quietly guided her gran into the memorial gardens next to the Tube station and through the secret entrance to the tunnel that led to the Keep.

27

UNDER SIEGE

To the Lord Chamberlain's surprise, it was Hayley and her gran who came to his rescue. He didn't want to hurt Yeoman Box, even though she'd become a rather horrible, foaming-at-the-mouth berserker. But nor could he afford to lose the Keep, not when Lock was just launching his shock attack on the country.

The other Yeoman Warders kept their screaming former colleague at bay with their long pikes, while others rolled the heavy Gatling gun into position. Just as LC was about to issue the order to open fire, Hayley and her gran burst into the Map Room.

"BRENDA?!" Hayley gasped, seeing her deranged former friend growl and bite a chair in half.

"Miss Hicks?!" LC shouted, shocked. "Keep back!"

He waved his arms, but Hayley had already sized-up the situation.

"Gran, have a seat!" Hayley said, easing her on to Herne's leather sofa. "Eshelby – chuck me some meat!"

The Ravenmaster was huddled in a corner of the chamber, trying to calm the *kaa*-ing ravens he'd just evacuated from the courtyard. Hearing Hayley's order, he pointed at himself, *who me?*

"NOW WOULD BE GOOD!" yelled Hayley.

Startled into action, he tossed her a slab of raw steak, much to the irritation of his birds. Realizing that she had a plan, LC signalled for the beefeaters to hold their fire.

"Hey, Brenda!" Hayley shouted, holding the dripping meat up so the berserker could get an eyeful. "Come and get it!"

Brenda screamed a Norse oath and, drooling like a hungry dog, she lumbered after Hayley, pushing over desks and shoving Yeoman Warders out of the way.

Hayley let Brenda get closer and then threw the bloody steak across the Map Room. It landed with a *squelch* next to the hatch to the Archives. A second later, the transformed Brenda was on top of it, pulling at the red strands of flesh with gnashing yellow teeth. With the berserker distracted, Hayley inched close enough to slip the bolt to the hatch across and ease it open. Taking their cue, the Yeoman Warders rushed forward and booted their colleague hard up the backside. Berserker Brenda clawed at the air, but couldn't stop herself tumbling forward into the dark of the Archives. Before she shut the hatch, Hayley kicked what was left of the steak down after her and heard a distant belch, which she took as a sign that Brenda had survived the fall.

The Yeoman Warders broke into spontaneous applause, gathering round Hayley and patting her on the back.

"That was a very brave thing you did, Hayley," said Chief Yeoman Seabrook.

"It's good to see the Keeper of the King's Arrows back where she belongs," LC added.

A little embarrassed, Hayley bowed.

"Right then," announced Hayley's gran from the

sofa, "which of you nice young men is going to make me a cup of tea?"

"Although you might need to be reminded of the rules around bringing visitors to the Keep," LC said to Hayley with a wry smile.

A few minutes later, Hayley's gran was enjoying her cup of tea (plus digestive biscuits) and watching some of the Yeomen reinforce the main doors of the Keep with iron girders, while others handed out pikes and swords.

"All tourists have been evacuated," shouted Chief Yeoman Seabrook. "Draugar have penetrated the White Tower!"

"Then we are under siege," LC said, glancing at the ceiling, as if he could see the rampaging Vikings above them.

"It's all right, Gran. We'll be safe enough down here," Hayley whispered, even though she didn't quite believe it herself. If the Raven Banner's magic could penetrate the Keep, of all places, then surely nowhere was safe.

"Don't you worry about me, child. I'm still batting," Gran replied, miming a cricket stroke.

Her eyes were bright, and she squeezed Hayley's hand good and tight. Guilt stabbed at Hayley's heart

323

like a knife. She felt terrible that she'd ever doubted her remarkable gran; she'd saved their lives down there in the Tube tunnels.

"I'm sorry," Hayley said.

"Whatever for, child?" asked Gran.

"I'm sorry I . . . you know . . . made you walk all this way."

"Nonsense. I could do with another cuppa, though," Gran said, shaking her empty mug.

On her way to the Mess Hall, Hayley stopped by the ops table, where LC was watching as Yeoman Warder plotters added more and more models of berserker Vikings to the map.

"What's going on out there?" asked Hayley.

"Bedlam, that's what, just as Lock planned it," said LC. "I fear the cunning professor has outwitted me once more. Only he could have thought to create his own army out of innocent people like this. Turning them into his slaves."

"To do what?"

LC looked up at her. His eyes were red, haunted by age and fatigue.

"To take the kingdom, Miss Hicks. He means to overthrow King Alfred and place his puppet, Prince Richard, on the throne. And with this force of berserkers at his disposal he might just do it. The Defender is all that stands between us and disaster."

Hayley looked to the monitor showing the video link to the Defender's helmet. Static still filled the screen.

"Where are you, Alfie?" said Hayley.

"Have we re-established communication with His Majesty?" barked LC.

"Working on it, sir!" came Chief Yeoman Seabrook's tense reply.

CLANG... CLANG... CLANG...

Everyone froze. Something was pounding into the other side of the main doors, shaking clouds of dust from the thick wood. Vikings bellowed as they tried to break through.

"STAND AT ARMS!" LC shouted, and the Yeomen Warders scrambled to arm themselves, grabbing pikes and wheeling over the Gatling gun.

"Will the door hold?" Hayley asked.

"We can but hope, Miss Hicks," LC replied.

"Bring me my bow!" shouted Hayley.

Yeoman Gillam hurried to the Arena.

"Very good, Keeper of the King's Arrows," said the Lord Chamberlain with a nod.

"SIR!" It was the Yeoman at the communications desk. "I HAVE THE DEFENDER!"

There was no sign of Guthrum or Ellie by the time the Defender made it outside. The high street of Wimbledon Village was littered with abandoned shopping bags and empty pushchairs. Panicking pedestrians ran to and fro, fleeing the crazed, hulking forms of those who had recently turned berserker. The only thing that made Alfie feel better was that Guthrum clearly wanted his sister alive – no doubt under instructions from Lock, or perhaps even their own brother, Richard. He would find her, but first he had to deal with this outbreak of Norse mayhem. He raised an arm and produced a shield from one of his bracelets, flooring a galloping berserker that was chasing a woman carrying a baby. She stuttered a "Thank you", her eyes wide with horror. Alfie realized there must be thousands like her out there – millions even – scared and confused, helpless in the face of an enemy they never knew they had until today.

"No problem." He smiled to reassure her, then realized that was stupid, as she couldn't see his face. "Um, maybe find somewhere to hide till all this blows over?"

A whine of feedback rattled Alfie's eardrums as the Lord Chamberlain's voice came over his helmet-radio. "Majesty? Come in, sir?"

"I'm here, LC," Alfie replied, whacking another passing berserker over the head with his sword as she tried to roar at him.

"Thank goodness. Where are you?"

"Wimbledon. Guthrum was here. He took Ellie. I couldn't stop him. I don't know where he went."

Hayley took the radio. "Alfie, it's me. Guthrum's men are here. They're trying to break in to the Keep. We could use some backup."

Alfie summoned Wyvern from his spurs and hovered off the ground. "I'm on my way."

But just then, Wyvern reared up and flew backwards. A jet of fire washed across the street, setting cars and shopfronts aflame. With a scream, the Black Dragon descended, casting a shadow across the rooftops. He landed, cracking the soot-blackened pavement beneath his clawed feet.

Alfie tried to speak, but choked on his words at first. He had seen this creature up close before, but that was before he knew it was his brother. Despite what he'd witnessed at St Paul's, the very idea still seemed impossible.

"Richard. . ."

The Dragon's forked tongue flicked out and another torrent of fire burst from his jaws, washing over Alfie's hastily deployed shield. He spoke with a guttural reptilian hiss. "That is no longer my name."

"What have you done with our sister?" asked Alfie, being careful to keep out of range of his brother's swaying, spiked tail.

"Don't worry about her. She is under my protection now."

"What, the same way you protected Dad?"

The Black Dragon shrieked and flapped his wings, tearing the tiles from the roofs on either side of the street. "He was not *my* father. He never cared about me. Only for you, his firstborn." He spat the words at Alfie, smoke pouring from his nostrils.

A people carrier weaved through the wreckage behind the Dragon and screeched to a halt when it saw the monster filling the road ahead. The driver, a pale-faced man in his forties, clutched the wheel, frozen in fear, while his wife turned round to comfort the three crying children on the back seats. The Dragon swiped the vehicle with its tail, rocking it off its wheels for a moment. Alfie could hear the screams of the occupants rising in pitch as the Dragon leant down to sneer through the windscreen.

"Stop it, Richard! Leave them alone!"

The Black Dragon hooked a claw underneath the people carrier and dragged it along the tarmac until its jaws touched the bonnet.

"Why do you care about these ... peasants?" he chuckled. "All they ever did was sneer and laugh at us royals. They're not laughing now, are they?"

He arched his neck and opened his mouth. Alfie could see the orange glow building inside his throat as the Dragon prepared to engulf the car in fire. The Defender leapt at the Dragon, slashing at him with his sword. It bounced off his rock-hard scales, but the attack was enough to make him release the car, which veered away through the rubble.

Alfie flew straight up on Wyvern. He might not be able to reason with this thing that used to be his brother, but if they were going to fight, at least he could try to take him somewhere it would cause less damage.

28

BROTHERS IN ARMS

"GO ON, WYVERN!" Alfie yelled.

She'd never galloped so hard or fast. Did magical ghost horses have a top speed? He was sure she'd smashed the record. He chanced a look over his shoulder to see if the Black Dragon was still following him and got his answer in the shape of an eruption of fire blazing inches from his back. He spurred Wyvern on even faster. Ahead he could just make out the churning waters of the North Sea beneath the setting sun.

"Majesty, where are you going?" LC shouted in his earpiece.

The old man sounded breathless, but there wasn't time to ask him what was going on back at the Keep; Alfie had his own hands full.

"Somewhere he can't hurt anyone!" Alfie yelled over the onrushing wind.

"You must engage the Dragon! Draw your sword, sir! End this, NOW!"

Alfie didn't know what to do. He could barely deal with the fact that somewhere underneath those hideous black scales was Richard, let alone the idea that he was supposed to drive his sword into him.

As the Defender reached the sea, the Black Dragon pumping its wings in pursuit, another jet of flame fired past, missing him by a millimetre. In seconds the land was far behind them and Alfie tugged on Wyvern's reins, turning her round to face his brother. He drew the Great Sword of State from its sheath, lighting up the dark sky.

The Black Dragon wheeled high above him for a moment then stooped into a dive. Claws struck metal as the Defender parried the attack. But the beast's tail whipped against Alfie's back as it streaked by, making him scream in pain. And with the pain, came anger. He was sick of feeling guilty for something that wasn't his fault. Richard had killed their father and betrayed their country. Alfie hadn't started this, but if Richard wanted a fight, then he would give him one. The Defender gripped his sword and drove Wyvern into a gallop straight towards the Dragon. As sword and talons met again, Alfie steered Wyvern beneath the Dragon, cutting him across the belly. The wound was not deep, but the message was clear: the Defender was not afraid to spill blood.

Dragon and Defender wheeled around each other in the sky like World War Two planes in a dogfight. They hammered each other with everything they had. Alfie's heart was pounding as he existed only in the moment, not even thinking as he reacted to every move, looking for an opening. It was like his mind was closing down, filtering out all but the essential information that would keep him alive. Swinging his sword, ducking under the Dragon's tail, deflecting a fiery blast with his shield.

Duck, swing, parry, thrust. A blur of scales, fangs and flame. Duck, swing, parry, thrust. Claws sparked across his chest plate. Wyvern whinnied in pain, but Alfie barely heard it. The Defender's sword flashed in the sky like a beacon.

Hundreds of feet below them, in the dark North Sea, overall-clad workers on a giant oil platform crowded at the rusty safety railings, watching in awe as the supernatural battle raged overhead.

Exhausted, the combatants collided with each other. The Black Dragon grabbed the Defender's throat in a scaly claw. The Defender grabbed the Dragon's tail right back. Wings tangled with spectral horse's hooves as together they tumbled from the sky. For a moment they were face to face, spinning through the air head over heels, neither prepared to release their hold on the other. Just before they hit the rig Alfie saw the Dragon's eyes change – no longer the burning eyes of the rage-filled beast, but the terrified eyes of a young man, his brother, Richard.

Workers dived for cover as the Dragon and Defender hit the oil rig and crashed through floor after floor. Steel buckled, gantries collapsed and cables snapped as the Dragon's bulk tore a ragged hole through the rig's accommodation block and he disappeared, leaving a trail of twisted metal, ruptured power lines and punctured pipes.

Alfie was thrown clear, landing on his back on a walkway with a hefty *clang*. The armour had saved his life, but the air was knocked out of him. When he opened his eyes, a weathered-looking foreman, his face stained black, was looking down at him.

"FIRE!" the foreman yelled.

Thick black smoke billowed across the oil rig as a fire raged out of control from the gaping hole where the Dragon had fallen. But this wasn't Dragon flames, it was burning oil. As he struggled to his feet, Alfie could smell it and feel it sting his eyes even through the visor. Alarms sounded. Warning lights flashed. Workers scrambled to launch an orange lifeboat. But the winch, which would lower them from the platform to the sea, had buckled in the impact of the crash.

Back in the Keep, they had seen the whole thing. Audio had cut out some time during the aerial battle, but the Defender's helmet cam was still beaming back pictures, giving them a Defender's-eye view of the plummet on to the rig.

"Majesty? Can you hear me?" shouted LC as Yeoman Gillam worked on re-establishing communications. Meanwhile, Hayley was busy on her laptop, hacking into the CCTV feed from the rig itself, searching every camera for any sign of the Black Dragon.

On the rig, Alfie extended his hand towards the sea and tried to command the waters to rise and douse the fires. But every time he thought he had done it, his mental connection with the water would break, like he was trying to tune a broken radio.

"Majesty? What are you doing?" LC was back.

"The sea..." said Alfie, straining. "I can't command it..."

"That's because the currents are too mixed out there," said LC. "It's not British water alone. King Canute had much the same problem."

"Do you know what happened to Richard?" yelled Alfie over the sound of the rig's metal groaning in the heat of the fire.

"Nothing yet!" Hayley called out.

The foreman grabbed Alfie by the shoulders and shouted in his face. "We gotta get off here before she blows!"

"Get your men inside the boat," Alfie said. "I'll launch it."

The foreman nodded and herded his men to the orange lifeboat, pushing them into the spacious cabin and shouting at them to stop gawping at the Defender and move.

An explosion shook the rig. The entire platform

lurched like a groggy giant. The men inside the lifeboat cabin screamed in fear. Alfie had to launch this thing before the rig collapsed on top of it. Gripping a metal beam with one hand, Alfie drew his sword.

The foreman poked his head out of the cabin and looked up at the Defender, alarmed. "You can't drop us from this height, we'll break apart!"

Alfie looked at the rolling sea far below and saw it was true. They were far too high up. Another explosion sent debris tumbling on to the roof of the lifeboat. Now or never.

"Hang on!" Alfie shouted and, with a slash of his sword, cut the ropes. The lifeboat plummeted towards the sea. "SPURS!"

Wyvern emerged and they dived down, racing the boat to the ocean. At the last second, the Defender zoomed under it and braced himself. He hoped the armour could take the impact. For the second time that night, the air was punched from Alfie's lungs as the fully laden lifeboat hit him square on the shoulders and slid over him into the sea like he was a ramp.

The workers' screams turned to cheers as the lifeboat's engines started and it powered away from the burning rig. Alfie flew behind it for a short way, seeing it clear. The foreman stuck his head out and waved at the Defender; his men were safe. Alfie waved, then galloped back to the collapsing rig, landing on what looked like the most stable part of the platform. Smoke bellowed as he unclipped his scout orb, sending it down into the raging fire. Had the Dragon, his brother, fallen straight through the platform? Had he drowned in the sea below? Alfie had to know.

"Richard?" Alfie called.

The scout orb showed him nothing but fire and smoke; there was no sign of his brother. Alfie commanded it back to his hand. The platform shook again, but still he searched on, pushing aside a girder, ignoring the pulsing heat, sweat pouring down his face inside the helmet. Was Richard lying in here somewhere, broken and alone? And if he was dead— Alfie flinched from the thought. He couldn't leave him here. Maybe he'd survived and retreated?

"There's nothing you can do, Alfie," said Hayley over the radio. "Get out of there!"

With a screech, the Black Dragon rose through the smoke, his wings beating. The creature's body was slashed and battered from their fight and the fall, but he was still very much alive. Alfie retreated out of the fire, backing out along the great metal gas flare tower that stuck out from the oil rig like a crane arm. At its far end, flames shot out of the gas vent into the night sky.

The Black Dragon stalked along the tower, hissing at him. "The Defender, so noble, such a hero. But what good has it done you?"

"I'm sorry. I didn't know how you felt," said Alfie. "You should have told me."

"Run crying to big brother?" scoffed the Dragon. "Sorry, not my style."

He breathed out fire, the flames licking at Alfie's feet. The Defender drew his sword.

"That's it, sir," shouted LC, watching from the Keep. "YOU MUST SLAY HIM!"

Alfie looked around. The rig was falling apart. If he was going to do something, he had to do it now.

"No," said Alfie calmly. "I can't."

He dropped his sword, which clattered on to the gantry below, then reached up and removed his armour.

"NO! MAJESTY! WHAT ARE YOU DOING?" yelled the Lord Chamberlain, as the pictures from the Defender's helmet went dark.

"We've lost the link, sir!" shouted Yeoman Gillam.

"Here!" said Hayley, spinning the laptop with the CCTV feed from the rig still playing live, showing the two figures standing on the walkway, smoke and flames rising all around them.

Alfie stood in his crumpled clothes before the Black Dragon. He removed the Ring of Command and tossed it on to the Shroud Tunic along with his spurs and other regalia.

"I know you're still in there, Richard. I saw it. We'll find a way to get rid of this thing! Together."

The Dragon's head rocked from side to side, as if wrestling with Alfie's words. He craned his neck and roared out a sheet of flame into the sky. "It is too late for that," he croaked.

Alfie took a step towards him. "No, it's not. Whatever Lock's promised you, it's all lies. Just look what he's done to you!"

Their eyes met again and Alfie could see Richard fighting to be free of the creature that possessed him, the poison clearing, the sickness receding.

Alfie reached out his hand. "I won't fight you, brother."

The Dragon closed his eyes as if contemplating it. But when they opened again, they were burning red and filled with hate.

"I'm not your brother!"

The Black Dragon reached forward and picked up the regalia in his claws, except for the spurs, which he left where they lay.

"You can keep the horse. I don't think we'd get along."

"Richard, wait—"

Unfurling his wings, the Dragon flew up, opened his jaws wide and blasted the tower arm where Alfie stood with a relentless gust of fire. Wave upon wave of flames, until the entire rig was engulfed.

In the Keep, LC, Hayley and the Yeoman Warders watched in horror as the rig exploded with incredible force and the camera feed was obliterated. Herne threw back his head and howled.

The Dragon flew above the debris as plumes of oil-black smoke billowed into the sky. There was no sign of his brother below. Nothing could have survived such an inferno. He circled once more, shrieking in triumph, then flew away, back towards the mainland. Back to the kingdom that was now his.

29

THE KINGDOM FALLS

Buckingham Palace was on fire. That is the sort of thing that can easily happen when one of the royal chefs suddenly turns into an insane, angry Viking warrior and starts hurling pans of hot truffle oil around. While most of the staff fled through the palace gates on to the Mall, three more berserkers ran rampant on the roof. One of them, who until an hour ago had been an especially unpopular head footman, kicked down the flagpole and ripped the Union Jack to shreds with his new jagged, yellow teeth.

The BBC, the last news organization to go off air

that day, just managed to broadcast the stark image of the burning palace to the nation before it too was overrun by berserker cameramen, canteen workers and at least one well-known game-show host.

On the Holy Island of Lindisfarne, Yeoman Burgh Keeper Rodney "Sultana" Raisin valiantly confronted Trisha Harald, the landlady of the Ship Inn, as she went crazy, interrupted a darts match and started throwing her customers out of the pub ... through the windows. Sultana managed to lock her in the beer cellar where he could hear her draining the beer kegs dry and letting out belches that shook the walls.

At Harrow School, Mr Lang had just started his assembly on "Respecting One Another" when he turned berserker and started chasing teachers and pupils around the school hall.

Panic and confusion, along with a desire not to hurt friends and family, even when they had become slobbering monsters, led most people to run and hide.

At the Tower of London, Guthrum and the draugar Vikings were still pounding the great doors of the Keep with the help of an iron cannon they had found outside.

On the other side of the buckling doors, Hayley pulled on her Yeoman's tunic for the first time and nocked an arrow on to her bow. Her mind was weirdly blank, as if watching the Black Dragon kill the Defender – *her* Defender, Alfie – on the oil rig had wiped away all thoughts except one: revenge. If this was the end, then she was going to take down some Viking scum with her. The Yeoman Warders, some with tears streaming down their faces, gripped their weapons tight. The Lord Chamberlain was slumped over, his face white with grief.

"Our king . . . is slain. Not another. . . Not young Alfred," he muttered.

Hayley pulled LC to his feet. "Look after her," she said, pushing him towards Gran, who was hiding behind a thick stone pillar.

With a terrible groan of metal and wood, the main doors to the Keep gave way and the maniac gang of Vikings charged inside.

"OPEN FIRE!" Hayley yelled.

The Gatling gun spat shells at the first line of draugar, felling them all. Hayley stepped up, drew her bow and shot an arrow right into the forehead of the largest Viking warrior left standing. She screamed with rage, spearing arrow after arrow into their attackers. She had known grief before, but she preferred rage, and right now it was the more useful emotion. But the fallen Vikings started to move again, grunting as they got back to their feet, plucking bullets and arrows from their rotting flesh and advancing once more.

"How do we kill them?" Hayley yelled, backing off.

"With great difficulty," replied Seabrook, impaling a Viking on his pike. "That's the problem with the undead."

Forced to retreat into one corner of the hall, the Yeomen fought the Vikings hand to hand, desperately fending off their swinging axes. As if that were not bad enough, one of the Vikings sounded his war horn, and several of the draugar began to shake and transform into devil dogs with bristling black fur and gnashing fangs.

Hayley shot her last arrow and found herself pinned to a wall by one of the foul-breathed dogs. She whacked at the beast with her longbow, but the hound snapped it in half and reared up, closing in for the kill. But suddenly Herne leapt on to the back of the devil dog, sunk his teeth into its neck and clung on. The devil dog thrashed and howled and transformed back into a Viking.

Hayley took her chance to reach her gran and LC behind the pillar. "We can't stay! You need to order the retreat!"

LC looked appalled. "And abandon the Keep, His Majesty's secret base? Never!"

"Alfie's not coming back!" Hayley shouted through tears. "And I don't want to lose anyone else I care about today."

Yeoman Gillam fell towards them. Blood was pouring from a wound on his head. Hayley pulled him away from the fighting. LC looked aghast at the battle raging around him. "Very well. Chief Yeoman, full retreat!"

Seabrook gave the order and together the Yeomen heaved over the heavy ops table into the path of the Vikings, giving them precious seconds to fall back to the stairs with their injured. Hayley helped her gran into the evacuation tunnel and risked a look back into the Map Room. Herne was still fighting bravely, holding the Viking squad at bay with ferocious snarls and bites.

"HERNE! HERE, BOY! COME ON!"

The grey dog turned his shaggy head to look at her, but as he did, two devil dogs fell on top of him and they rolled out of view.

"MISS HICKS!" LC was beckoning from the tunnel.

Distraught, Hayley pulled the tunnel door closed and ran after them.

As they emerged at street level, blinking into the light, the extent of their defeat was obvious. There were no police cars, no ambulances, no soldiers restoring order. Just the last few people to find shelter running blindly from door to door. And the grunts and howls of the berserkers not far off. The city belonged to them tonight. The Yeoman Warders stood to attention.

"What are your orders, sir?" asked Seabrook.

LC bowed his head, solemn. For a moment, Hayley didn't think he would reply at all. Then he spoke, even and commanding once more.

"Yeomen Warders of His Majesty's Royal Palace and Fortress the Tower of London. You have fought gallantly, but the Keep is lost. Now, you are to remove your uniforms and conceal yourselves among the population."

There was much muttering and grumbling, but he continued:

"Tend to the injured, lie low. When the time is right you will be contacted in the traditional manner. Now leave. God save the King."

"GOD SAVE THE KING!" came the cry.

A wretched growl rose from the end of the street as several berserkers appeared. The fearless beefeaters readied their weapons. But LC shook his head at the Yeomen, who bowed their heads and dispersed.

Hayley put a hand on LC's arm. "What about you?"

"Me?"

"Where will you go?"

"Oh. I, um, hadn't given it much thought, Miss Hicks. I imagine I will find lodging at an inn or hostelry."

Hayley's gran was peering at the group of drooling berserkers who were getting closer. "Look at that lot. Drunk as skunks," she tutted.

Hayley ran over to an abandoned black cab and checked the ignition. The key was still in it. She hopped into the driver's seat and started the engine. LC helped Hayley's gran into the back.

"You're coming too. Get in!" ordered Hayley.

The fight seemingly gone from him, LC obediently climbed in and Hayley drove off.

"HOLD UP!" cried Gran.

Hayley screeched the cab to a halt and spun round. "What is it?" she asked.

Then she saw him, running towards them, over the bridge from the Tower, a Viking's arm dangling from his mouth.

"HERNE!" shouted Hayley, relieved.

The grey dog was being pursued by the angry owner of the arm, who was wielding an axe with his remaining hand.

Hayley flung open the passenger door as Herne ran up. "Good boy. Um, you can leave that outside, thanks."

Herne dropped the arm and jumped on to the passenger seat. Hayley pulled the door closed and was surprised to receive a lick on the hand from the dog. *CRUNCH*. The Viking's axe planted itself in the roof, which Hayley took as her cue to hit the accelerator and drive them away. She looked in the rear-view mirror as the Tower of London shrank from view. She wondered if she would ever see it again.

"What now?" asked Hayley as they pulled on to the main road, heading north out of the city.

The Lord Chamberlain gazed out at the battle-scarred capital. Berserkers were rioting with no one to stop them. Smoke from a hundred different fires rose above the office blocks and houses.

"We must find Princess Eleanor," he said. "All our hopes now rest with her."

Guthrum tossed Ellie on to the cold stone floor of the cell deep in the Tower of London's dungeons. She wiped blood from her lip and scowled up at the Viking lord.

"You're a real tough guy, aren't you? Throwing girls around," said Ellie.

Guthrum snarled and raised a fist, but seemed to think better of it and walked out with a grunt. The heavy cell door swung shut behind him, magically locked by the mysterious key bundle hanging in the middle of the antechamber. The Yeoman Jailer lay nearby, unconscious.

Ellie hauled herself to her feet. The cell was small and entirely bare, the only light coming from a tiny barred window too high up to reach. She tried not to think about what it would be like to spend a whole night here. Or longer. Had they captured the rest of her family? Were her brothers prisoners too? She spotted a small grate in one wall and leaned down to it. An odd smell like copper coins hit her.

"Hello?" she called, not expecting a reply.

"Good day to you, young mistress," came Colonel

Blood's lighthearted voice through the grate. "I would offer ye my acquaintance, but I am newly hopeful that my incarceration shall soon be at its end."

"Come again?" said Ellie, baffled.

"Sweet freedom, princess, for me and my kind. For there has been this day ... what shall one call it? A changing of the guard!"

His shrill laughter filled the dungeons, and was soon joined by a cacophony of yells and growls from the other cells. Ellie retreated to a corner and held her hands over her ears.

In Westminster, Lock gazed around in satisfaction at the fear and confusion his transformed berserkers had unleashed. But now it was time to rein them in. Grabbing the Raven Banner, Lock stalked out of the abandoned building and his berserkers fell into line behind him, compliant. Marching through the devastated streets, more and more new berserkers stopped rioting and joined his growing army, ready to do his bidding. The United Kingdom was now at his mercy.

Professor Lock smiled as he crossed the bridge into the Tower of London. The last time he had come here it had been through Traitor's Gate. Now he strolled inside as a free man, an army at his back, the victor in a new Battle of Britain. He set a bag of clothes down behind a wall and waited. The sound of leathery wingbeats grew closer until the Black Dragon swooped down and landed behind the wall.

"Is it done?" asked Lock.

Richard stepped out wearing the trousers and shirt the professor has left for him. His face was pale, hair slick, eyes tinged red. His voice was hoarse, his throat still hot from breathing fire. "Yes. He's gone."

Richard held out the regalia to show the professor – the soaking wet Shroud Tunic, the Orb and Great Sword of State. He was already wearing the Ring of Command. Guthrum and his Viking raiders marched from the White Tower to join them as Lock bowed to Richard.

"Then congratulations, *Your Majesty.*"

Lock kneeled and after some prompting, Guthrum and his men reluctantly did the same. Behind them, the new berserker army bowed their heads in respect.

"My sister?" asked Richard.

Guthrum growled a curt reply.

"Her Royal Highness is comfortable," Lock translated.

Richard smiled, satisfied, and looked over the Tower. *His* tower. *His* kingdom.

"We should have a great victory feast tonight, don't you think?" Richard said. "Just like in the good old days."

A deep *GRONK!* drew their eyes to the top of the White Tower. A raven was flying out from the battlements, flapping in a circle before gliding away, high into the distance.

"NO!" shouted Lock, running for the tower steps, as two more ravens launched themselves into the air.

On the tower roof, Yeoman Eshelby was shooing his great birds away, encouraging them to fly. Only Gwenn, his favourite, remained. He had left her for last, as he knew she would take some coaxing to leave him. And if he was being honest, he didn't want to say goodbye either.

"Now come on, Gwenny," he whispered, tickling her under the beak. "We've all got to do our duty, you included."

The door flew open and Professor Lock burst on to the roof. "What are you doing? Who are you?!" he shouted at the beefeater.

Yeoman Eshelby released Gwenn and she spread her wings, rising high above the tower. Issuing a throaty call, she glided over the outer wall and disappeared into the distance.

"I'm the Ravenmaster," he said, finally turning to Lock with a look of sheer contempt. "And if I were you, mate, I'd hold on to something."

Lock felt the roof shudder beneath his feet. Alarmed, he looked out over the towers and turrets of the ancient fortress. A gargoyle crumbled and fell from the top of the Beauchamp Tower. Far below, the Viking undead roared and covered their heads as chunks of stone and masonry cascaded towards them. The battlements all around Lock and the Ravenmaster disintegrated and tumbled away. At the last moment, the Black Dragon dived past, plucking Lock from the roof as the entire White Tower collapsed in a billowing plume of dust.

Moments later, Professor Lock, his battered, undead Vikings and the new King Richard surveyed the fresh ruins from the safety of the road. Richard seethed with rage. The flight of the ravens had turned the taste of victory bitter in his mouth. He might be king, but the Tower and the kingdom had fallen.

"Don't be concerned with a few dusty old rocks, Your Majesty." Lock smiled, reassuring. "Such things can be rebuilt. Britain is yours."

30

EXILE

I'm drowning, thought Alfie.

He had held his breath for as long as he could, but now his every inhalation was seawater. He didn't know if he was freezing cold or burning hot, and he had no idea which way was up or down. Everything was black. Besides, he did not have enough strength left to swim to the surface. The oil rig was still collapsing, sending pounding shockwaves through the water with every girder that fell. But there was something else, a familiar sound at the very edge of his mind. Somewhere, Wyvern was calling for him, a desperate, whinnying cry. The last thing Alfie saw before he passed out were the spurs, glinting as they sank towards the seabed.

Alfred the Second, King of Great Britain and Northern Island, Defender of the Realm, slipped into unconsciousness, his body shutting down sense by sense.

His last thought was of his brother.

Alfie didn't see the red-robed figure of Qilin materalize next to him in the churning, rust-stained water. He didn't feel him grab his arm. He didn't see the dark shadow of the mini submarine passing by below them, nor feel the rush of air as Qilin teleported them inside it.

"Come on, breathe!" Brian shouted at Alfie as he pumped his chest.

"Is he dead?" a sopping wet Tony asked as Brian pinched Alfie's nose and blew air into his mouth. "Is he?"

Brian didn't answer, but continued to work on Alfie as water ran off him on to the floor of the submarine. Suddenly Alfie coughed up a fountain of seawater and took a long, ragged breath.

"Turn him over!" Brian shouted at Tony. "Pat his back. Hard."

Tony did as he was told, slamming his fists into his friend's back. Alfie heaved and spluttered like a faulty motor.

"Sorry, Alfa-bet," said Tony. "Doctor's orders."

"Prepare to surface!" Brian said, flipping a switch that filled the little sub's ballast tanks with air.

Within a minute they were bobbing on the surface of the North Sea and the communication mast was raised. To the west, beyond the wreckage of the burning oil rig, night had fallen over Britain. Brian punched numbers into a console, and picked up an attached phone handset.

"We have him, ma'am," Brian said. "We're coming to you. Stand by."

Queen Tamara's voice filled the submarine through the tinny speakers. "Thank goodness. I'll be waiting."

Hearing her, Alfie rolled over, not sure if he was living or dead. "Mum?" he croaked.

"You just rest up, matey. Get your strength back," Tony said and patted Alfie on the shoulders. "You're going to need it."

Brian charted a course north, keeping a watch through the sub's conning tower. Outside, a small flock of black birds was approaching from the mainland. It was the Tower's ravens. They cried out their *gronk*ing call and dived out of the sky, flying above the submarine. A loyal escort, following their king into exile.

ACKNOWLEDGEMENTS

To every reader who told us they enjoyed the first book, posted a review, or recommended it to a friend or customer, our heartfelt thanks. We hope this sequel lived up to your expectations.

Thank you to everyone at Scholastic, who continue to bring Alfie, Hayley and their adventures out into the world. Especially to Rachel Phillips and Lucy Richardson, who guided us through the whirlwind that was our first publicity tour, and our editors Linas Alsenas and Peter Matthews for their thoughtful and perceptive notes. Huge thanks again to the one and only David Stevens, who may have changed in name, but remains the same in his boundless support and wisdom.

Our immense gratitude, as ever, to our tireless team at Independent Talent Group, Cathy King, Ikenna Obiekwe, Alex Rusher and Sam Kingston-Jones.

Huge thanks to Chris Skaife, the Tower of London's real Ravenmaster, for generously giving us an unforgettable tour of the ravens' favourite hangouts, and for introducing us to the wonderful Merlina, who served as inspiration for Gwenn (whose name he also suggested).

Thanks also to Dr Erika Sigurdson of the University of Iceland, who kindly provided the Old Norse dialogue translations for the fearsome Guthrum.

Thanks to our old friend Olivier Hein for taking time out of his busy cider-sampling schedule on holiday to speed-read the early draft and give us his feedback.

Extra special thanks go to our brilliant new events manager, Melanie Ostler.

Above all, we would like to thank the hundreds of amazing teachers, librarians and students from all over the country we have met this year. We are honoured to have been invited into your schools to talk about what we do, and inspired by your dedication and enthusiasm. This is for you.

For details of school visits and author events, go to: www.ostlerandhuckerby.com

Photo courtesy of Sarah Weal.

Nick Ostler and Mark Huckerby are Emmy-winning and BAFTA-nominated screenwriters best known for writing popular TV shows such as *Danger Mouse*, *Thunderbirds Are Go!* and *Peter Rabbit*. *Defender of the Realm* is their first novel.

Follow Nick on Twitter @nickostler
Follow Mark on Twitter @Huckywucky

Visit their website
www.ostlerandhuckerby.com

www.instagram.com/defenderoftherealm